THE DNA
MURDERS

John Clark Wagner

Long Branch Cabin
Press, LLC
11414 N. 109 Avenue, Sun City, AZ 85351
Copyright © 2016 John Clark Wagner
This is a work of fiction. Any similarity to actual persons living or dead
is purely coincidental
All rights reserved
ISBN: 0996907017
ISBN: 9780996907019
Library of Congress Control Number: 2016904687
Long Branch Cabin Press, LLC, Sun City, AZ

THE DNA MURDERS

John Clark Wagner

Dedicated to my Parents:

Elisha Botner Wagner
And
Flossie Smith Wagner

CHAPTER 1

OLD INDIAN BONES

Daniel Burke, Chief Detective of the town of Stanton, Ohio, rarely drank to excess anymore, not since Vietnam. But he enjoyed a cool one occasionally, like after a hard day at City Hall, or when he went fishing, or when he played poker. Thursday night was when he and a few of the boys got together in the back room of Schiller's Bar and Grill down on River Road for a friendly game, since Friday was generally a slow day. The game usually started around eight and broke up around eleven thirty, during which time Burke typically had two or three beers. But on that particular Thursday night—it was the day the kids found the old decrepit skull in Bealer woods—Burke was on a rare winning streak, and every time he yawned, stretched and started to rise from the table with his parting comments on the tip of his tongue such as, "Well boys, it's past my bed time." the other guys would whine and complain and demand a chance to get their money back. Naturally, in the heat and passion of such an exciting, protracted game, they had all stayed longer and drunk more that was good for them.

Of course, Daniel's wife, Marge, and their two kids, Sam and Linda, were asleep when Daniel finally got home. He very quietly slipped inside the house and into bed.

It was difficult for him to get out of bed the following morning, being hung over and sleep-deprived, and just about all he could do to get through breakfast without giving himself away. He knew he wasn't a pleasant fellow when he was hung over, so he smiled weakly at everyone at the table and mumbled a few pleasantries and hid behind the newspaper as much as possible. Then, all he wanted to do was get to the office and fix himself a seltzer for his headache and to head off a sour stomach. After that, he wanted to put his feet up on the corner of his desk and be left alone.

He always arrived at the Police Department, an annex of City Hall, no later than 7:45, which allowed him enough time to stop by the break room for a cup of coffee, nod hello to whomever he might encounter there, and get to his desk before starting time.

On this particular morning in April, 1983, when he arrived at the break room, instead of his usual cup of coffee he plopped two white quarter-size seltzer tablets into a cup of cold water, and listened to them fizz as he walked on to his office. As usual, his subordinate, Detective Elmo Dempsey, was already there, sitting at his desk across the office he shared with Burke with *his* feet up on the edge of *his* desk reading the newspaper and sipping *his* coffee.

Chief Newman hired Dempsey three years earlier and put him under Burke's supervision. Burke had not been consulted in the hiring, and did not interview the candidate; in fact, nobody even asked him his opinion. He was not sure there had been other applicants. The whole thing had gotten under his skin. Obviously Dempsey was somebody's nephew, or cousin, or had worked in someone's election campaign. Dempsey, a rather tall, slender, rail of a man, with brown eyes and hair, which he wore short in the military fashion, had only recently returned to Stanton, from six years in the Air Force.

When Burke wasn't feeling well, he tended to get a little petulant and spiteful. This morning, it irritated him to an irrational extent that Dempsey was already there, as he was every morning, in fact. Burke had always suspected that Dempsey came to work early so he could snoop through all the in-boxes, read the mail and memos on everyone's desks, and get all the gossip from the patrol officers and secretaries. Invariably, by the time Burke got there, Dempsey would have completed his reconnaissance and would be right where he was now, his feet up, reading the damn newspaper and sipping his coffee. Besides all this usual early morning aggravation, and the debilitating effect his hangover was having on him, it irritated Burke further that Dempsey's coffee cup was a stainless steel thing (unbreakable) whose bottom flared out to twice the width of a real cup. Burke was not sure why that bothered him so much.

He went straight to his desk without even acknowledging Dempsey, who had his nose in the newspaper, anyway. Indeed, Burke didn't even look over his way as he came in the door. He sat down with his back to him pretending he didn't know he was there, and turned his chair around to the window that looked out over the city hall parking lot and a little municipal park beyond. He drank his seltzer and began mentally counting off the seconds: One, two, three... At the mental count of nine, Dempsey said, "Morning, Boss."

"Oh, morning, Elmo," he said. "I didn't notice you there. You're here early again today. Finding anything interesting in the paper?"

"I'll let you have it when I'm finished with it, Boss."

"That's all right, I glanced at it at breakfast this morning. Anything happening around here?"

"Chief was by looking for you."

Burke perked up. "Already? What did he want?"

"Didn't say. He left you a note. It's there in your in-box."

Burke felt a tinge of hatred for Dempsey. He knew that Dempsey already knew the contents of the note and he felt certain he had caught a glimpse of Dempsey smirking just now. He snatched up the note from atop the other papers in his in-box.

It read: "Daniel, please retrieve contraband Indian artifacts at 734 Elm Street."

Burke recognized the address as that of Ed and Sarah Moore. He knew that Chief of Police, Newman's "contraband Indian artifact" was a human skull, since his wife, Marge, played bridge with Sarah Moore and friends at the country club on Thursday afternoons, and Marge had mentioned the skull at breakfast, describing it as an old decrepit thing. In fact, Burke felt confident there wasn't a housewife within twenty miles of the center of town who didn't know about the skull. He was not overly excited about it. It was a common thing to find old bones in that part of Ohio, where Indian Mound Builder cultures had lived for thousands of years before the arrival of the White Man. Burial mounds were an important tourist attraction, and there was a little museum off the town square which was popular. He chuckled at the chief calling it a "contraband Indian artifact."

With Dempsey momentarily forgotten, Burke fumbled through all the papers on his desk, and then checked his basket for anything else he might have missed. There was only the usual interoffice busy-work, which was no surprise to him. In fact, Burke mused, he would more than welcome a surprise. When a crime of any significance was committed, everybody in town knew who did it, unless it was some bum come in from the highway to knock off a service station or a minute-market. Everybody knew where the cathouses were, who was selling the dope, who was buying it, where to get after-hours booze, and who was romancing whom among the better classes. It was unusual, though, now that he thought about it, how things had been so slow all winter, crime wise. The two-man detective squad, indeed, the whole police department, had spent more effort on traffic accidents caused by a lousy winter. Most of the serious crime was in the larger cities, downstream at Cincinnati, Covington and Newport, and on up river in the West Virginia towns, like Huntington, Parkersburg, and Wheeling. There were times when Burke envied big city detectives whatever excitement they had. In a typical week, Stanton usually had a few DUI, a brawl or two at a beer joint down on River Road, maybe a little petty thievery, a little dope, that sort of thing, even an occasional uncomplicated killing, over a woman or a card game usually, or just drunken meanness. And certainly, nobody was complaining about the slow pace of crime in his little town, really, except him, the Chief Detective of the two-man detective squad, who was about, finally, to go out of his mind with boredom and frustration. *How much can a man take?*

I'd just once like to have me something to sink my teeth into, he thought.

He swung his simulated black leather chair around to the window once more. Right below his window were the assigned parking spaces of the mayor and his staff. The mayor's secretary, May Ellen Posey, pulled in just then in her red convertible. Not seeming to be in any big hurry about it, she languidly exited the car, dropping her left leg outside, then her right, revealing a goodly portion of thigh as she did so.

"Uh, uh," said Burke, under his breath.

As she walked toward the building entrance she glanced up at Burke at the window, and flashed him a smile, causing him to flinch involuntarily. He suspecting that she knew he was watching her all along. He absent-mindedly took a last little swig of seltzer and screwed up his mouth. It was the sour, gritty dregs of the antacid tablet.

He glanced at his subordinate across the office, who seemed to be oblivious to him. The moron, he thought, sitting there with his feet up, reading the financial section. He didn't like having Dempsey in the same office with him. It was just something else which kept Burke on the point of despair most of the time. How was he expected to maintain any kind of discipline and respect for the authority of his position when he had to sit there all day long with this asshole subordinate watching his every move, for crying out loud?

Burke swung his chair around to his desk, straightened up, and cleared his throat. God, I'm really negative this morning, he thought. I've got to get with it. He leaned back in his chair, took several deep breaths, and said, "well, Elmo, this looks like an assignment for a crack detective."

"What?" Elmo said absently, without bothering to lower the paper.

"Contraband Indian artifact," Burke said.

"What's that, Boss?" Elmo asked, his feet still comfortably elevated on the desk, not bothering to lower the newspaper to respond to his superior.

"Contraband Indian artifact," Burke repeated.

"Huh? Contraband Indian artifact? What does that mean?"

"This note the chief left me, kids found a skull in the woods over by Bealer Street. That's what he called it, 'contraband Indian artifact.' I got to go retrieve it."

Dempsey peered, grinning, over the top of the paper. He was apparently studying the stock market reports. "Want me to handle it, Boss?"

"No, no, I'll take care of it, Elmo. You stand by the radio here in case I need backup."

Elmo smirked, and mumbled to himself as Burke went out the door, "Everybody is a comedian."

Burke cruised slowly up Third Avenue, then right on Elm Street. He knew most of the people on Elm. Ed Moore owned a hardware store, and Sarah was a close friend of Marge's going back to grade school.

He sighed as he drove along, noting the beautiful spring day. Deep down he really was grateful that little hard crime existed in their little river-port town, for Marge's and the kids' sake. That was the reason they lived there in the first place. She had asked him to promise before they got married that they would live there near her family. Nevertheless, there were times, as he watched the cop shows on television, that he projected himself into the roles of the super-cops, and imagined himself living a life of danger and excitement.

Burke pulled up in front of 734 Elm Street, a white two story colonial house with windows bordered with neat grey shutters. Burke had always liked the house. It was in a better section of town than where he and Marge and the kids lived, because Burke couldn't afford a house like that on his salary.

He rapped on the glass door with the white curtains, through which he could see the foyer and part of the living room. The furnishings were clearly a cut above the norm. Immediately, Sarah came from the back of the house and flung open the door. "Daniel!" She said. "What a surprise."

"Hi, Sarah, nice to see you, how are you?"

"Fine," he said. He leaned over and gave her a peck on the cheek. "How is Ed?"

"Ed is fine, also. Everybody's fine." Sarah suddenly registered concern. "Is something wrong, Daniel? Why are you here?"

"We have a report that somebody in this household is harboring a cache of illegal Indian artifacts, Ma'am, is this true?"

"Oh, you," she giggled. "You frightened me. You're here for that skull, aren't you?"

"Yes."

"Hold on, and I'll get it for you." Sarah hurried down the hallway to the kitchen in the rear of the house, the scent of cookies baking filled the air, and low music came from somewhere. Sarah returned with a brown paper bag containing the skull.

Burke removed it from the bag and examined it.

"The boys were playing in Bealer Woods when they came across it." She said. "It was mostly uncovered, sticking out of the dead leaves."

"No lower jaw?"

"No."

"Did they find anything else? —other bones, objects, clothing?"

"Nope, that's it."

"Okay, fine, but I'll need to speak to Bobby and the other kid. Would you mind asking them to come by the station after school this afternoon, if possible? Otherwise, Monday will be okay."

"I'll tell them."

"Thanks. Say, you and Ed and me and Marge, we have to get together, go out and do something, like we used to."

"Yes, it's been a long time."

⚊⧏⧐⚊

Back at the station, Burke removed the small skull from the paper sack. Dempsey sauntered over and they gave it a going over.

"Boy, that thing is old," Dempsey volunteered.

"Yeah."

"It's so small. A kid's skull, you think?"

"Looks that way, the boys found it on the surface, nothing else around."

"Old Indian skull, maybe?"

"Probably is," Burke replied, "but what was it doing on top of the ground like that, though?"

"Dogs dug it up somewhere nearby. Sure is pitted. I would say it has been in the ground an awful long time. It sure ain't no recently dear departed."

"You're probably right, Elmo. I asked Sarah to send the boys by after school. When they get here, we'll take a run out there and let them show us where they found it. Say, is there any fresh coffee?"

Bobby and Will, ten and nine years old respectively, came to the police station after school that afternoon and guided Burke and Dempsey to the place where they had found the skull. They went in Burke's unmarked police car. The boys rode in the back seat, enthralled by the radios and police paraphernalia. They pointed out the exact spot among the trees where they had found the skull. Burke and Dempsey turned about in all directions, studying the lay of the land. There was evidence of erosion at the site. A rotting tree, which had uprooted further up the shallow slope long before, had channeled the run-off water in such a way that it had contributed to the forming of a "v"-shaped ditch. It meandered through the trees and undergrowth all the way down to the river, some seventy yards away.

Dempsey picked up a stick and poked around, scraped away the rotting matt of leaves in several places revealing the bare earth beneath, looking for evidence of disturbed earth. Burke walked in a wide arc all around the site, studying the terrain for either indentations or mounds. Then the two men followed the ditch all the way to the river, but found nothing.

"I see what's happened," Burke said. "Erosion has washed the cover off of the skull so that animals could get to it. The rest of the skeleton should be around here somewhere."

"You think we ought to rope this area off, Boss?" Elmo asked, as they prepared to leave the site.

"No, not yet, that would only arouse curiosity if someone came across it. It's better we leave it just the way it is for now. You boys don't talk about this to your friends, okay?" Burke said, "We don't want people out here stomping around."

"Do you think somebody's been murdered?" Bobby asked.

"No, just old Indian bones, I imagine," Burke answered absently, although it did occur to him that no Indian graves had ever been found in that area to his knowledge. He could understand why. The riverbank was subject to periodic flooding.

After Bobby and Will had departed for home, Burke reported his findings to the chief. Newman sat behind his desk, and seemed to be uncharacteristically relaxed. A cigar smoldered in a large

amber glass ash tray on his mahogany desk. He was in his early six-
ties, although he looked a bit older than that. Burke always thought
Newman looked rather like a man who hadn't taken good care of
himself, with excess flab, a florid complexion, and a bulbous red
nose, from drinking too much bourbon, most likely. His hair was
thin and grey, with a bald spot at the crown.

"What have you got, Daniel?" the chief said, holding out his
hand for the paper bag containing the skull.

"A rather decrepit looking little skull."

The chief removed the skull and turned it over in his hands.
"Hmm, animals dug up an Indian grave, huh?"

"Could be. Elmo and I walked all over the site. We didn't find
anything else."

"Well, take it over to Professor Ripley at the College and let him
take a look at it to be sure."

"Okay, Chief. Do you have any objections if I get a couple of
boys from Public Works to go out there and do a little digging
around where the kids found it, though, see if we can find any
more bones?"

"No, I don't care, but be sure and let Ripley check out the skull,
and anything else you come up with."

⟨✦✦⟩

The Stanton Police Department was too small to have a well-
equipped and staffed crime lab. On those occasions when a matter
required complex lab services, they used the State Police Lab, and
in rare cases, sent evidence to the FBI lab in Washington. Though
Burke had never had occasion to do it himself, he knew that there
had been times over the years when the professors and their tech-
nical staffs at Stanton College had helped. The issue at hand
seemed to be right up their alley. The Archaeology Department
at the small liberal arts college was something of an anomaly, and

had come into existence because of its proximity to the Indian burial grounds. From what Burke had heard around the police station, they often called upon Dr. Robert Ripley whenever skeletal remains were involved in any kind of investigation.

Burke placed a call to Ripley, and the following morning, he, Burke and Dempsey, and two backhoe operators borrowed from the city's Public Works Department, converged at the Bealer Street site. Ripley instructed the men to begin digging concentrically outward, while Ripley and the detectives examined each shovel full of earth. After an hour or so, having found nothing, they started up the backhoe and dug to a radius of some twenty to 30 feet. It was slow work, because Ripley insisted on small cautious bites with the bucket. By mid-afternoon they had turned up a few additional bones, all found near the surface, and in no particular arrangement. Ripley examined the bones as they were found.

When they had dug enough to satisfy both Ripley and Burke that no other bones were to be found, the two workers filled in the holes, gathered up their tools, and departed, while the two detectives and the professor discussed the find.

"These are unquestionably the bones of a young child," Ripley said. The acid and moisture concentration are high here, so I can't begin to guess how old they really are. Best thing we can do is run tests at the lab."

"Good," Burke said. If they are old Indian bones it will save us a lot of time and trouble by not having to send them off to the Crime Lab. He took a bag from the trunk of his car, put all the bones in it, and handed it to Ripley.

"In the meantime," said Ripley, "I recommend you rope off the area until we know what we have here."

Burke took a roll of yellow tape used for police barriers out of the trunk. "Here, Elmo, you do the honors."

"How did it go today, Dear," Marge asked, when Burke came in. She had heard him drive up and met him at the door. He brushed a few strands of light reddish hair from her forehead and kissed her cheek.

"Fine," he said. "How was your day?"

"Uneventful."

"Are the kids home?"

"Yes, they're in the den watching TV, waiting for dinner."

"What are we having tonight, I'm starved?"

"Your favorite, roast beef and all the trimmings."

Burke smiled and patted his substantial stomach. Marge did everything she could to guide her husband to a better diet, but in the end he ate what he pleased.

⟨⟩

The following day, a story appeared in the Stanton Daily News, a small one-column item below the fold on page two. It read, "Skeleton of Child Found in Bealer Woods." Burke saw it when he unfolded the paper at the breakfast table. He frowned and emitted a mild expletive when he read it. Everyone turned to look at him. "What's wrong Dad? Sam said. "Something go down wrong?"

Burke managed a smile for his nine-year-old son, who, with his sandy hair, freckles and blue eyes, was the image of Marge. "No son, only something I read here in the Daily Rag."

"That's cool, Dad, the Daily Rag!" said Linda, who was two years older than Sam, and whose facial features were closer to her father's. "Why do you call it that?"

"Don't get your father started on that newspaper, sweetheart," Marge said. "What happened with the skull, dear?"

"That's what this article is about. Look at this." He held the newspaper up to each of them in turn so they could read the headline of the article. "See that?" he said. He read it aloud for effect.

'Skeleton of Child Found in Bealer Wood' I didn't put this in the paper. I didn't tell this reporter Barton about it."

Marge could see that Burke's face was a bit flushed. "Now, don't get yourself worked up about it. There's a reasonable explanation for it."

Burke glanced at the kids. They were still, interested, looked at him, waiting for the climax of the little drama.

"You're right," he said. "What's the big deal, anyway?" He resumed his breakfast, and everyone else did the same.

But, later, he charged into the office clutching the paper. "Elmo, did you talk to this damned reporter, Barton, about the bones?"

"Me? No! I haven't talked to anyone. Is there something in the paper?"

"Yeah"

"I haven't seen it yet. Where is it?"

"Right here," Burke grumbled, as he tossed the paper on Dempsey's desk. "I guess it's too much to ask that I be consulted around here."

Burke had made no particular effort to keep the matter secret. However, as the investigating officer, he was the one the press should have contacted for their story. "This headline is misleading, anyway," he said in disgust. "And that's typical of this stinking paper."

"Looks like they pretty much got the story right, though, Boss," Dempsey quipped.

"Don't make any damn difference," Burke said. But when he read through the whole story, he grudgingly acknowledged that it gave a fairly accurate account, noting that the remains were old, thought to be from an Indian burial site that had escaped previous notice, and that the remains had been turned over to the college for laboratory examination.

"Maybe it was Dr. Ripley, told him about it." Dempsey said.

"Why would he do that, a professional man like him? It was some smart ass here at City Hall, and I have a good idea who it was."

"Who?"

"Never mind," Burke said. He had in mind the man in the department with whom he had unknowingly competed for the Chief Detective job years ago, but he didn't want to acknowledge that to Dempsey. Everybody in the department knew of the rivalry, if not hubris, between the two men.

"You really believe someone here did that to irritate you?"

"Well, yeah. You find that so hard to believe?"

"I don't know. It could have been the backhoe guys. Did you tell them not to say anything about what we were doing?"

"No. They ought to know not to go blabbing to the press about a police investigation."

Dempsey shrugged and busied himself with papers on his desk, while Burke continued to fume.

That very afternoon, just as Burke had anticipated, calls began to come in about the bones, and they would continue for several days, mainly from out of town readers who were parents and other relatives of missing children, people who had not quite understood what they had read, or people who had heard about the article second hand.

"See what I mean?" Burke said.

"I guess you're right, Boss."

"Get the callers' information," Burke said, "Tell them we'll get back to them later when we know something. I'll do the same. Set up a folder."

"Roger, Boss," Dempsey said. He had been an airman first class in the Air Force, and he often worked a "Roger" or a "Wilco" into the conversation.

—❈—

Three days passed without notable incident, and Burke was busy at his desk with administrative work. A school break-in had occurred overnight, and Dempsey was out working the case. The phone rang. Burke answered it. The caller was Professor Ripley, reporting on the test results of the bones.

"It's our conclusion," Ripley said, "that the bones are those of a Caucasian child between three and five years of age at the time of death. We were unable to determine the sex of the child. The bones have been in the ground between twenty and forty years. I know that seems like a wide spread, but it is not possible with our facilities to be more precise than that."

"Twenty to forty years? That rules out the old Indian bones theory, "

"Looks that way."

"How about the cause of death?"

"No way to tell. There's no evidence of trauma to the skull. By the way, the other bones we found were a few rib fragments, a couple of vertebrae, and a piece of the left femur. Animals probably carried off the rest."

"Uh, huh, well, thanks for the help, Professor. I'll swing by and pick up the bones later."

"Your welcome. I'll have you a written copy of the test results when you come by. In case I'm not here, my secretary will have them. Call me anytime you need me, and keep me in the loop on this one, it might prove to be interesting."

"Will do," Burke said. He put down the receiver, wheeled his chair to the filing cabinet and removed the folder containing the names of the people who had called about missing children. He reviewed the notes, then called the person and explained why the skull could not be that of their missing child. While he was at it, he opened his personal address book, in which he kept the names and numbers of police officers from surrounding towns and began calling them. He couldn't finish in one setting, he knew, but he would keep it up in spare moments. When Dempsey returned to the office, Burke told him about Ripley's call, and asked him to go by the college for the bones and then have the technician in the evidence room get them off to the State Police Crime Lab. "I don't expect anything to come of it, but one never knows."

The following morning, before breakfast, Burke went outside for the paper as usual, and was startled when he opened it and saw another new item about the bones. It was a recap of the original story followed by a summary of Ripley's report. Burke experienced a sense of outrage. When he got to the office he charged into Newman's office "Chief, there's a new story in the paper this morning about the skull. I want to know who's running his mouth off to the newspaper without checking with me."

Newman was taken aback by Burke's agitated state. "Jesus, Daniel, I don't know. I thought you did it. It seemed like a good article to me. I thought you did it yourself."

"No, I didn't do it. Did you see my name mentioned? Did you see a quote from me? No, you didn't. I don't know who the joker is, for sure, but I have a pretty good idea, and I don't like it, Chief. It's one thing for someone who wants my job to take shots at me now and then, to try to make me look bad, but this is interfering with my duties. There's no justification for getting the towns-people stirred up over nothing. How am I supposed to conduct an investigation with this kind of crap going on behind my back?"

"Calm down, Daniel, calm down," Newman said. "I agree that someone is yanking your chain. You tell me who's doing it, give me some evidence, and I'll deal with them?"

Daniel strongly suspected the culprit was Marty Sullivan, his main rival for the detective job, and he strongly suspected that Newman knew this, or strongly suspected it himself. When anything in the least screwy happened to Burke, he automatically assumed Sullivan was behind it. Sullivan was the only other lieutenant in the department. He had been a sergeant back then, when he coveted the detective position. Soon after Burke was hired, they promoted Sullivan to lieutenant also, and put him in charge of the newly organized Operations Division. Burke figured it was a pay-off to keep him from raising a stink. It was common knowledge around City Hall that when Newman either died or retired, Sullivan was the man in line to succeed him, even though Burke technically had seniority, and would, theoretically, be entitled to first dibs on the job. Burke knew he didn't have a chance in hell of getting the job, and accepted the inevitability of that. After all, Sullivan was a political ally of Newman from the same local political faction.

"I'm sorry, Chief," Burke said. "I didn't mean to come in here and jump down your throat, it's just that things are getting to me lately." Newman seemed relieved at Burke's show of contrition. He looked him over for a few seconds. "When was your last vacation, Daniel? Maybe you need to take a couple of weeks off and go fishing. I ain't had a good mess of your catfish in a long time. You're not neglecting it, are you?"

"Funny you should mention that, Chief. I was just thinking the other day how I'd like to put my trotline out again, about a quarter-mile up Birch Creek, like I used to do every year. I caught some real fine cats on that trotline."

"Yes, I know you did—mighty good eating, as I remember, mighty fine."

"You know, maybe I'll do that, Chief, maybe I'll run up there Saturday and check things out."

"That sounds like a good idea to me. In the meantime, I'll put out a memo to the department, directing all personnel to run anything concerning your investigations by you first before anyone talks to the press, okay?"

"Okay, Chief, thanks."

Burke walked slowly down the hall toward his office, his shoulders slightly hunched. Tiny beads of perspiration glistened on his upper lip. As he passed the break room he glanced inside, realized he had not prepared his usual cup of coffee, yet, went in and did so. He was alone in the room. He sat down at the table, and grabbed up part of the newspaper, the sections of which were scattered on the table where other had left them. Absentmindedly, he reassembled the sections, then read the article on the bones on page one again. He had been so angry at breakfast he hardly remembered what he had read. The chief was right, it wasn't a bad article, really, it was just … not his article. Someone had stolen it from him. Whoever did it was getting his goat. He was playing into the SOB's hands. He took his coffee and walked wearily on to his office. Dempsey was at his desk, seemingly busy. He didn't look up as Burke entered.

Within the hour, Newman's secretary, Louise, came in and handed Burke a sheet of paper. She smiled briefly and said, "The chief said I should bring you your own, individual copy of this memo. I've put it up on all the bulletin boards."

When she left the room, Dempsey raised his head from his work. "In case you think I had something to do with that newspaper story, Boss, I didn't."

"Well, Elmo, it might surprise you to learn that I never suspected you."

The second newspaper story, which described the test results on the bones, caused a flurry of speculation all over the town, since it raised the possibility that a murder had been committed many years ago—the murder of a child, but nobody got much beyond that. Nobody could guess the identity of the victim, since nobody was missing. In a few days the excitement subsided, but it didn't go away entirely, it continued to simmer below the surface. Some people were clearly intrigued and suspicious, and looked askance at others, thinking back, trying to recall something they might have heard or seen at some earlier time. When asked about it, Burke replied that there was no evidence of any murder. He continued to fume and complain about the press releases, which tended to excite the public.

A week after his flare-up with the chief over the newspaper articles, Burke and Dempsey were in the office early. Burke had calmed down, and had pushed Sullivan's transgressions to the back of his mind. He was giving serious thought to the skull. It certainly had ignited the interest of the public. He shared that interest, though he expected nothing to come of it. How could anyone hope to solve the mystery of the bones after so long a time, with so little to go on, and with no one missing in the community?

"You know, Elmo," he said "It really gets to me, to think of that innocent child out there in the woods like that. No telling how long people been stepping over that skull there in those rotting leaves."

"Yeah, fascinating, ain't it?" Dempsey said.

"That's not my point. What kind of scum-bag would do something like that to a child? A toddler"

"There's a lot of bad people in the world."

"I been here over twelve years. I never heard of any kid going missing," Burke said.

"Me neither, and I been here all my life."

"Forty years is a long time. Lot of people come and go. Lot of transients, people off of barges, off the highway."

"Yeah." Dempsey said absently.

"You remember the Lindbergh baby?"

"No, I don't think I was born then." Dempsey said.

"I don't mean, did you remember it personally, I mean, you know about it."

"Yeah, I know about it. What about it?"

"Well, according to reports, the kidnappers killed the child and buried it right away, close to the Lindberg house. Projecting that line of reasoning to the present case, if the dead child was kidnapped, it probably was from somewhere nearby, since the kidnappers wouldn't risk hauling the child around for a long time or over long distances for fear of being caught. One would think that a file search of the regional police departments would turn up any kidnapped or missing children, even from that long ago."

"Uh, huh." Dempsey said. "You would think so.

"Yet we have received no information back from the cities and towns we called. What do you make of that, Elmo?"

"Every body's busy? I don't know."

Burke gave up on having a meaningful conversation with Dempsey, but he continued to mull over in his mind, the questions of the bones: *Was there a murder? Or was it a tragedy of another sort?* The questions excited his imagination, snagged him and pulled him in like one of his catfish caught on a dough-ball, and motivated him to want to solve the mystery. This could be what he had been yearning for, something to get his teeth into. He could get Dempsey involved, too. They could work on it together, and maybe even establish a proper working relationship.

He glanced over at Dempsey, who was bending over his desk, doing the paperwork on a burglary he had investigated down at the bakery. Burke had always told Dempsey what he wanted him to do, then exercised a minimum of supervision, and that seemed to work out reasonably well. Dempsey, he had always figured, was part of his curse—to have to make a living in a small, political town, where a man's prospects were so limited. But now, he was considering involving him, seriously asking him his opinion.

"Elmo?"

"Yeah, Boss."

"I'm still thinking about the bones. It occurs to me that we are kind of stuck in the middle, here. On the one hand, if the bones were very old, the issue would be closed. There'd be nothing to do, because we would assume they were old Indian bones. On the other hand, if they were fresh, we would treat it as a probable crime, and go out and try to solve the crime. But the way it is, being as how the bones are twenty to forty years old, and the fact that we got nobody missing around here, and from no place nearby, apparently, it kind of puts us in a no-man's land. See what I mean?"

Dempsey put down his pen, clasped his hands in front of him on the desk, and stared at Burke for fifteen or twenty seconds before he answered. "Not yet, Boss, keep talking," he said.

"Well, what is our obligation, here? That's my first question. We don't know that a crime has been committed. I doubt that anyone, including Newman, would fault us if we put the matter in the dead case file. We've notified the State Police and other law enforcement authorities around about. Maybe we ought to leave it at that, unless something turns up. What's your opinion?"

A quizzical expression came over Dempsey's face, a mixture of surprise and amusement. He hesitated, and then said, "Hell, Boss, I think we ought to solve it. We should dig into it a little more. Trouble is, like you say, I don't know what we could do that would likely get us anywhere, other than what we've done already. I guess bottom line, I don't expect much to come of it, either, but it wouldn't hurt to try."

"Yeah? Well, I have to agree with you there, Elmo. We could take a stab at it in our spare time. I mean, it's not like there is some urgency. We'll have to work around our routine duties. Who knows? We might get lucky and solve the damn thing."

"What does the chief think about it?"

"I know he's been getting a lot of inquiries. He awful sensitive to the public, as you know. I'll talk to him about it."

Dempsey went back to his paperwork, and Burke continued thinking about it, out loud, more or less. "The first thing we need to do is research the old files here at City Hall, and the second thing is to research the archives at the newspaper office. They have microfiche records over there of old editions."

"Do they?"

"Yeah. You should know that, you been here all your life."

"Do they go back forty years?"

"Now, that I don't know. I don't even know how long that paper has been in existence.

"It's been here as long as I can remember."

"Yeah, and you've been here all your life, haven't you?"

"That's right, I'm a native."

"And you're, uh…what, thirty-one, thirty-two?"

"Yeah."

"Yeah, what?"

Dempsey glanced up at him quizzically. "Yeah, Sir?"

"No, no, Elmo, which is it, thirty-one, or thirty-two?"

"Oh. I just turned thirty-one."

Buck continued to glare at Dempsey, incredulously, for several moments after Dempsey went back to working on his report. Burke sighed, shook his head slightly, and said, "I'll talk it over with the chief, Elmo, and we'll see what happens."

CHAPTER 2
CHIEF DETECTIVE BURKE

Unlike Elmo Dempsey, Daniel Burke was not native to the town of Stanton, he was originally from Pontiac, Michigan, where his father had spent his entire working life on an auto assembly line. Burke might have followed his father's example had he not gone into the Marine Corps right after high school, and had he not met and befriended a Marine in his unit named Chris Schilling, who often spoke fondly of his home town on the Ohio River. Schilling's father owned a bar there, he said, right on the riverbank. Schilling told Burke appealing stories of his home town, small and quiet, but near enough to larger cities if one had a yen for excitement, and how it was noted for its hunting, fishing and boating on the Ohio. The town also had a small college, and Schilling told Burke that he planned to attend college there on the GI bill when he got out of the service.

When Burke completed his military obligation in 1970, he spent a few weeks at home in Pontiac with his parents, mulling over what he had been through and what he wanted to do. What he needed was a job. The idea of a job on an assembly line did not appeal to him. In fact, nothing that he imagined as being readily available to him appealed to him, and he, too, considered college on the

GI Bill. Then Chris Schilling wrote him a letter inviting him for a visit. Burke was eager to look over the town on the river, and the college, and consider whether he was cut out for college life. While there, however, he met and became enamored of a young woman named Margie Belden, who, although four years his junior, was already in her third year at Stanton College.

Burke never really left Stanton after he met Margie: he briefly returned to Michigan to get his things and to tell his parents of his plans to attend Stanton College.

Over the next year, the ensuing intense courtship came as a shock to Margie's parents, Samuel and Penny Belden. In fact, they were alarmed and angry that this audacious young Marine veteran, this nobody, this freshman (when Marge was already in her senior year), had stormed into town and swept their only daughter off her feet. They had hopes and plans for their daughter, plans now tromped upon, pushed aside, like the storming of an enemy position. When the subject of marriage came up, Margie's parents, with as much civility as they could muster, urged the young people to wait, not to act hastily. They said the usual things to their daughter which parents say in such a crisis, that she didn't know what she was getting into, that she should wait until Daniel finished his education, that she should get her teaching credentials as she had planned to do since she was a little girl.

Naturally, she didn't listen, and neither did he. They eloped, thus alienating the father more, and disappointing the mother and friends, who would otherwise have looked forward to a formal wedding, with all the excitement and trimmings.

The Beldens were well-to-do by the standards of the community, and clearly were offended and humiliated by what they must have considered an act of cruelty and indifference to their feelings, and their standing within the community, especially when they had to explain the situation to their friends. There was some quiet speculation that it was a "shotgun" wedding, which no amount of

disclaimer could dispel. Marge's pregnancy soon thereafter forti-
fied the speculation.

Three years later, in 1973, when Burke was in the second semester of his junior year, and Margie was eight months pregnant
with their second child, and working part time as a teacher's aide
at the elementary school, they slowly and painfully come to the
realization that they could no longer make it on the GI Bill and
their part-time jobs. Pride kept him from accepting the proffered
subsidy from Marge's parents, so Burke decided there was nothing
to do but drop out of school and get a full-time job. It would only
be for a semester or two, he thought, and then he would go back
and finish up. After depressing weeks of looking for work, Burke
applied for a job on the city police force, and they granted him an
interview. He had no expectation of success, but to his surprise,
the city offered him the job. He would fill a vacancy created by the
retirement of the department's detective, the only one the town
had ever had. Even though he lacked police experience, they said
his military experience and college had strongly influenced their
decision. He found out soon afterwards, however, that other men
had wanted the job (there are always others who want the job—no
matter what it is), and because of that, and the obviously political
nature of government, people assumed that favoritism had come
into play on his behalf. Consequently, he had a rough time with
the little city's bureaucracy in the beginning. Oh, nobody had the
balls to come right out and give him a really bad time, but they
had their ways of making him uncomfortable. He never said anything to Margie about it, nor complained to anyone, with the ex-
ception of his friend Chris Schilling. Schilling knew all his secrets.
However, Burke felt bad about the situation in general, and felt
that he had somehow let Marge down.

Not long into his tenure with the city, Burke started to suspect, based on comments and insinuations, primarily from
Marty Sullivan, that Marge's father, Samuel Belden, a prominent

attorney in the town, had intervened on Burke's behalf to get him the job on the Police Force. Burke became angry and incensed at what he believed were malicious lies from the man whom he had beat out for the job, and invited Sullivan out to the parking lot to sample Burke's expertise in hand-to-hand combat. Sullivan wisely declined. However, after that, Sullivan kept his mouth shut around Burke.

Even so, Burke came to believe that what Sullivan had said about Belden's role in his hiring was true, even though he could not prove it. Burke was embarrassed by the prospect and a little ashamed, but he never allowed himself to dwell on it. He had his family to think about. He wasn't going to ask anybody about it, either, to find out if it really was true—certainly not Belden.

His new job was nothing to sneeze at, especially for a new man in town in desperate need of employment. He was a police officer and not just a lowly patrolman either, but a detective. No starting at the bottom of the stack for the son-in-law of Samuel Belden, even if the son-in-law had no experience, or knew nothing about the job. As to Belden, if he had wanted Burke to know about his efforts, he would have told him, or, better still, he would have asked him first. He was sure Marge knew nothing of it. It probably wouldn't occur to her, she was such a sweet and trusting soul. But Burke's relationship with his in-laws after that was politely frigid.

It made perfect sense that Belden had a hand in it for the sake of his daughter and grandchildren. Burke finally came to realize, that without the influence of his honcho father-in-law, he would have been lucky to get a city job as a meter reader or as a grunt in the street department. He would have taken such a job if that was all that was available, he was that desperate for work at the time. And if Belden did it, people at some level within city government would know about it. That would explain the hostility directed at him by certain individuals within city government, the reason being that Belden and the Chief of Police were from opposing political factions.

It was all very ironic: he could have gone to Columbus, Cincinnati, or Wheeling and gotten a better paying job. But Marge made him promise before they were married that they would make their home in Stanton, so that she and their children could be near her parents, and so that they could live in a nice, pleasant community, rather than in a busy, dirty, crime-infested city. He had agreed. So, he was a cop in a small town. But if you intend to live in a small town, being a cop is a fairly prestigious position, one of responsibility and trust. *Why wasn't he grateful? Why wasn't he happy with it?*

The thing that puzzled Burke most about it was how Belden got Newman to hire him in the first place, considering that they were political adversaries. Burke knew that he owed Belden something for that, owed him a little respect, maybe, but that sentiment was chilled right out of Burke's bones by the first real run-in he had with Belden.

It was about a year into his tenure with the city. He, Marge and Linda had gone to the Belden house for Sunday dinner, and the old man called him into his study, and lit right into him, without preliminaries.

"Daniel, I have received some disturbing news about you. I've been told you have a police record up there in Pontiac, Michigan, and, further, that your decision to enter the Marine Corps when you did, right after high school, was not entirely your own idea, that you were helped along in your decision by a judge of the Municipal Court."

An icy chill traveled up Burke's spine and enveloped him. He was speechless. A cool rage gripped him, a feeling of intrusion, violation."

"Well," the old man continued. "Is there any truth to this?"

"Where did you get that?"

"Never mind that, please answer my question."

"To hell with you, mister," Burke growled, as he rose from his chair and moved quickly toward the door.

"Wait!" Belden shouted.

Burke froze with his hand on the knob.

"Look, son," Belden's manner softened, "I'm sorry I came at you like that. I've been thinking about this for a few days, working myself up, I guess. I'm only looking out for my daughter and her child—your child—trying to, anyway. Please come back and sit down. Let's talk about this."

Burke hesitated, and then said. "It was teenager stuff, pranks and mischief. I was underage...that file was sealed." He opened the door to leave."

Belden rushed over and grabbed him by the arm. "Please, please...don't upset the women folk. Let's keep this between us. Come back and sit down."

Burke gave in and sat down again with his teeth clenched, staring into Belden's eyes."

"Somebody down at City Hall is spreading this stuff about you. Someone doesn't like you, it appears."

"Do you know who?"

"I don't know who started it," Belden said. "It doesn't matter now. Whatever they were up to, I've quelled it."

"You've quelled it?" Burke said, incredulously. "How did you quell it?"

"That doesn't matter. It wouldn't hurt you, Daniel, to try to be a little friendlier with the people down there, your coworkers. Try to make a few friends. Learn how to get along with them."

"Play ball, you mean. That'll be the day. I'm not for sale, Mr. Belden."

"Nobody is suggesting you are, Daniel. Try, that's all. Try to get along, for all our sakes. Will you do that? That's not an unreasonable request, is it?"

Even though Burke considered the charges leveled against him by some anonymous detractor to be baseless and unfair, he did try harder in the weeks that followed, and, things did get better, for a while. Belden had practically admitted that he had gotten Burke his job, so even though that knowledge was actually painful to Burke, he swallowed his pride and tried to show gratitude without actually saying anything. He forced himself to be friendlier to the Beldens. They did many generous things for the family. However, each one cut another chunk out of Burke's manhood, whether it should have or not.

Two more years passed, and Burke grew progressively more resentful of what he considered Belden's interference with his family. He got up his nerve to talk to Belden about it during one of their Sunday visit. Burke and Belden went into the study, and Burke, with characteristic candor, got right to the point. "Look, Mr. Belden, I know I'm a disappointment to you, and you can't see what your daughter could possibly have seen in me. Am I right?"

Belden registered surprise, which quickly transitioned to a wry smile. "Well, Daniel, since you put it like that, yes, that pretty much sums it up. I haven't tried to keep it a secret from you. You are a disappointment to me. But it's not because you come from humble origins and have few prospects, as you probably think, and it's not just that you got my only daughter pregnant and felt you had to marry her." His voice raised an octave when he said that. "I respect you in spite of that, because I'm convinced you love her. And it's not that you've showed no gratitude that I got you your job at City Hall, where, by the way, you have yet to distinguish yourself. No, it's not for any of those things."

"So you did get me the job?"

"That's right. That was a hard one to figure out, wasn't it?"

"Well, since you're at it, why don't you mention the down payment on our house you put up," snarled Burke bitterly, and the Country Club membership, and the clothes and stuff you and Penny have been lavishing on my wife and child. My wife and child! Not yours! How do you think that makes me feel?"

"Whatever it is, Daniel, it's not gratitude."

That one got to Burke. He clenched his fists and turned a deep shade of red. "If you weren't my wife's father—

"If I wasn't your wife's father you wouldn't do a damned thing, and you know it. You're a whipped dog, boy, that's all you are. Any time you want to step outside, you just let me know."

The old man rose from his chair then, rather wobbly, and stood there unsteadily for a moment, then slumped back in the chair. His seemingly weak condition caught Burke off balance. He didn't know what to make of it. He had never seen Samuel Belden display any weakness, or any frailty at all. "What's the matter Mr. Belden, are you sick?

"It's nothing."

"It's not nothing. You look sick to me."

"Thanks you for your concern," Belden said grudgingly. "It's nothing, really, I'm just coming down with something—the flu, probably."

Neither of them spoke for a minute. Burke was chewing on what his father-in-law had said.

"I don't understand you," Burke said. Why do you disrespect me so much?"

"I can respect a man who takes his turn at bat, even if he strikes out, but I can't respect a man who won't step up to the plate."

Once again, Burke struggled to understand what the old man was jabbering about. *Won't step up to the plate? What the hell does that mean? Have I failed to meet some obligation? What is he talking about?*

Belden turned back to his desk. "Now, Daniel, if you don't mind, I have things to do. Why don't you go on out and rejoin the rest of the family? I would appreciate it if you would not trouble my daughter—your wife—or my wife with our issues. Whatever they are, they are between you and me. Agreed?"

Burke gave a grudging noncommittal wave of the hand and stomped in exasperation out of the study. He was smoldering with offence, too much for him to ask Belden to elaborate on his statement, to explain what he meant. He had not achieved his objective of persuading Belden to leave his family alone and allow him to care for his own. Belden had skillfully managed to defuse him, and turn the tables on him.

For the rest of the day Burke continued to mull it all over in his mind. It was easy, he reasoned, resentfully, for a man like Belden to criticize him. Belden had it all given to him. His family money went back generations to the time of the big lumber crunch during and after the Civil war. That was when a handful of exploiters had denuded the hills of their timber. They had slashed, profited, and moved on to the next hill. There was no such thing as environmental protection then, there were no tree replanting programs to replenish the forest. He had heard the stories.

That's how the town of Stanton had begun. It was because of its location at the mouth of Birch Creek. The logs were floated down from the hills, sawed into rough lumber there, and then stacked on barges and floated down the Ohio River to the big, growing cities.

So Belden, to Burke's way of thinking, was little more than the spawn of robber barons. He would not permit Belden to tell him anything about responsibility. He had done his time in Vietnam. He had won the Bronze Star for bravery under fire, he had the Purple Heart. Did Belden know that? Burke had never told him.

Nevertheless, he honored Belden's request and never mentioned his conversations with her father to Marge. But knowing how Belden felt about him chilled family relations for him even more, so that over time he participated less and less in family activities involving Marge's parents, and was never at ease around them. He seldom went to the country club, and only grudgingly, about once a month, accompanied the family to a Sunday dinner at their house.

⇥⇤

Back to the present, with Burke sitting in the office, following his not so inspiring conversation with Dempsey about making a project out of solving the mystery of the bones, Burke picked up the phone and dialed the chief's office to see if he was in. He was, so Burke went to talk it over with him.

"Come on in, Daniel, what's up?"

"I want to talk about the bones, Chief, get your ideas about what we should do with the situation."

"Have you come up with anything new?"

"No. We sent everything off to the crime lab, and I called the police departments of the surrounding town and got them to looking for missing children, but that's about it. I'm aware there's an awful lot of public interest and curiosity out there, so how do you want to play it?"

"What do you think?"

"I think it would be a good idea for me and Elmo both to put in a good effort as our time will permit."

"How do you propose to go about it?"

"I thought we would start with the old police records down in the basement, and the newspaper archives, and look for any kind of suspicious events or comings and goings back there in that time-frame. I know it's not much, but it's a beginning. You have any ideas?"

Newman thought about it. "I don't recollect a damn thing, myself, and I've lived here all my life. There are a few old-timers around here who would know more about that time than anybody else. Wouldn't hurt for you to talk to some of them. I'll make you a list. The first one that I think of is old man Potter, Boyd Potter. You know him don't you? He's out at the nursing home now."

"I know the name. I certainly would appreciate that list, Chief, and I'll go out there and see Mr. Potter right away."

"Yes, Daniel, I think that's a good idea. You go ahead with it. Keep me advised of everything, and try to get along with the newspaper reporters."

"Yes, Sir. Thank you Chief." Burke rose from his chair and left the office. On the way down the hall, as he passed the break room, he saw Marty Sullivan sitting at the table alone, reading the paper, a half-full cup of coffee on the table before him. Burke couldn't resist. He went in and stood gazing hostilely at Sullivan, whose face was concealed behind the spread newspaper which he was holding up in front of him. Burke stood that way for half a minute, until Sullivan apparently sensed his presence, and put down the paper. "Well, something on your mind, Burke?"

"Yeah, you're on my mind, Sullivan. You know that offer I made years ago, about you and me stepping out to the parking lot? Well, that offer still stands."

Sullivan said nothing, went back to his paper, and Burke turned and strode out of the room, and back to his office where Dempsey sat with his legs stretched out and with his hands clasped behind his head, staring vacuously up at the ceiling, as if in deep thought. He put his hands down and turned toward Burke as he entered, and said, "Well, what did the chief say?"

"He said to go ahead and do it. Just keep him advised."

"Okay, so what do you want me to do first, then, specifically?"

"Why don't you take on the newspaper office, and I'll tackle the old city files? Just work it in between things whenever you can. We'll get together once a week or so and talk over what we're doing."

"Sounds like a plan," Dempsey quipped.

"Keep an open mind, now, Elmo," Burke admonished. "It may not be something obvious. It may be something totally unexpected."

"Like what?"

"I don't know. That's why it would be totally unexpected, maybe stories of family troubles, people moving away suddenly. There must be a dozen things that would catch one's eye. You know what I mean?"

"Yeah, I think so."

"All right, then."

⊶ ⊷

Burke postponed his planned examination of the old police files for a few more days to interview the people on the chief's short list of names starting with Boyd Potter. He asked Marge that evening at dinner if she knew him.

"Old man Potter? Sure, everybody knows Mr. Potter."

"How is it that you know him, exactly? He was already an old man when you were a kid."

"Yes, he has to be in his mid-eighties. All of us kids knew the Potters. He had that big farm on the edge of town. You know where it is. The Bradfords own it now. We used to go there as guests of Wendell Potter, Mr. Potter's grandson. I went to school with Wendell."

"I see. I'm going out to the nursing home to talk to him about missing children, to see if he remembers anything. According to the chief, if anybody knows anything around here, it ought to be him."

"I asked Mom and Dad about that, if they had any recollection of a missing child."

"What did they say?"

"They didn't remember anything."

"Let me tell you what I heard," Linda began, "about these people that used to live in the west end, this trashy bunch—

"Uh, oh, here we go." Sam said.

"Sam, let your sister talk."

"Okay, sorry."

"All right, children, be nice."

The children were nice. If Burke had legitimate cause for his discontent, it was not the fault of his family. He knew this profoundly. He was still in love with his wife, and he believed she was still in love with him. His two children were nice kids, for lack of a better description, and the joy of his existence. They were good students, happy and adjusted, and doted on by their grandparents, just as Marge had anticipated. Burke tried not to say or do anything in their presence which his family would pick up on of a disparaging nature, especially concerning their grandparents. He carried it all inside him.

Burke made an appointment to see Mr. Potter at the Green Hills Rest Home. When he arrived there, he was directed to a table by the pool. While he waited, Burke studied the surroundings. The place was clean and well-maintained The large swimming pool was roped off into three sections. A half-dozen old people with sagging body parts walked back and forth from one end of the pool to the other in the shallow section, the water up to their waists. Most wore brimmed or billed white hats and sunglasses, and some had zinc ointment on their noses for protection from the sun. Swimming lanes ran on the other side of a blue and white rope, supported on the surface by grapefruit-size floats. A lone swimmer with a deep tan, gray hair, and tiny eye-goggles, steadily and strongly did the Australian Crawl—obviously one of those serious swimmers who can do fifty laps, Burke mused. They know how to pace themselves. He could never do that. He would go too fast, too early, and burn himself out.

Background music played from strategically placed speakers: A young Mary Martin, backed up by a perky group, sang, "...I'm in love with a wonderful guy...."

"Detective Burke?"

Burke turned to see an ancient, stooped gentlemen, seemingly all bones and parchment, dressed in swim trunks, a loose fitting, open terrycloth robe, and clogs, carrying a tall glass in his hand. Burke leapt up as the man approached. The man extended his hand, and said, "I'm Boyd Potter." He motioned Burke to sit and he sat opposite him. "Something to drink, Detective Burke?" he asked. "I'm having iced tea."

"I'll have the same."

The man summoned to a male attendant dressed in white slacks and short-sleeved shirt to take the order.

"I don't think we've met before, Detective Burke, but I've heard of you. You married Sam Belden's daughter, didn't you?"

"That's right."

"Yes, Margie is a real sweet girl, used to come to the farm with my grandson."

"Yes, she mentioned that when I told her I was coming to see you."

"You have children, too, don't you? I apologize … my memory, you know."

"Yes, two. Sam is ten—we named him after Mr. Belden—and Linda is eleven."

"That's wonderful. You're a very fortunate man, Mr. Burke, I hope you realize that. Now, Sir, what can I do for you?"

Burke explained his mission, while Potter listened intently, looked him in the eyes, nodded frequently to show his interest and understanding. Burke completed his remarks as his tea was brought to the table.

"I read about the skull in the paper, of course," Potter said, "and I've thought about it quite a bit since then, and since you called, but I'm afraid I'm not going to be any help to you."

"I am disappointed. Chief Newman said you were my best bet."

The old man took a sip from his tea. "It occurs to me," he continued, "as I'm sure it has to you, that this dead child was most likely brought in from someplace else. In my opinion, you need to broaden your search. I'm sure you have inquired of the State Police and the FBI."

"Yes, I have. They would have records if they know about it. I have also contacted the police departments in nearby towns. So far, I haven't gotten anything back from anyone."

"What do you mean when you say, 'if they know about it'?"

"People disappear, or are murdered, and the authorities may never know. It is partly due, I think, to the mobility of the population, people moving back and forth across the country. Five people leave point a, and four arrive at point b, you know what I mean? People could be dead for years without the right people missing them. Neighborhoods are not what they used to be."

"I see what you mean. You know, when I was a kid, people often lived their whole lives and didn't even venture more than a few dozen miles from home. It sure isn't that way anymore."

"You have certainly lived through some mighty profound changes," Burke said.

The old man's face took on a wistfulness, his eyes staring sightlessly at some phantom remembrance from his long past. "I was born in 1897," he said, pausing momentarily, then pulled himself back to the present with a start, and a guilty little smile, as if nostalgia were a sin, and he had been caught. "I don't get around much anymore. I have to stay close to my doctors. When I had my business in Stanton, I was involved in everything, and knew people from all over the state and the region. I still maintain contact with many of them. If you like, I could call around and ask about missing children from three or four decades ago. You never know what might turn up."

"It couldn't hurt. I would appreciate that very much, Mr. Potter."

"Not at all. If I learn anything I'll give you a call."

"Thank you. Now I'll let you get back to your swim," Burke said, as he rose from the chair, and extended his hand to the old man. "I hope I haven't messed up your schedule too much."

"Not in the least. I swim every day; it keeps me limber. Say hello to that sweet wife of yours for me, will you, and the children too. Come by and see me again. Bring your swimming trunks next time."

"Good day, sir."

<hr />

Burke often took his lunch at Schilling's Bar and Lounge with his friend Chris Schilling. He was there having lunch the Monday following the interview with Mr. Potter. The half dozen names Newman had given him had turned up no additional leads.

"You still parking in the garage?" Schilling asked. He was refer-ring to the three story parking garage three door down.

"Yeah, old habits die hard," Burke answered, grinning, re-membering how the two of them had parked in the garage and taken the "nice" girls they were dating in the back way and up the stairs to their rooms on the third floor of the building, rooms which Chris' father, August Schilling, had made available to them when they were in college, and which they had fixed up and furnished nicely.

"I park there so the stuffed shirts down at City Hall won't know I'm hanging around the bar with you, since they consider you to be a bit on the shady side," Burke said with a grin.

"You're smiling, like you're making a joke, but you really mean that, don't you, Corporeal?"

"Don't start pulling rank on me, now, Sergeant. You know I wouldn't think anything like that."

Burke's favorite lunch was an open-faced roast beef sandwich, on rye, with mashed potatoes and brown gravy, and a side order of green beans or some other green vegetable, followed by apple pie with vanilla ice cream. The meal not only superbly satisfied his palette, it was also hot and quick, and in a man-sized quantity. Today, as he often did, Chris Schilling sat across from him while he wolfed down his roast beef. He was having a BLT and coffee.

"You seem a little out of sort today, sport, is anything wrong?" Schilling asked, as he studied his old friend's body language.

"I'm okay."

"Everything all right at home? You and Margie getting along okay?"

"What are you getting at?"

"Nothing. Don't get sore. I was only asking."

"It's city government," Burke said wearily, "I don't know how much more of it I can stand."

"What is it now?"

"Nothing new, nothing I can put my finger on. I used to shake it off, but it's getting harder and harder for me to do. I don't know what's wrong with me."

"You're out of shape, pal, that's all. You're letting yourself go. Look at you, how much do you weigh now?"

"Hey, I can take my lunch business somewhere else."

"I'm happy to have your business, pal, but you're sitting there right now putting on another ten pounds. When you are not eating these hefty, delicious, calorie-laden lunches of mine, you've got your paws in the boiled eggs and pickled pig's feet jars at the bar."

"Don't start on me. That's Marge's department."

"No, seriously, how much exercise do you get."

Burke sighed, and pushed his not-quite-empty plate away (he had not yet sopped up the last traces of the dark, rich gravy from his plate with the last crusts of bread). He smiled at his long-time friend, the only one he would allow to talk to him like that. "Not nearly enough, not nearly enough. However, it is rather simple-minded of you to think that is what is bothering me. Give me a beer, will you?"

"Aren't you still on duty, Detective?"

"Yeah, get off my ass and get me a beer."

Schilling got up and got him a draft beer.

"You know, Chris, it's frustration, that's all. Nothing more exotic than that."

"Okay, my friend. So, what's happening with your skull investigation?"

"Well, since I have no expectation of success, the fact that I seem to be getting nowhere doesn't bother me in the least. I've just finished interviewing old timers, people who have lived around here a long time, to see if they remember anything. That was the chief's idea."

"The chief is supporting you in this effort?"

"Yeah, how about that? I talked to old man Potter first. He didn't know anything, but he offered to use some of his connections around the state to make some inquiries."

"Anything going to come of it, you think?"

"I don't know. It's something to do. I even have Dempsey over at the newspaper office researching old editions on their microfiche. Me, I am starting to go through old police files in the basement of city hall. In fact, that's what I'll be doing this afternoon."

Chris sipped his coffee while Burke finished off his apple pie and ice cream, then Burke stretched, scratched his belly, and said, "Well, I got to be on my way. I'll see you at poker on Thursday."

"Yeah, okay. Don't let those bastards get to you down there at City Hall."

Back at the station, Burke dug into the files with something akin to enthusiasm. Current records were on the city's new mid-frame computer. The older ones that had not been lost or purged were in long cardboard boxes in a dusty room in the basement. Burke examined the labels on the boxes, selected one and carried it to a wooden table under the glare of stark florescent lights.

Neither his nor Elmo's efforts turned up anything useful. Their activities, however, aroused the interest of the newspaper staff, who wondered what Dempsey was doing there, searching through their microfiche files. Burke received a call from Jake Barton, the reporter, who had covered the first two stories of the bones, who wanted to come by the office to talk with him.

"About what?" Burke asked.

"I'd rather discuss it in person, if it's all the same to you, Detective. I can be there in five minutes."

Barton seldom came to him for anything, as evidenced by the two articles about the bones. In the beginning, when Burke first came on the force, Newman wanted all matters to do with the press referred to him. He allowed as how there was only one official voice of the Police Department, and that was him, unless he said otherwise. However, the chief had become trapped between two of his pet considerations: on the one hand, he was in control, and he wanted everyone to know it. On the other hand, he had come to value his peace and quiet. Consequently, he gradually relegated such matters to his subordinates, including Burke, even though Burke was not of his "faction." Burke had known then that he was on safe footing in dealing with the press if he didn't say anything which would embarrass the chief, the mayor, the city council, or the city in general. Even so, Burke and Barton had not hit it off, and the less contact Burke had with him the better. It was particularly galling to him, when he was in charge of an investigation, to have a reporter go around him and get his information from an "unidentified source" within the department. That was what had just happened to him, twice. He figured the only reason Barton was calling him now, was that his usual source had dried up after the chief published that departmental memorandum.

"All right, if you come right now."

Barton arrived six minutes later.

"Hello, Jake, have a seat," Burke said. "What can I do for you?"

"Thanks for seeing me, Detective Burke. I'm doing a follow-up on the skull," Barton said. "I was hoping you could bring me up to speed on that case?"

"Hey, I could have told you over the phone, there's nothing new to tell you. Besides, why are you asking me? Why aren't you asking your snoop here in the Department?" Burke blurted it out in spite of his intention to restrain himself.

"Oh, so that's it, huh?"

"That's what?"

"Your hostility to me and to the paper. Look, I'm doing my job, same as you. I've been covering this beat since before you were even here. I have friends and sources all over town, some who might even surprise you. Look, I don't want to fight with you. If you don't want to talk to me, I'll go to Newman. Maybe he will talk to me."

"I have already told you, there's nothing to tell you about the damn bones, there never was, really. However, your paper managed to blow the story up and distort it, and get people riled up over nothing. That's why I don't want to talk to you. You people never get anything quite right, even when you try, which in my opinion is not often. You are irresponsible, interested only in the buck, in selling papers."

Barton ignored Burke's tirade, and responded only to the "there's nothing to tell" part.

"That's not what I heard, I heard you're digging through old police files, and researching the newspaper archives. What are you looking for? It's been suggested there may be a cover-up going on over here—a conspiracy. What's do you say to that?" Barton held his pad and pencil poised on his thigh as if he were about to record the scoop of the century.

"What? Why that's ridiculous, even for a dumb ass little rag like yours. What possible conspiracy could there be?"

"That's what I intend to find out."

"Who suggested a cover-up?"

"That is privileged and confidential information."

"Oh, I see, an unidentified source that preferred to remain anonymous. Isn't that the way you say it?"

Barton rose and walked out of the office.

Burke called after him: "I'd be careful what I wrote if I were you."

No sooner had Barton left than Burke began to feel remorseful about how he had behaved. The reporter was doing his job, as he had said, even if the way he did it didn't please Burke. He sat with his thoughts for a while, looking out beyond the parking lot to the little park where children were playing. Presently, he got up and went down the hall to the chief's office and rapped on the doorframe. The chief was at his desk, fumbling with papers. He looked up at Burke. "Yes, Daniel? What is it?"

"I stopped by to tell you that I just had a little row with that reporter from the paper. I expect somebody will be calling you."

"Already have."

"Look, Chief, I..."

"Don't sweat it, Daniel, just take care of it. You guys sort it out. Okay?"

"Okay," Burke said with a surge of gratitude.

⚊╫╫⚊

Now that Burke and Dempsey were working harder than usual, probing into the issue of the bones, a few of the other police officers took an interest in the search, and stopped by Burke's office for updates. Burke had nothing to report. He was not certain whether they were serious, or if they were having sport at his expense. He suspected the latter. One patrol officer observed to another as they walked away from the doorway, that he hadn't seen that much energy expended by the detective squad in years. Burke thought he heard a chuckle. But no matter, Burke was busy at the moment expanding the investigation throughout Ohio, and across the river into Kentucky and West Virginia. He and Dempsey were writing letters and making phone calls. They also sent a request directly to the records section of the State Police in Columbus, asking them to initiate a search of their records similar to their local effort. They enclosed photographs, diagrams, a map of the location where they found the bones, and test results from the college.

"What do you think, Elmo? Are we spinning our wheels?"

"I don't intend to hold my breath."

Columbus acknowledged the letter about ten days later. The acknowledgment gave no commitment as to when they would initiate the search, since the bones were so old, and they had more current and pressing matters. It only indicated a willingness to have a go at it, when time and resources permitted. Clearly, the matter was not given any kind of priority.

⚊╫╫⚊

Weeks passed without further word from Columbus, and nothing came in from neighboring police departments. The stories in the newspaper dwindled to an occasional brief reference to the skull and then finally stopped altogether. Burke returned the skull to the evidence room, and his thoughts turned to more pleasant things. It was summer, and Burke still had not put his fishing boat in the water.

Burke's fishing boat was an eighteen-footer, a flat bottom aluminum craft with a sixty-horse outboard motor. It was in every sense a fisherman's boat, with folding seats, storage boxes, non-skid vinyl covered floorboards, built in bow fuel tank, bilge pump, fish boxes—the list went on-and-on. The boat was his one and only extravagance, and he had been neglecting it because of his pre-occupation with the bones. The weekend after he put the skull back in the evidence room, Burke and Sam pulled the boat from under the shed behind their detached two-car garage and parked it in the drive where they proceeded to give it a real going over. They took everything off the boat, including the motor. The two of them wrestled the heavy and awkward motor onto a fifty-five-gallon drum filled with water, where it could be test run with the prop removed.

Linda pitched in and they all gave the boat a long, sudsy wash followed by a coat of wax. Then they oiled every moving part. After lunch, Sam helped his father reinstall the motor onto the boat, and then he quit helping to attend to his own affairs. Burke continued for the remainder of the day, sorting and cleaning his lures and baits and oiling his reels, completely oblivious to the world around him.

Sunday, when the rest of the family returned from church Burke backed the station wagon into the driveway and hitched the boat trailer to it. After a quick lunch, the entire family drove out to the boat launching ramp two miles up Birch creek from its confluence with the Ohio. They took a leisurely boat ride farther inland then returned. Sam drove the boat, while Burke got in some practice casts toward the banks, laying them right in there, around tree roots and grassy overhangs. He caught a couple of keepers, which generated some enthusiasm. They stopped the boat on several occasions, and Linda and Sam threw a few casts. Burke had provided each member of the family with his or her own rod and reel and tackle box, even Marge, who rarely used hers. The children, however, enjoyed fishing and boating with their father.

In late June the family loaded into the station wagon and headed for Florida. Burke had sworn after their previous visit to Disney World that he would never do that again, yet here he was.

CHAPTER 3

THE FUNEREAL VISITOR

It was a Wednesday morning in July, with the day not yet hot and sticky, as it was bound to be in the afternoon. Burke sat at his desk daydreaming and piddling with Newman's monthly report to the City Council, when the telephone jangled and startled him alert. It was Chief Newman.

"Right away, Chief," he said into the phone. He put the receiver down, rose from his chair, and headed for the door.

"What's up?" Dempsey asked, looking up from the financial news.

"Chief wants to see me. Say, would you put that damn paper down and do some work? Why have you always got your nose in that paper?"

"What do you want me to do?"

"Find something. Go out and write a few traffic tickets, or something."

Upon entering the Chief's office Burke saw that he had a visitor, a plump man in his mid-forties, wearing a dark, pin-striped suit and a fancy white shirt with French cuffs. He had thick, well-oiled, black hair, which was combed straight back and framed a flushed face atop a thick neck, which bulged over the collar of the fancy shirt.

This guy has to be a lawyer, Burke thought.

"Come in, Burke. Have a seat," Newman said. "I want you to meet Mr. Markowitz. He's an attorney from Brockton. I'll let him tell you why he's here."

Burke suppressed a smile of satisfaction, extended his hand to the funereally-attired stranger and said, "Hello, Mr. Markowitz."

"A pleasure, uh, Mr. Burke," the stranger responded, rose slightly from his chair, and then settled himself again. "I was just explaining to Chief Newman here that I represent a client who is interested in the matter of the child's remains which were unearthed here some months ago."

Burke glanced at the chief who was in process of taking a cigar from an old-fashioned rosewood humidor on his desk.

"Cigar?" the chief asked, proffering the humidor to his guests.

"No, thanks," said Markowitz, and continued on with what he was saying before Burke could respond. "You see, uh, what is your title, again, Mr. Burke?" Markowitz looked confused, deferential, as if he did not wish to offend.

"Detective," Burke said.

"Well, Detective Burke," Markowitz continued, "my client's infant son disappeared twenty-eight years ago, and just yesterday he became aware of these two news articles which appeared in your local newspaper back in April of this year."

The lawyer produced the two newspaper clippings from his inside coat pocket.

"Your client only became aware yesterday?" Burke asked, immediately thinking of Boyd Potter's promise to check with his old friends around the state for any missing children.

"I frankly don't know how it happened that he only learned of it yesterday. I didn't ask him, and he didn't volunteer to tell me. Is it important? I'll ask him—"

"No, no, just curious," Burke said. "Your client has reason to believe the remains might be his missing son's from twenty-eight years ago?"

"Possibly," Mr. Markowitz answered. "His kid was abducted from a shopping center in Brockton, from right under the noses of his parents, as it happened. My ex-law partner, Wilfred Berry, now deceased, was this gentleman's attorney at the time of the disappearance. Since Mr. Berry's death, I've assumed the relationship of counsel to the old gentleman, and among my duties is assisting him in his efforts to find his child, or at least to learn his fate."

"Whew! Twenty-eight years is a long time to keep looking," said the chief. "No success at all, I take it?"

"None, certainly nothing on my watch. Oh, Mr. Berry used to tell me what was going on with the old man. Seems there have been a few leads over the years, but nothing ever came of them. I suspect that will be the case here, as well, but no matter. The old gentleman expended enormous effort and a great deal of money hiring detectives. He has not done much in recent years, though. I, frankly, have done what I could to dissuade him from it, but, like I said, just yesterday he got hold of these clippings. He called me first thing this morning and insisted that I drop everything and rush right over here. He also insisted that I pursue the matter quietly, find out what I could. He wants no publicity if it turns out there's nothing to it."

Newman leaned back in his chair and puffed slowly on the cigar. "We'll be happy to give you what information we have. You realize that the case is still ongoing?"

"Oh, certainly, I do," said Markowitz.

"Good. Then I'll let Lieutenant Burke fill you in."

"I don't have much to tell you," Burke said. "Our investigation to-date has been a dead end. We know little more than what you read in those two newspaper articles. In fact, you've brought us our first real promising lead."

"That so?" the lawyer seemed mildly surprised, but Burke had already sized the man up and concluded that he had little faith or interest in his mission, and was obviously simply pandering to the whims of his client.

"The time period certainly fits." Burke observed, more to himself than to the other men.

"Yes," agreed the attorney. "And wouldn't it be wonderful? I don't mind telling you, gentlemen, that nothing would make me happier than to see an end to this matter. Even though I'm well paid for my services, the whole thing gives me the willies, if you know what I mean. I'd as soon forgo the fees and have an end to it once and for all."

"A clumsy silence followed. Burke studied the man, a dislike for him growing in his belly. He said: "Why didn't your client contact us himself, or come with you, at any rate?"

"He's not well, Lieutenant Burke, not well at all. He seldom leaves his home anymore except to get medical attention. He is very frail, any real excitement or exertion would probably kill him, he's more or less an invalid, you see."

"No wonder. Poor fellow has had this awful thing hanging over him for twenty-eight years," the chief said, seeming to be preoccupied with the man's persistence over the span of so many years.

The lawyer shrugged.

"Who is your client, then?" Burke asked.

The lawyer hesitated.

"It's going to be necessary for us to talk to him directly," said Burke. We'll respect his privacy as much as possible. In fact, I'll be happy to drive up to Brockton to interview him at his home," Burke turned to face Newman, "if you have no objection, Chief."

"Fine by me."

The lawyer shrugged again. "His name is Clarence Hanford. He's a life-long resident of Brockton. He was quite prominent in his day." The lawyer paused, thinking. "When would it be convenient for you—

"Tomorrow," Burke said, perking up, suddenly pleased at the possibility offered by the stranger. A tiny surge of enthusiasm lifted his sprit.

"I'll arrange it, then. Meet me at my office in Brockton at ten? Here's my card." He produced a card from his vest pocket. "We can drive out to his home together."

"Ten it is, then," said Burke, extending his hand to the plump attorney as he rose to leave. He said over his shoulder, "You have any other thoughts, Chief?"

"I'll leave it up to you, Daniel. Whatever you think," Newman said as he rose and escorted the two men from his office.

⇌ ⇋

Burke left at seven-thirty the following morning for the 120 miles drive to Brockton. It was a pleasant drive, he listened to classical music on the radio. He arrived at the lawyer's office with a few minutes to spare, and Markowitz joined him and directed him to the outskirts of the city. On the way, Markowitz gave him additional details of Mr. Hanford's story:

"Twenty-eight years ago, on July 4th, 1955, Mr. Hanford and his wife Susan set out with their infant son, Carlton, to attend a picnic. They stopped at a market to buy refreshments. Inside the store, the child was riding in their shopping cart, and Mr. Hanford swears they couldn't have had their eyes off him for more than a few seconds. The child simply disappeared. They made a thorough search of the market and the parking lot outside. Then they called the police, who canvassed the entire area. Not a trace of the child was found. Then the FBI took it on, and since the Hanfords were prominent in the community and well off financially, they immediately suspected it was a kidnapping for ransom. But no ransom demand ever came, no calls, no nothing."

"That's odd," observed Burke.

"Yes. After that, the Hanfords went crazy with worry and grief. I mean really went nuts. That's what my law partner said. They sent out notices all over the country, hired private detectives, and offered a large reward, which, by the way, is still in effect."

"It is?"

"Yeah, still in effect after twenty-eight years."

"How much is it."

"One hundred thousand bucks."

"Whew! That's a chunk of money, even today."

"That's right."

"Never any takers, though, nobody sniffing around?"

"Not a soul, to my knowledge."

"That's a very significant bit of information."

The attorney looked puzzled. "Why is that, exactly?"

"Because a reward like that obviously will flush out information not otherwise obtainable by the police. That's what rewards are for. The fact that no one has come forward in all these years to take a shot at that reward is bad news."

"Oh, of course, how stupid of me."

Burke tended to agree with him. *How could he not have thought of that?* Burke was beginning to believe that this attorney thought about the problem of the missing child as little as possible, if at all.

The lawyer picked up where he had left off. "Mrs. Hanford died some fifteen years ago, and poor Mr. Hanford, who all his life had been a vital, robust man, began to fail in health, too. Now, as I said, he's an invalid, a recluse, he seems to hang on to life by a thread. I suspect the only thing keeping him alive is this hopeless quest to find his son. Sad, very sad, smacks of mental illness, truth be told."

"I don't know," Burke muttered. "It may be a sounder reason for living than a lot of people have."

"Why, Detective Burke," Markowitz said, "You have a philosophical streak."

The Hanford house was in a grove of trees, and wasn't visible from the highway. At Markowitz's direction, Burke turned the car onto a winding poorly-maintained lane. It was necessary to negotiate around potholes, and the trees and shrubs along the way were overgrown and dense. The lane proved to be s-shaped—a stratagem no doubt intended to maximize privacy. As they rounded the second turn, the house came into view, a large red brick, two-story house, typical of a successful upper-middle-class merchant of twenty or thirty years ago, but was now shabby from neglect. Shutters were randomly closed, particularly on the right side of the house, and one hung slightly out of alignment from a faulty hinge. To the left was a three car garage connected to the house by a covered walkway. Ivy grew wildly over much of the facade of the house and garage.

As they approached the entrance, Burke observed that the paint on the wood trim was chalky and peeling, and that the wood here and there had deteriorated from dry-rot and general lack of maintenance. Mr. Markowitz rang the bell, stepped back a pace, and looking at the house. "A real shame," he whispered conspiratorially. "Especially since Mr. Hanford once owned a construction company. He lost interest in the business after the tragedy and sold it to his employees."

The door opened slightly and a gray-haired woman peered at them through the opening. "Yes? What is it?" she said coldly. "Oh, it's you Mr. Markowitz," she added, as she opened the door wider and stepped aside to allow their entry. Though perhaps nearing seventy, she was a straight, slender, determined-appearing lady with clear, piercing hazel eyes. Her steel-grey hair was done up neatly in a bun.

The inside of the house belied the exterior, it was clean and well-ordered.

"Mrs. Halper, this is Detective Burke from the Stanton Police Department. Mr. Hanford is expecting us."

"Yes, I know," she said. "See that you don't upset the old gentleman, Mr. Markowitz. You know how delicate he is these days. And don't raise any false expectations. This foolishness has got to stop."

Mrs. Halper did not acknowledge the detective, did not extend her hand to him, and barely glanced in his direction.

"Of course, Mrs. Halper, we'll be as considerate as humanly possible, I assure you. If you wouldn't mind announcing us ..."

Burke concluded that there was no love lost between the housekeeper and the attorney, and Mrs. Halper continued to registering her disapproval with a stoic and stolid demeanor, even as she led the men through the hallway toward the rear of the house.

"Mrs. Halper has been with Mr. Hanford for, how long has it been, Mrs. Halper?"

"A good deal longer than you," she said sarcastically. "Over thirty years, in fact."

Markowitz ignored her sarcasm, and turning toward Burke, gave a slight smile and a shrug of the shoulder. Then he whispered, "She doesn't approve of all this."

"I gathered as much," Burke whispered back.

At the end of the hallway, they followed her through double doors into a large room. Though comfortably appointed it had the flavor of an earlier period. In reality, two rooms had been combined by removing a partition between what had been a library and an adjoining sunroom. The library portion of the room was lined with filled bookshelves and rich walnut paneling, and had a handsome walnut desk and side chairs. Opposite the doorway, between two sets of double French doors which opened onto a veranda, was a magnificent fireplace. The sunroom portion of the combined room had floor to ceiling windows on three sides, and an outside doorway that led to a patio and garden. Near the windows stood a hospital bed with a commanding view of the garden and the woods beyond. The rear of the bed was cranked up so that the occupant was in a sitting position. The old man in the bed wore a loose fitting garment, and a crumpled sheet covered his lower body. Beside the bed was a rack holding a bottle of clear liquid. A tube running down from the bottle was taped to his arm. In the corner, behind the bed, stood a large, green oxygen cylinder, which the patient was not currently using.

Mr. Hanford, a gray emaciated apparition, appeared much older than his reported age of sixty-eight years. His face was deeply lined, and parchment-like. His mottled skin and thin, grey, wispy hair, stretched over a skeletal skull. He raised a palsied hand slightly toward them, and said, "Come in, Gentlemen."

Burke was shocked by his appearance.

"You must be Lieutenant Burke," the old man said as he extended his hard, which Burke accepted. "Please sit down. Mrs. Halper, bring in some refreshments, won't you. What would you like, Gentlemen? Coffee? Tea? A soft drink, perhaps?"

"Coffee for me," said Markowitz.

"Coffee will be fine," Burke said as he and Markowitz took the chairs by the bed.

Mrs. Halper departed and then returned shortly thereafter with a coffee service and some light sweet rolls on a tray, which she placed on a low table between the two men so they could help themselves. She then retreated to a chair near the big walnut desk in the library section of the large room, and sat quietly throughout the remainder of the visit.

"If you don't mind, Lieutenant Burke, I will begin while you gentlemen enjoy Mrs. Halper's refreshments. I'm sure that my attorney, Mr. Markowitz, has filled you in on the basics of my child's disappearance, these many years ago. Has he also given you biographical information on me and my family?"

"Only that you were a successful businessman, a contractor."

"I will try to add any needed details, and respond to any questions you might have."

A small elongated table stood on the opposite side of the bed within Halper's easy reach, upon which were stacked an assortment of papers. Mr. Hanford indicated the table and said, "I have accumulated here all the information I have, photographs of my son, newspaper clippings, notes which I and others made at the time, and a list of mine and my wife's friends and acquaintances from back then. So, tell me, Detective Burke, how do you wish for me to proceed?"

"First, sir, tell me in your own words what happened that day, in as much detail and completeness as you can. Use your papers and photographs as you see fit. Obviously, we are looking for anything which might connect the disappearance of your son with the skeletal remains found in Stanton. Also, think of anyone you knew in or around Stanton, any business relationships, any competitors, rivals, enemies, anyone at all."

The old man seemed to hesitate for an instant as if to steel himself, then he began. "That day is burned into my memory, Gentlemen. It was a clear, bright day. The Independence Day picnic in the municipal park was a big event here in Brockton. It was a free-flowing kind of affair, with something going on all day and into the evening, culminating in the firework display. There were all sorts of games and amusements, and the children all loved it. I remember it from my own childhood. Little Carlton—we called him Carl, of course—had been looking forward to it all week. Even though he was such a little tyke, he remembered from the year before, the fireworks in particular. He would run around the house, his arms flailing about, trying to make noises like the bursting fireworks in the sky." Mr. Hanford stopped talking, a wistful, far-away look in his eyes. "If only I had not stopped at that market."

Suddenly his features contorted, his shoulders began to heave. He brought his hands to his face and wept piteously.

So abrupt and unexpected was it, that Burke was caught unprepared and unsure of what to do. He glanced at Markowitz, who looked solemn and shook his head slightly, and placed his hand on Burke's forearm, as if to indicate for him to remain seated, while he rose to his feet, turned, and motioned for Mrs. Halper to come, then said, "Are you all right, Mr. Hanford? Would you like for us to leave?"

Halper came over. "May I get you something, sir?" she said.

Hanford took a tissue to his eyes. "No," he said, "Please, I sorry, I'll be all right. Why don't you take the tray away, Mrs. Halper?" He turned and looked from Burke to Markowitz. I'm sorry Gentlemen, and embarrassed. Let us continue."

As the morning wore on, Burke marveled at the stamina and determination of the old man. But he sensed that the visit and the stress of recounting remembrances were taking their toll. At noon they departed with his account of the disappearance of the child, and its aftermath. Burke carried with him all the accumulated information on the affair. Hanford demanded assurances from Burke that he would protect the items and return them safely to him.

"Well, what do you make of it all?" Markowitz asked, as they drove back into town.

"Everything fits," Burke said, "time-wise, and the age of the child. The main thing I got from Mr. Hanford was that he desperately wants these bones not to be those of his missing son."

"What do you mean?"

"The old man wants his son to still be alive, of course. That's why he's never given up all these years. He does not want the dead baby found in the woods to be his child. He believes his son is still alive out there, somewhere."

"Of course, but how could you ever prove that one way or the other—whether or not it is his child?"

"How, indeed," said Burke, "At this time, I don't have the foggiest."

As soon as he got back to the station, Burke set in right away examining the photographs and newspaper clippings from the time of the disappearance and afterwards. He began to appreciate more fully the devastating, life-altering drama and tragedy. However, while it provided him with background information, it did not contribute to the solution of his problem, which was to identify the decades-old, moldy bones, and tie them in with the child. He turned his attention to that problem. It seemed insurmountable.

He needed some way, some chemical way of comparing the bones of the old man with the child's bones. But that was impossible! Or was it?

He remembered reading an article in a law enforcement journal which had to do with a means of testing and comparing genetic traits of individuals. The procedure had been touted as a possible means of identification at least as reliable as finger prints. At the time he had considered it in the same sense that he regarded other futuristic notions such as "a helicopter in every garage." Sometime later, though, he had seen an article in the local paper, something about Stanton College being involved somehow in the new genetic testing. That was all he could remember. Maybe Ripley could help him out with that. He dialed the professor's office number. The phone rang, and Ripley answered.

"The case of the bones has taken a strange turn, Professor," Burke said.

"Oh? How so?"

Burke told him about Mr. Hanford and his missing son. "It looks very promising, But the problem is proving the bones are his son's. I recall reading an article about genetic testing of some sort going on there at the college. Do you know anything about that?"

"You're referring to DNA analysis. Yes, there is a small group on campus. I'm not very familiar with their activities, though, but I'll be happy to look into it for you and get back to you, possibly this afternoon."

"Thank you Professor. I'll wait for your call."

Burke breathed a small sigh of relief. It was almost as if he could feel the pressure ease. That was what Burke had come to appreciate about Professor Ripley, he got down to cases. No pussy-footing around for him.

After the telephone conversation, Burke called across the room. "Elmo, you ever heard of DNA analysis?"

DNA analysis? Yeah, sure."

"Oh, yeah?" Burke was surprised. "What do you know about it?"

"There were these scientists in England, at Oxford University, I believe, a few years ago. They learned how genes work to pass on human traits. Now, they're trying to use this to identify people, because each person genes are supposed to be different."

"No kidding, Elmo. How come you know all that stuff and I don't?"

Dempsey peered across the room at Burke for several moments, as if weighing how he should answer such a question from his supervisor, the man who gave him his performance evaluation each year, upon which depended, in theory at least, whether or not he got his annual salary increment. Suddenly, his face cracked into a rare, wide grin. "Boss, you tell me. I just work here."

Burke had to smile, too. "Well, does it work?"

"I don't know. My understanding is that it's still experimental. But I seem to remember that there was a case somewhere where it was accepted as evidence in a rape case, or maybe it was murder, and there was a big legal to-do about it. It was in the news."

Burke checked his watch. "I've got a call in to Ripley at the college. I'm going to take my lunch early so I'll be here when he calls back."

"Okay, Boss. See you later."

Ripley called at two o'clock in the afternoon. "I have good news for you Detective Burke," he said, "Doctor Smithers, who heads up the research project I mentioned to you, has agreed to meet with you and discuss your problem. When can you be here?"

"How about right now?"

Ripley chuckled. "Come on over. I'll wait until you get here, then we'll get up with Smithers."

Burke hurried over to Ripley's office, and plopped down in the proffered chair. Ripley picked up the phone and dialed. He spoke briefly into the phone and then replaced it on the cradle. "He'll be right along. You'll enjoy Doctor Smithers. He's a fine young man."

With a few minutes to kill, Ripley asked, "You like sports, Detective?"

"Yes, I do."

They talked sports, and had got around to Ohio State football, and the career of Woody Hayes, by the time Smithers arrived.

Smithers looked to Burke to be in his late twenties, although he could have been older. He was slightly built, with a pleasant face, and thinning blonde hair. After introductions, he led the detective back through the corridors toward his office in another part of the large building. As they walked along, Burke explained his problem and the chronology of events since the discovery of the bones to the present.

"Did Doctor Ripley mention to you that our lab people did the carbon dating for you back in April?" Smithers ask.

"No, you were involved with that?"

"Not me directly, but the lab people we work with were."

"Are you a medical doctor?"

"No. My field is the Biological Science. I hold a Ph.D. I provide general oversight on this small research project, but I spend the bulk of my time teaching Biology and Physiology. My partner in this research project is Sheila Vann. She also holds a Ph.D. Hers is in the Medical Sciences. She is something of a computer whiz to boot. She also teaches. The two of us call upon various specialists within the academic and medical areas here at the college and at the hospital as needed. For example, Mark Hamilton is an M. D. who works at the City Hospital, teaches a course or two here, and devotes maybe ten to fifteen percent of his time on our project. However, Sheila devotes the most time and effort. She does the heavy lifting, since she mainly handles the computer work."

"I see. Who is this research for?"

"We have a small NIH grant which pays some of the bills.

"NIH?"

"National Institutes of Health. They fund research in health related areas. How familiar are you with DNA, Detective Burke?"

"I'm embarrassed to say I know nothing about it."

"Then, I'll give you my short version of the subject."

"Okay."

"DNA is short for deoxyribonucleic acid. That's a mouthful, huh? Well, this substance is in every cell of our bodies. It carries the genetic blueprint of the individual, and, except for identical twins, we believe it is unique to each individual. That's where its value for identification purposes comes in. DNA exists as long, coiled molecular strands. You've probably heard the term 'double helix.' The amount of genetic information contained on these strands is enormous. Each of these coiled molecular strands, if straightened out, would be approximately a meter long, and, if all the molecules of DNA in the human body were placed end-to-end, they would stretch to the moon and back, several times." He paused, glancing at the detective for evidence of comprehension.

"If the particular pattern or arrangement of the DNA of an individual can be determined, we believe this produces identification as reliable as fingerprinting. Patterns from different individuals can be compared to determine relationships between them. Briefly, that's it. That's all there is to it. I have to point out, though, that there isn't universal acceptance of this procedure, not even in the scientific community."

"What does that mean?"

"It means that the process is not foolproof, not yet, at any rate. Nothing is black and white. We must state our conclusions in terms of probabilities."

"What about my bones? Will you be able to tell if they're related to Mr. Hanford?"

"Maybe, maybe not. First of all, there is a problem with the age of the bones and their badly deteriorated state. It is difficult and sometimes impossible to get good DNA samples from old, deteriorated bones. That's the first and greatest hurdle we have to overcome. If we get a good sample, then we're off to the races."

"I see," said Burke. "Assuming that you get a good sample, will the test stand up in court?"

"Some courts are starting to look at DNA evidence, especially in cases involving rape and murder, but those cases haven't worked their way through the appeals process yet. Your guess is as good as mine as to how that might work itself out. There are other factors at play other than purely scientific. Many people, for example, do not trust the fact that results are stated in probabilities rather than absolutes."

Smithers stopped walking, and swung his arm around. "These are our offices here, and this is our computer laboratory where we do our analysis." They glanced in through the glass door of the computer lab. No one was there.

"Sheila isn't here," he said. "Let's see if she's in her office. He rapped on a door next to the lab, opened it and peeked in. "Not here either," he said. They went to a door on the other side of the lab. He repeated the process. "Come in," a voice sounded from inside.

"Ah, we're in luck. Mark's here today."

They entered the small office as a young man rose from behind the desk. "Hi, Adrian. What's up?" he said, pleasantly.

"I have someone I'd like you to meet. Doctor Mark Hamilton, this is Detective Burke, from the Stanton Police Department. He's trying to identify that skull that was found down by the river a few months ago. He's interested in DNA testing."

"Oh, I see. Come on in, Detective Burke. Have a seat. It's a pleasure to meet you."

They shook hands, and the two visitors took seats in front of the desk. Smithers explained Burke's mission. "I've given him a very brief description of our capabilities, but I am running out of time. I need to be somewhere in about five minutes." He glanced at his wrist watch. "Would you mind taking it from here and answer any other questions he might have?"

"Be happy to."

"Well, then, perhaps I'll be talking to you later, Detective Burke. If you'll excuse me, I'll be on my way."

"Thank you very much, Doctor Smithers."

"So, what else can I tell you, Detective? Hatfield asked.

"I'm afraid I still don't understand exactly what you do. You don't actually run the DNA tests yourselves, is that correct?"

"The lab technicians here at the school or at the hospital run the tests under Doctor Smithers' supervision. He is the boss of the project. I'm a consultant on medical matters. Did you meet Sheila?"

"No, she isn't here, but Doctor Smithers told me about her."

"Well, these are two very intelligent scientists, and we enjoy a cooperative relationship. The main reason we're geared up as we are, is because the two of them are developing and testing computer programs to be used to evaluate large amounts of DNA data. The work is statistical, a computer science project more than medical one. It's not as interesting and exotic as the basic research being done by others."

"What's the purpose of the computer programs?"

"To detect and evaluate degrees of similarities between DNA mappings in large populations, and then to test the reliability of the results, statistically."

Burke stared blankly at the young doctor. He felt terribly inadequate. His two and one half years of college education acquired years ago at Stanton College were doing him little good. "Look, Doctor, this is way over my head, but it's very important to my case."

"I understand. Ask me anything."

"Why do you need to know that kind of information?"

"It has application in such things as the migratory patterns of populations over thousands of years, including human. It can tell us where we come from, and how we got from there to here. But, more importantly, it has uses in the treatment and understanding of genetic diseases and problems of aging. But in your particular case it is simply to determine if two individuals are related to each other, and, if so, the degree of the relationship. And one step beyond that, the degree of the reliability of the conclusion. That's where probability and statistics come in. But the first obstacle is getting viable genetic material from the bones. So, do you want us to take a shot at it?"

"Absolutely."

"Okay. We can get started as soon as you bring us the bones, and a sample of blood from the gentleman in question, Mister, uh..."

"Clarence Hanford is his name. But please keep the name confidential. I'll arrange to have the sample drawn. He's not in good health, so we will draw the blood at his home."

"Where is that?"

"Brockton"

"I could draw the blood myself," Hamilton said. "That way, I could control the integrity of the sample. In fact, I'd prefer it, if you have no objection."

"That's fine with me. I'll drive you there. I'll set it up with Mr. Hanford's attorney and get back to you with the date and time. When's good for you?"

Hamilton thought. "The sooner the better. Tomorrow would be fine if you can set it up that quickly."

"I'll go back to the office right now and see if I can." Thank you Doctor, I'll be in touch.

As soon as he returned to the office, Burke placed a call to Markowitz, Hanford's attorney, and briefly explained the DNA testing to him and about their need to draw blood from Mr. Hanford.

"I'm sure it's okay, but let me explain it to him and I'll call you right back."

While Burke waited for Markowitz's call, he resumed his examination of the materials he had obtained from Hanford. He scattered the documents and photographs on his desktop. There was a picture of a laughing child lying naked on a blanket. There was another of the same child in a carriage wearing a cap and wrapped in a blanket. Another showed a park-like setting, with leafless trees, with the child held in the arms of an attractive, smiling, young woman, Mrs. Hanford, he had been informed. Her radiant smile belied the tragedy soon to befall her family. The old man had hardly mentioned his deceased wife. *What could that mean?* Could it be that the tragedy had become Hanford's alone now, jealously guarded even from the woman with whom he had shared it while she lived? Burke checked himself, noting that he was letting his imagination run away with him. He picked up another photograph. It showed the child, now a toddler, standing on a grassy lawn in front of the house, which Burke and the attorney had visited. The house appeared new in the photo. The child was wearing a white, short-sleeved, short-pants sailor suit with dark trim and brass buttons, and he was looking back over his right shoulder, smiling, presumably at someone or something not in the picture. The old man had said the picture was taken just shortly before the child's disappearance. Burke put the photographs aside and reread the newspaper clippings. He examined the child's birth certificate.

The phone rang, it was the attorney. Mr. Hanford would see them the following day. He said, also, that Hanford had insisted his private physician be present. Burke called the doctor and plans were set for the trip to Brockton.

⇌ ⇋

The following morning Burke swung by the campus and picked up Hamilton, who was waiting on the curb. He carried a traditional black doctor's bag.

"Been a long time since I've seen one of those black bags," quipped Burke, as they got underway.

"My mother gave it to me when I graduated from medical school. It comes in handy now and then."

"How is you mother, by the way?"

"You know my mother?"

"Not very well, but my wife plays bridge with her and some other ladies at the country club on Thursdays. I've met her once or twice, and see her picture in the papers sometimes. She seems to be a very busy lady, active in community."

"Yes, that's my mother, all right, she makes the paper right regularly. She enjoys being active in things that interest her. That's her idea of a good time, but she has earned the right. She was a nurse when I was a kid, and that's hard, grueling work."

"I suppose she was your inspiration to become a doctor, then."

"You would think so, but actually, that was my own idea, although she certainly encouraged and supported me."

"Was your father a doctor?"

"No. I didn't know my father. He died when I was an infant. He was a sales representative for a manufacturing company."

Burke changed the subject. "I was one of your fans when you played high school basketball."

"Oh, really? I appreciate that."

"Did you play any college ball?"

"No, I was too small. those big boys would have eaten me alive."

"You got your share of glory in high school, being a sports hero in your hometown. Doesn't get any better than that, does it?"

"I had a great time then. But each stage of life brings its own excitement. How about you? I imagine being a police officer is exciting work."

"It has its moments."

Their conversation petered out after a while, and they drove on in silence, with the young doctor studying the scenery out the window.

When they arrived at the Hanford house they were greeted at the door by Halper. As Burke expected, she treated them coolly. Markowitz was already there, as was Hanford's regular physician, a Doctor Samuels. After introductions and a few moments of polite conversation, Hamilton prepared to draw the sample of blood. "I'd like to wash my hands" he said.

"There's a bathroom off the hallway," said Markowitz.

As Hamilton walked across the room toward the door, Markowitz called across the large room to Halper, "Mrs. Halper, will you show the doctor the way, please?" She was standing by the double French doors observing the proceedings. Her expression conveyed disapproval of the goings on, and she seemed to start at hearing her name spoken. She followed Hamilton with her eyes for a moment as he crossed the room, then hurried toward the door, but stopped short and just stood there, saying nothing as Hamilton proceeded on down the hall. Her face was pale and gaunt.

Hamilton called out, "Never mind, Mrs. Halper, I have it."

She hesitated, once again, as if confused, retreated a few steps back into the room, and sat on the arm of a chair beside the big desk.

Hanford was watching her closely. "What is it, Mrs. Halper? Are you ill?" he asked her.

"I—I'd like to go to my room, if you don't need me, sir."

"Certainly, Mrs. Halper, but are you ill?" he asked again.

"I'll be fine, if I can lie down for a minute."

"Of course. We can do without you. Take all the time you need. In fact, you need not come back at all unless you wish to do so."

Halper left the room.

What a strange woman, Burke thought, as he watched her depart. Hamilton returned, nodded to her in passing. He turned and watched her for a moment as she walked unsteadily down the hallway. "What's wrong with Mrs. Halper?" He asked. "She looks like she's seen a ghost."

"She isn't feeling well, I'm afraid," the old man said. "I'm such a burden to her, but I would be lost without her."

"Maybe I should look in on her, Mister Hanford, once we are finished here." Doctor Samuels said.

"Yes, I think you should."

Hamilton collected two small, cylindrical vials of blood, which he placed carefully in a container and placed the container it in his bag. He covered the tiny wound with an adhesive bandage. "Well, that's it, Mr. Hanford. Thank you very much."

"No, thank you, Doctor," said Hanford, his voice feeble. "You don't know how much I appreciate this effort."

They all said their goodbyes, and Burke and Hamilton returned to Stanton. They talked briefly about the visit, with Burke asking, "What did you make of Mrs. Halper?"

"I don't know what to think. She was obviously distressed, or ill. I'm glad Doctor Samuels was there to see after her."

Three days later, Hamilton called Burke to report the results of the tests. "Hanford's DNA was mapped satisfactorily, Detective Burke, but, as I feared, we haven't been able to get a viable sample from the bones."

Burke's voice reflected his disappointment as he said, "Is that it, then?"

"Not necessarily, we won't give up yet. Did you happen to notice any hair at the site where you found the bones?"

"No. But I'll go back out and scratch around a little,"

"Okay. Call me if you find anything."

It was mid-afternoon when Burke entered the woods. It was a cloudless day and a bright sun filtered through the canopy of green, casting geometric shadow-lines and patterns over the bed of brown, rotting leaves. Everything was oppressively still, with no sound beyond the crunch of his feet on the matt—not as much as the chirping of a bird. The utter stillness gave him the creeps. He stood a few yards away from the excavation site, filled in now, yet it disrupted the symmetry of the woods, like a wound not yet scabbed over.

His eyes sweep the terrain. Nearby a large beech tree was literally covered with carvings of names and initials. The bark had grown over earlier ones, until they were barely legible. It was evident that Bealer woods had been, and perhaps still was, a lover's lane. For several moments, he stood idly studying the carvings, distracted and absorbed in his own musings and the eerie peace of the place, while noting that by the degree to which the carvings were overgrown, one could sense the passage of time. Perhaps decades of lovers had dallied there.

Abruptly a whistle sounded in the distance, followed by the faint chug of a diesel engine, as a barge made its way upstream against the river current, and his reverie was broken. He walked around the dig once again, studied the ground, stooped and raked the soil with his hand, crumbled it in his fingers, searching for hair. He walked in a wide circle around the disturbed earth, observed the lay of the ground, and considered, once again, how the uprooted tree had apparently set a process of erosion in motion. Suddenly, his face brightened. "Well, I'll be damned!" he said, as he turned about and hurried to his car, as if he had had a 'Eureka' moment. He drove back to the station, found Dempsey there, and blurted out excitedly that the dead tree was the key the mystery of the bones. "I've got it! I've figured it out!" he said exuberantly.

"What?" Elmo asked, startled at seeing Burke so uncharacteristically excited.

"That rotting tree, the one that uprooted, it wasn't there when the child's body was buried. How large was that tree, huh? A foot or so in diameter, right? That's not a thirty-year-old tree."

"I'm not following you, Boss. You'll have to make it a little plainer for me."

"That tree grew there after the child's body was buried," Burke said. "Maybe years later. It grew right over the grave, or very near it. When it went over, probably in a storm, the root system dislodged part of the child's skeleton, and deposited some of the bones, including the skull, farther down the hill from the original burial site. Then dirt and debris washed over the bones, giving them a shallow new burial. That's why the bones were found near the surface, and kind of helter-skelter."

"That makes sense."

"Yes. We didn't see any evidence of a grave where we were poking around out there. If there was one, we should have been able to find it. A grave is hard to conceal, no matter how carefully it's filled in. It'll sink on you, or stay mounded up, one or the other."

"That's right, we didn't see either, did we?"

"No, we sure didn't."

"I want to get Joe Benson back out there with his backhoe," Burke said. "Have him dig further up the slope where that rotting tree uprooted."

"You want Dr. Ripley out there again?"

"Yes. I'll call him right now."

The following morning, Joe Benson from Public Works arrived with his backhoe and a couple of helpers, and they maneuvered their way through the trees once again. Ripley, Dempsey and Burke were present. Benson maneuvered to the new site up the hill, positioned the outriggers to stabilize the machine on the slope, and gingerly took a bite out of the earth at the place indicated, and then swung the arm around and deposited the extracted soil on the ground at the feet of Ripley and the two detectives. They examined each bucket of soil carefully before allowing Benson to proceed. On the forth such operation Ripley waved his arms and shouted for Benson to stop. Protruding from the soil and debris was an assortment of bones, including another human skull. Burke bent over and grasped the skull and wiped away the dirt. There was an enormous gash in the forehead, right between the eyes.

"Wow! Would you look at that!" Elmo exclaimed.

Ripley's expression was grim. "I think it's safe to say we know the cause of this poor creature's demise."

CHAPTER 4
MORE BONES

"Gentlemen, can we all agree that we have come upon a crime scene, so that we need not worry ourselves about getting in trouble with the preservationists of ancient burial sites?"

"I think we are on solid ground, in that regard." Ripley said. Dempsey smiled, and the workmen nodded, solemnly.

"Then, I propose that we continue digging here, and collect the evidence. But we must do that carefully, with a little more finesse than that magnificent piece of machinery, the backhoe, affords. I would like to finish up by hand. I don't expect that we will have to dig farther out. I believe we have us a conventional-sized grave here, though it perhaps was not dug as deeply, nor as carefully as one at the Green Hill Cemetery."

"Want me to take the backhoe back to the yard, Daniel?" asked Joe Benson.

"Yeah, Joe, but you and your boys stay on this with us. Bring back more hand tools, like trowels, and so forth, so we don't miss anything. I don't know how long it might take. It could be the rest of the day, or maybe longer."

"What we need out here," offered Ripley," is a screen to sift the soil like I use on archaeology digs, otherwise something important might get overlooked."

"Good idea. You don't happen to have one available, do you?" Burke Asked.

"Yes, I do, back at the college."

"Great. Let's go get it." Burke said. "How big is it? Do we need a truck?"

"It's not all that big or heavy, but it won't fit in a car. We'll need a pickup truck."

Burke thought a moment. "Elmo, you go with him, and swing by the Street Department and find us a pickup, okay?"

"Okay, Boss."

"If you like, Detective Burke," Ripley said, "I'll see if I can find one or two of my experienced students to help with the excavation."

"Sure. One other thing, fellows, I want to have a talk with Jake Barton, at the Daily News. I want to bring him in on this early and try to keep things under a little better control than the last time. So, I'm going to give him a call, and see if that works any better. Everybody keep our find to yourselves for now. Let me do it my way, okay? Let's meet back here in two hours."

Joe Benson and his boys left to take the backhoe to the Public Works equipment yard, and get hand tools. Dempsey and Ripley left in Ripley's car to get the screen, and Burke went to his car to use the car phone to call the Stanton Dailey News.

Everybody reassembled at the site two hours later, Joe Benson with his two men, Dempsey and Ripley, accompanied by two male Archaeology students, and Burke, with Barton in tow. Burke had had a good talk with Barton, and they had come to an understanding. Barton was to have a free hand to present the story, but in a professional manner, with no sensationalizing. He could take all the pictures he wanted, and he agreed to share them with the Police Department if need be.

Burke had also called and notified Chief Newman of their find, and asked him to contact the Coroner's Office. There were quite a few people there in the middle of the afternoon. Newman came out, and Barton took his picture standing by the hole where the workmen were digging.

"By God," Burke mumbled to Dempsey, "now, let somebody accuse me of being uncooperative."

Ripley Summoned Burke to the screen where he and his students had found fragments of cloth, several buttons, and three item the size of finger tips, which appeared to be corroded, encrusted metal. "I want to call your attention to these items, Detective," Ripley said. "I can't be certain until they're cleaned, but these look like metal buttons."

Burke examined the small objects, the encrusted metal, and the cloth fragments. "These are important clues," he said.

They finished around six, and Burke left Dempsey to secure the site, while he and Ripley packed up the bones and other articles, and each drove his own car back to the college, where Smithers met them. They arranged to extract samples of bone material for the carbon dating and the DNA tests. Ripley, being the most experienced at it, volunteered to see to the cleaning of the metal buttons, and the fragments of cloth.

"We've had quite a day of it, eh, Professor Ripley?" Burke quipped with satisfaction as he prepared to leave.

"I would say so," Ripley said, smiling

Burke drove home with a real feeling of accomplishment. On impulse, he stopped and bought his wife a bouquet of flowers and a box of her favorite chocolates.

The next day, the story made the headline in the Daily News. The headline read, *Second Skull Found in Bealer Woods.* Underneath the headline, beside the story, was a picture of the skull, with the vertical gash in the middle of the forehead. The continuation of the story on page four had several other pictures, including the picture of Newman standing authoritatively beside the dig. The story mentioned that the college was running test of the bones, which were found in a common grave with the bones of the child. They were thought to be equally as old. The story caused a sensation, and was the main topic of conversation all over town. Those who were old enough racked their brains to remember something from the past which might shed light on this new development. For three days, Burke and Elmo cooled their heels in the office and tried to catch up on their paperwork, while they waited for the results of the tests on the bones. Burke had not told Barton about the DNA tests, in deference to the wishes of Hanford, and to avoid speculation, so he had been deliberately vague in speaking with Barton. It was deception, he realized, but he thought it justified. Everybody at the Stanton Police Department and at the college who were knowledgeable had agreed to keep that aspect of the matter confidential for the present.

Burke and Dempsey didn't get a lot done, the phone rang continuously. The newspaper story had attracted regional news outlets and reporters were calling for additional information. Something about the story had obviously struck a chord with the public, generating interest disproportionately to its importance in the overall scheme of things. Because Chief Newman's picture was in the paper, many of the calls came directly to him.

Two days after the story appeared, rumors began to circulate that the police had uncovered a clandestine graveyard where murder victim's bodies were buried. Burke first heard it when he stopped at the barber shop for a trim. Fred Vincent, his barber, asked him flat out if there was anything to it. "No, there is nothing to it, Fred, where did you ever hear such a thing as that?"

"From my customers, where else?"

"Shortly after Burke got back to the office, Newman rushed in, excited. "My phone is ringing off the hook," he said, "and, the mayor is on his way in to see me. What the hell is going on out there, Burke."

"Nothing that I know of, Chief. What are you referring to?"

"Rumors, but we'll talk later. I don't have time right now. I have to see what the mayor wants."

"The phone rang again. It was Barton at the Daily News."

"Have you heard the rumors circulating around town?" Barton asked.

"You mean about a graveyard for dead criminals? Yeah, I heard that. How ridiculous is that?"

"So then there's nothing to it?"

"What do you think? Of course not."

"Well, I had to ask. And, there's no police cover up of any kind going on?"

"No! Jesus, Jake! Have you forgotten our talk three days ago?"

"All right, thanks. Anything new to report?"

"No. We're performing our regular duties, and waiting for the lab report on the bones."

"Okay Burke, thanks. Good bye."

Burke could hardly wait to leave the office. He had a queasy feeling that something was really going awry. When he got home, he told Marge about the rumor. "Have you ever heard anything so utterly stupid in your life?"

"Don't worry about it dear. You know how people are. They'll forget it by tomorrow."

But morning came, and Burke opened the newspaper to another headline story *Police Deny Cover up in Bealer Woods Murders* "What the heck is this?" Burke asked."

"What is it, dear."

"It's another story about the skeletons. I'm reading it." Burke read rapidly through the article, the expression on his face turning from surprise to disgust then to incredulity. "I just can't believe this!" he exclaimed, as he handed the paper to Marge."

"Somehow these morons have got it in their heads that there is something fishy going on concerning the skeletons," Burke said. "Apparently, according to this, people have been calling around anonymously, including to the newspaper and to the mayor, spreading lies. I need to get to the office and assess the damage. I'll tell you all about it tonight."

As Burke pulled into the parking lot he saw a van from a Cincinnati TV station parked there. He walked inside through the back entrance as he always did, and on into his office, bypassing the break room and his usual cup of coffee. Dempsey was there. He said, "Morning, Daniel. Newman said I should tell you to come see him as soon as you got in this morning."

"Thanks. I suppose it has to do with the story in the paper?"

"Yeah, I think so."

Daniel walked down the hallway to Newman's office. The door was open; he could see that the mayor was with him."

"Good morning, Chief, morning Mayor."

"Come on in, Burke," Newman said, "have a seat."

"Good Morning, Detective Burke," the mayor responded.

Burke sat down, and looked passively expectant first at the chief, then at the mayor.

The mayor's name was Clifton Stover. He was a fixture around Stanton on the political scene, having served on the City Council several terms before he became mayor. He earned his living selling office supplies. Burke did not care for him for a variety of reasons, including the fact that he reminder Burke of a weasel, both in his actions and his appearance. Appearance-wise, it was the way his face was shaped, coming up to a point, as it did. He had a long, slender nose, and small eyes set close together, and a receding chin and forehead. But it wasn't just his face, he was also short and stooped, and his hair was thin and wispy, and he hunched his shoulders when he walked, and bent a little forward, like he really had somewhere to go in a hurry, or he was facing a headwind.

And that wasn't all, he also wore a perpetual simpering grin, and displayed a penchant to shake hands with every voter he encountered. Everything about him, in its totality, caused Burke to be repulsed by him. Now, here he was, staring into Burke's face, with something on his mind.

"What do you think about the story in the paper this morning," Newman began.

"Oh, that," Burke grimaced. "I've heard of some stupid ideas in my time, but that one ranks right up there with the best of them."

"What idea are you referring to, Detective?" Stover asked.

"Why, the idea that Bealer Woods is a burial ground for murder victims, that there are other bodies buried out there—a lot of bodies. That's for starters, then—"

"I don't think it's a stupid idea," Stover interrupted. "Chief Newman, do you think it's a stupid idea?"

"What? Well, I, uh ..."

"Neither do a lot of people who have been calling me the last three days," the mayor continued, looking from one to the other. "And what is this thing about you covering up something, Burke?"

"Covering up what, Mayor? There's nothing for me to cover up."

"Well, don't you think that it would be a good idea to do a little more digging out there, seeing as how so many people are concerned about the situation?"

"No, I don't. And, I don't know that many people are concerned. Sounds like a few trouble-makers to me."

"Well, I do," Stover said, emphatically

"Wait a minute," Burke said, his temperature starting to rise. "What is this, Chief? What's going on here?"

"Now, hold on, Daniel, don't get excited. Don't jump out of the starting gate, yet. There's some concerns being expressed, and we, the mayor and me, we are trying to get to the bottom of it, that's all."

"All right, sir. Pardon me. How can I help you do that—get to the bottom of it?"

"Daniel, is there anything about any of this that I don't know about, that you're not telling me?

"No, Sir, absolutely not," Burke said. "I don't even know what you're talking about," he added. He hesitated for a moment, thinking, searching his memory, and then he said, "you know about Mr. Hanford. We haven't told anybody about that, because the old man is ill, and he asked us to keep that confidential. You're not talking about that, are you, Chief?"

"Wait a minute," Mayor Stover interrupted, "what are you talking about, now. Who is this Mr. Hanford?"

"Look, Mayor, I shouldn't have even mentioned him." Burke said, he has nothing to do with any more bodies being buried out in the woods. It's something else which has to do with my investigation, and I told this man we would treat it confidentially. Can't you trust me on this one?"

"Trust you? I'm having difficulty deciding in my own mind whether you're handling this investigation properly. Do you know there is a TV reporter and a camera crew cooling their heels in my office right now, waiting for some explanation from me as to what the hell is going on around here. I don't know what to tell them. Chief, I want to know what Burke is talking about. Who is this Hanford person?"

Before Newman could answer, Burke spoke. "Mayor Stover, why is that TV guy interviewing you in the first place. Seems to me he should be over here interviewing me, or the chief."

"I don't need your approval to talk to the press, Burke."

"Yeah? Well I don't like the implications of your questions, and I don't need you telling me how to do my job, either. If you ask me, Mayor, you're out of line here."

"Dammit, gentlemen, calm down," Newman said. We aren't getting anywhere like this. Burke, you go on to your office and let me and the Mayer talk this over. I'll get back with you."

"Yes, sir," Burke said, as he jumped up from his chair without looking toward Stover and hurried out of the room and down the hall to his office. He plopped down in his chair, and wheeled it around to the window, and sat there fuming, not seeing what he was looking at."

"What's wrong, Boss," Dempsey asked.

"I probably just got my ass fired, that's all, and I haven't even had my morning coffee yet."

"I'll get you your coffee. You try to calm down."

Dempsey came back with the coffee, put it on the desk.."

"Thanks. I don't want to talk about it right now," Burke said, anticipating Dempsey's questions. "I'll tell you about it later."

Burke sipped his coffee. For twenty minutes he rocked back and forth gently in his chair, looked out the window, waiting to find out if he still had a job. Newman came in, walked over, leaned over his desk, and spoke softly. "Daniel, I'm going to take care of this matter here with Stover. You just go on about your business, but do me a favor: in a couple of days walk over to the mayor's office, and kind of make up with him. You know, tell him you're sorry about losing your temper. Will you do that for me, Daniel? Let him save a little face?"

"All right, Chief. I'll do it. In fact, I do usually feel sorry when I lose my temper, even when I'm right about something."

"That's fine. The mayor and I are going to talk to that TV reporter. Maybe we'll even take him out to the woods and let him get a picture of the mayor out there. That ought to placate Stover. You know how politicians are." Newman grinned and winked at Burke. "Maybe we'll even get the Public Works crew out there again to poke around a little more, look for more bodies, to get these nutcases of the mayor's back, you know. What's the harm?"

"Won't do the trees any good, Burke said."

Newman chuckled. "Well, you don't need to worry about it. Just get back to work."

After Newman left, Burke filled Dempsey in on what had transpired between him, Newman and Stover.

"Unbelievable," Dempsey said.

With further prompting from the mayor, and over Burke's objections, the chief ordered serious earth moving equipment dispatched to Bealer Woods, and the area all around the site was devastated. The paper was filled with photographs and commentary and speculation. But no more bodies were found. Not so much as an old steak bone buried by a neighborhood dog was unearthed.

This high-level intrusion by the mayor and chief of police left Burke livid, though he managed to control himself pretty well in public. Marge heard about it, though. Even Elmo Dempsey rose to the occasion and murmured his disapproval, confidentially of course, well out of earshot of the chief and the mayor. However, interest declined quickly when no more bodies were unearthed. The newspaper stories abated, the mayor returned to hawking pencils, notepads and cheap electronic calculators, and the chief, who was long since incapable of mounting or sustaining a prolonged investigative effort, sheepishly left Burke to continue his investigation of the bones.

In the meantime, while the carnival atmosphere had prevailed at Bealer Woods, Smithers and his associates, and the laboratory personnel under their direction, had been laboring to extract viable DNA from the skeletal remains. With all the to-do in the paper, the laboratory technicians apparently developed a sense of proprietorship in the undertaking. In spite of several failures they persisted, and on the seventh attempt, someone got the bright idea of drilling into the teeth for DNA. Sure enough, the seventh attempt was successful.

Burke got a radio call from the dispatcher while he was out in his car informing him that that Smithers and Ripley wanted to see him. It was Wednesday afternoon, around two. Burke drove to the college, and found the two men in Ripley's office.

"Well, we've done it," Smithers began, enthusiastically. "We got good DNA, and we got results. First thing was the carbon-dating which verified the time since death of the adult, who was male, by the way, as being in the range of twenty to forty years, like before. And the DNA comparison of the infant's with Hanford's indicated that they were not related."

"Not related!" Burke was stunned by the news. "I am surprised to hear that, and disappointed as well."

"I thought you might be," Smithers said, "but the adult and the child were closely related to each other, probably father and child. Let me show you the test sheets."

Smithers took papers from a file, rose and stood beside Burke and held the sheets for him to see. They displayed groups of lines a fraction of an inch long and of different widths. The lines reminded Burke of the bar codes on product packages in super markets. He had never really understood exactly what the bar codes on packaging meant, he had not thought about it. Now he realized that they were a numbering system, in some new mathematical language. He studied the 8-1/2 by 11 inch sheets, compared them, and was able to see the similarities between the two patterns belonging to the two skeletons. He could also see clearly that the third one, the one from Hanford, was nothing like the other two.

"Is there any chance this is erroneous?" Burke asked.

"We're pretty sure of the results."

"Very well, then," Burke said. "Please continue to keep this confidential. I promised Mr. Hanford we would respect his privacy if the tests turned out this way. We have a continuing mystery on our hands, who are these two people, this father and child, who apparently were murdered and disposed of in Bealer Woods thirty years ago?"

"I don't envy you your job solving that one," Smithers said, as he rose from his chair. "But I wanted to let you know the test results right away. I'll send you a written report in a couple of days. Now, if you will excuse me, I must go. Doctor Ripley has additional information for you."

Burke expressed his thinks and Smithers departed. Ripley had been sitting quietly while Smithers gave his report. He said, "I was right about those three objects we found, they were metal buttons." He handed Burke a small manila envelope. Burke opened it and peeked inside.

"Two of them are in pretty bad shape, but the third one is fairly well intact." Ripley handed him a second envelope. "This contains the fragments of cloth. We managed to clean these but they are in delicate condition. I suggest you send them off to the crime lab for identification purposes.

"Okay, Professor thanks again. I'll send Detective Dempsey by for the bones."

"Listen, don't mention it. This is right up our alley, and we're happy to be involved."

Burke left Ripley and rushed to the office to call Hanford and give him the news. He stopped by Newman's office and told him. Newman didn't seem to be too thrilled about it one way or the other. Perhaps, Burke thought, he had had enough of the bones for a while. Dempsey was out. Burke sat down at his desk and dialed Hanford's number. The phone rang two times, and was answered by Halper.

"Mrs. Halper, this is Detective Burke of the Stanton Police Department. I have information for Mr. Hanford. May I speak to him please? It's important," he added, to forestall any objection from her.

"Very well, Sir, I'll inform him you are on the line."

"He heard her lay down the receiver. Thirty seconds later, Hanford came on the line. "Yes, Detective Burke," he said, "what do you have?"

Burke thought he detected fear in the old man's voice, or dread.

"I may be wrong, sir, but I think you will be happy to hear my news. Our DNA tests are concluded, and the bones from Bealer Woods are not your son's."

There was a long pause on the line, and then Hanford said, "Are you sure?"

"Yes. I have assurance from the scientist who did the tests. I don't have the documentation yet, but as soon as I do, I'll send you a letter to that effect. I thought you would like to know as soon as possible."

"Thank you, Detective Burke, thank you so much. And you are correct. I am happy at your news. I won't try to convince you of this, but I know my son is still alive out there somewhere."

"Well, I certainly hope you find him, Mr. Hanford. If we can be of any further assistance to you, please let me know. Good bye."

"Good bye, Lieutenant Burke, and God bless you."

Burke hung up the phone and pondered the situation. He felt a sense of relief that Hanford was removed from the equation, however, he felt rather empty, even let down. He had so thoroughly embraced the notion that the dead child was Hanford's long-lost son, that this new set of conflicting, complicating facts threw him into a state of confusion. He turned his chair around to the window and put his feet up on the sill. Several women, mothers one would assume, sat on benches in the little park and watched children playing on the swings and seesaws. He was still sitting there that way when Dempsey came in ten minutes later, and broke the spell. Burke turned his chair around to look into the inquisitive face of Dempsey.

"Okay, Burke said, "drag up a chair, and I'll tell you all about it."

When he finished he said, "we aren't just back to square one, we're back to minus ten. We now have two bunches of bones instead of one, and at least one of the people was clearly murdered. I say that, even as I realize how dangerous it is to draw conclusions—I'm learning my lessons. I would have bet anything that the dead baby was Hanford's kid, but if I had made that bet I would have lost my ass, wouldn't I? And you know something? It's scary to realize how wrong you can be sometimes."

"Yeah. I would have bet on it too. It looked like a safe bet."

"So," Burke continued, "I will say instead that, 'apparently one of the individuals was murdered, because he has this huge gash in his forehead right between his eyes,' and then I will leave it up to the reader of my report to draw his own conclusions."

"I wouldn't worry about being wrong on that one, Boss, unless someone thinks the gentleman committed suicide by striking himself soundly with an ax, after making arrangements with someone to drag him and his child out into the woods and bury them."

The absurdity of the image conjured up in his mind caused Burke to chuckle in spite of the gravity of the situation. "Seriously Elmo, look at what have we got here?"

"Like I've said all along, the bodies were brought in from somewhere else, either by road or water, and buried there in the woods. I tend to favor water. Somebody pulled a boat up to the bank, and dragged the corpses up there, dug a hole and buried them, it's as simple as that."

"That may be, but why do you suppose they didn't just throw them overboard and let the fish take care of them?" Burke asked.

"That's a good point, Dempsey said. I hadn't thought about that."

"Yeah, that's too simple to think about I guess." Burke got to his feet. I'm going in to talk to the chief. Want to come along?"

"Sure." Elmo put down his pencil, slipped the note pad he was writing on into a desk drawer, and followed Burke to Chief Newman's office. Newman motioned them inside, and said, "So, old man Hanson was real pleased to learn that wasn't his kid," Newman said.

"Hanford," Burke said.

"What?"

"His name is Hanford. That's right, like I told you before, he thinks his kid is still out there somewhere."

"Well, hope springs eternal. Now, what are we going to do about the man with the hole in his head, and his kid? You got any new ideas, Burke?"

"I'm debating with myself whether there is any use to send the bones off to the State Crime Lab this time, since the college has done such a good job. I want to send the remnants of cloth off, and the buttons, see if they can give us specific information on them. That might help us identify the bodies. Beyond that, I haven't worked anything else out yet. To tell you the truth, Chief, I'm sick of thinking about it. I think I'll go call Marge, and take he out to dinner and a movie tonight. Maybe even take the kids, too."

"Sounds like a good idea to me. Keep me posted, and try not to stir up any more controversies."

Burke was about to raise an objection to that last comment, but changed his mind when he thought he detected the slightest trace on a smile on Newman's face. "I'll try, Chief," He said instead.

—═┼ ┼═—

Burke decided to send the bones and everything to the State Crime Lab. The last week in August, he received the results. Along with a written report, there was an inventory of the bones, the buttons, the cloth fragments, and photographs. The lab confirmed the age estimates of the remains made by the university personnel, but refining it to around thirty years. The lab concluded that both the infant and the adult were male. How they were able to make the determination for the infant wasn't clear, and was not explained. No cause of death for the infant was stated, but the cause of death of the adult male was determined to be a skull-shattering blow to the forehead with a massive, sharp instrument, such as an axe or cleaver.

Burke read the report, handed it to Elmo, and then studied the inventory and photographs. The entire adult skeleton was accounted for, as were all but two lower ribs, a leg bone, and the lower jaw of the infant. The cloth fragments were dark blue serge, a twill fabric of worsted and wool, commonly used for men's suits, and scraps of linen, commonly used in the manufacture of shirts. The ordinary buttons were identified by size and type, as shirt and suit buttons, but without any manufacturer designation. The metal buttons were described as most likely from a child's play suit or jacket. Burke examined the items. When he got to the one metal button which was still in fairly good condition, he noted the faint imprint of an anchor, which good cleaning or chemical treatment had made visible, something clicked in his brain. "What the hell..." he said aloud. He opened his desk drawer and withdrew the envelope containing the Hanford materials, dumped the items on the desk, and pawed through them until he found the of the child standing on the lawn in front of the big house, looking back over his shoulder, smiling enigmatically at someone or something not in the picture. The child was wearing a sailor suit with brass buttons, on which he could discern the imprint of an anchor.

"Elmo! Look at this!"

Elmo jumped up and hurried across the room. "What is it?"

"What do you make of this?" Burke shoved the button and the photograph toward the edge of the desk for Elmo to examine.

He squinted at the ruined button, then at the photograph. He hurried back to his desk and returned with a magnifying glass. He studied them for a long time, going back and forth between the button and the photograph. "Well, I'll be," he said finally. "They sure look the same, don't they? What do you think, Boss?"

"I think they're identical."

"It has to be a coincidence, that's all," Elmo said. "What else could it be?"

"I don't know, but I want to verify what the Hanford child was wearing the day he disappeared." He handed some of the clippings to Elmo. "Read through these and see if they describe the kid's clothing. I don't recall that they did."

Elmo read through the articles. No mention was made of brass buttons, only that the child was wearing a white playsuit.

Burke was excited. "I want to follow up on this right now," he said. "But, I'm reluctant to disturb Hanford for something that could be a fluke."

"I imagine Mrs. Halper will answer the phone," said Dempsey.

Burke fumbled through the papers for Hanford's telephone number, found it and dialed. After three rings, Halper answered.

"Mrs. Halper, this is Detective Burke, Stanton Police Department."

Halper didn't speak, she was perhaps weighing whether to respond or hang up. Then she said, quietly, her voice sounded apprehensive. "Yes, Detective Burke, what is it?"

"A couple of loose ends, Mrs. Halper, I'm going through the material I got from Mr. Hanford, and I need to ask you a question. I'd rather not disturb him unless it's necessary."

"I appreciate your consideration, sir."

"Good. Thank you. Can you tell me what the child was wearing the day he disappeared?"

"Why, yes, I most certainly can. I remember it very clearly. I dressed him myself that morning. He was wearing a white play-suit with blue trim, and black patent leather shoes with little straps. It was his favorite outfit."

"A playsuit? Can you describe it for me, Mrs. Halper?"

"It was a sailor suit...white, with blue trim...."

"Is it the one in the picture Mr. Hanford gave me when I was there: The one with brass buttons, with anchors on them?"

"Why, yes...what...?"

"Thank you, Mrs. Halper, that all I need right now, thank you very much, goodbye." He hung up the phone before she could protest.

Burke gazed into space, a look of dark confusion on his face. The button on the playsuit in the photograph looked identical to the one he held in his hand, and Burke had great difficulty accepting as coincidental the fact that a button seemingly identical to the one on the clothing of the missing child should turn up in the grave of another child. It was simply too improbable. He pondered the facts, as he understood them, searching for a rational explanation, for something he had missed or misinterpreted. The first thing that occurred to him was that the DNA tests could somehow have been switched, or they could be wrong. Hadn't the scientists at Stanton College said that old samples were not always reliable? But, the State Crime Lab had agreed with the college's conclusions, had also agreed that the two skeletons were related, father and child, most likely, and that the dead child and Mr. Hanford were not related. Could it be possible that the tiny skeleton really was that of the abducted child after all, but that Mr. Hanford wasn't the biological father? Could he and his wife have adopted the child? Surely, if that were the case, Mr. Hanford would not have agreed to the test in the first place. It would have been pointless. Had his wife perhaps been unfaithful, and borne the child of another man?

Burke sat until the early afternoon pouring over the materials on his desk, attempting to resolve the conflicts and contradictions in his own mind. His confusion only increased. All of the scenarios seemed improbable, even absurd, and all he was getting for his effort was a headache. The ache behind his eyes, a dull throbbing ache, grew worse as he continued to read. He leaned far back in his chair and tried to relax, breathing slowly and evenly, as Marge had once taught him to do when he was worked up about something. Presently, still deep in thought, he left the office, drove to the college campus, parked in the visitors' lot, and walked to the offices of Dr. Smithers, on the chance that he might catch him there. The office was unoccupied. He glanced into the computer lab adjacent to the office and saw a young woman working alone at a computer terminal. Before her on the table were several printouts of wide, lined computer paper. He stepped inside. "Excuse me," he said.

Sheila Vann looked up from her work. "Yes? Oh, you're Detective Burke, aren't you?"

"Why, uh, yes, I am," he said, surprised that she knew him. "I'm looking for Professor Smithers, or Dr. Hamilton."

"Dr. Smithers isn't in today, and I don't know if Mark is here or not. I haven't seen either of them today. I'm Sheila Vann. I'll bet you're wondering how I knew who you were?"

"Yes, I was."

She stood, extended her hand, and said, "Nice to meet you. I missed you the first time you were here, but I saw you when you dropped off the bones and the blood sample. You've come about the tests?"

"Yes."

"I evaluated the test results. Maybe I can help you."

"Okay, thanks. I have a question. You might think it a strange one."

"Try me."

"I was wondering what the chances are that those test results could be completely wrong."

Ms. Vann arched her eyebrows as if she was indeed surprised at the question. "There's always a possibility, I suppose, but I really doubt it in this case."

"Why is that, Dr. Vann?"

"Call me Sheila."

"Okay, Sheila, if you'll call me Daniel."

She Smiled. "Okay, Daniel. The reason I say that is because the match was too good."

"Too good?"

"Yes, and besides that, I understand the state lab replicated our tests to a tee. I'm curious as to why you ask that question. Do you have reason to doubt the results?"

"Yes and no," Burke said. He quickly assessed the situation and decided to take her into his confidence.

"When we dug up the bones at Bealer Woods, we found a few tiny scraps of cloth and some buttons. Three of the buttons were of brass. One of them was in good enough shape to make out clearly that there was an anchor imprint on the button. Now, when I went to see Mister Hanford to interview him concerning his missing son, he lent me a photograph of the child wearing a playsuit. It had brass buttons on it, apparently identical with the one we found in the grave with the bones."

"Hmm, I see," she said. "That is very strange, isn't it? A coincidence, do you think?"

"Frankly, I find that very hard to get my mind around, Sheila. I don't much believe in coincidence. I'm wondering if the samples from Mr. Hanford and the adult skeleton could have been switched."

She thought about that at length. Finally, she said, "No, and here's why. We successfully ran the tests on Mr. Hanford's blood first. If you recall, we had the bones of the child before that, but we hadn't been able to get a good sample. We finally succeeded in extracting a viable sample from the child's teeth. The tests of Hanford and the infant were both completed, and the results recorded and dated, before we did the extraction from the teeth of the adult skeleton. Those tests were run two days later. I recall it exactly. All of this is properly recorded and the test sheets and log are dated. The test results we sent you will show that. No, Daniel, it is quite impossible. If you have the time, I will get your test results out and show you what I mean."

She walked across the room to a file cabinet and removed a folder, extracted the test sheets, spread them on the table side by side, and indicated the dates and test sequence numbers.

"I see. Well, that's that, then."

"Is there anything else I can help you with?"

He hesitated. "Yes, there is. Frankly, I am really over my head in this business, and I could use some help with it. I'd like to understand the mechanics of the thing better, the process you go through, so I can get a feel for whether it's telling me what I need to know, if you understand what I'm getting at. Dr. Smithers gave me a broad overview about the DNA, and genes, and so forth, but no details of the actual testing procedure."

"Yes, I understand. I'll be happy to explain it to you."

"I warn you, I barely scraped by high school biology."

"The test procedure isn't hard to understand. The DNA strands are extracted by centrifuge from blood or other body tissues that have been prepared in a liquid state. A centrifuge is used to separate out the DNA material. Then chemical substances called enzymes are used to cut the long strands of DNA into small segments. DNA has a negative electrical charge, so we place the fragments in a gel, and an electric current is passed through it. This causes the negatively charged fragments to separate and distribute along the gel as they migrate toward the positive electrode. The smaller ones move faster than the larger ones.

"After the fragments have distributed along the surface of the gel, we blot them onto a nylon membrane, after which they are exposed to, and absorb, a small amount of radiation. This nylon membrane is then placed on x-ray film. The absorbed radiation produces an image of the fragments on the film, just like a photograph negative. Then we produce positive photographic prints." She paused.

"Okay," said Burke. "Then what?"

"The patterns on these prints are compared with the patterns from other samples which have been processed in the same way. We look for similar, or even identical, arrangements." She picked up a sheet of paper and pointed to a cluster of lines, some darker than others. "The greater the number of similar arrangements between the two samples, the greater is the probability of a match. Of course, if the two samples are from the same person, they will be identical. That's about all there is to it."

"You make it sound so easy. What about the chances of it being in error?"

"The probability of error diminishes as the number of matching segments increases. For example, for five matching segments the odds of an error are roughly one in a million. With larger numbers of matches, the probability of error diminishes to as little as one in several billion."

"Several billion?"

"Yes."

"What about the probability of there being an error involving the two skeletons you tested for me?"

"Like I said, perhaps one in twenty or thirty billion."

"Twenty or thirty billion! Then it is virtually an absolute certainty that they are closely related."

"That's right."

"Okay, then, what's the catch?"

"The catch?"

"Yeah. It seems too easy, too certain, there must be a catch to it. Why isn't this process more accepted—by the courts, for example? According to Dr. Smithers, people don't have that much confidence in the results. I don't understand."

"Well, It's a brand-new science, for one thing, and I suppose there is a sort of catch. In the first place, bear in mind that we're dealing with probabilities, not absolutes. Another problem area is that of test reliability. There have been serious reliability problems in the past, such as questionable procedures, unqualified practitioners, that sort of thing. Like everything else, it largely depends on the integrity and skill of the people performing the procedure. But what else is new? It's the same with everything, isn't it?"

Burke smiled at the young woman's wisdom.

"Believe it or not, I think I understand, now." He rose, poised to depart when he noticed what appeared to be several other DNA test reports in folders on the table. He selected one and studied the lines and patterns. Sheila said, "There's another part of our work that I haven't told you about. You have a few more minutes?"

"Sure."

"Well, now I have to switch hats. I think Adrian mentioned to you that we were developing computer software."

"Yes, he did."

She picked up the folder and leafed through the photographic sheets, with the now familiar bar-code-like groupings of lines. "These are like the ones we sent you. We receive actual test data like this from various locations around the country. DNA is tested at some hospitals, clinics, and other types of labs. We need to use real data to test our computer programs. We are slowly building a real database for future applications. What I'm doing now is entering into the computer memory the data that came in this past week. This part isn't much fun, because it is slow, tedious work. We're looking into using optical scanners in the future to enter the data directly into the computer. That will make the process a lot simpler and faster. But in the meantime, I'll probably spend an hour and a half to two hours putting the data from these twelve sheets into the computer manually. After I do that, I'll run the program again."

"Sounds like a lot of work."

"Yes, it is. I'll be here late, but I only have to do it once a week."

"Then I better get out of here and let you get back to work. Thanks, Sheila," Burke extended his hand. "You've been a great help to me. I appreciate it."

"Glad I could help, Daniel."

Daniel was embarrassed by his ignorance as he left the young scientist. He didn't like the feeling. He was very much impressed with her. In fact, he was impressed with all the people he had encountered at the college. He recalled that he hadn't felt that way when he was a student. He had felt somehow superior to the college crowd then, students and teachers alike. They were the "soft bellies," as he sometimes thought of them, who had sat out the war in Vietnam, while other young men like him had fought and died, or had grown callous and bitter.

As a combat marine just back from Vietnam, he, like many others, was embittered by the treatment that returning veterans received at home. It had been difficult for him, as it was for others, to transition back to civilian life, to regain his civilian sensibilities, and to knuckle down to the hard work required to get an education and to prepare for a career. In his unsettled state, he, frankly, had not been that unhappy and disappointed at the time, when he dropped out of school to support his family. His frustration came later, as he realized his limitations. Now, ten years out of school, the sting of those limitations permeated everything, every facet of his existence, such as how people viewed him, how he and his family lived, their status within the community—everything. He hungered for the kind of jobs these people at the college had, meaningful, challenging careers that others respected and rewarded.

Even beyond that, he knew he had let himself slip too far. When a dodo bird like Elmo Dempsey starts spouting off to him about DNA analysis, he knows he has to be in trouble.

On impulse, he swung the car in the direction of the city's public library. He felt conspicuous as he walked through the entryway and up to the desk. He was sure all eyes were upon him. He felt a hot flash as the librarian turned to him and smiled. My God, I'm blushing, he realized. He managed to blurt out that he was interested in reading about DNA.

"Have you looked in the card index, sir?"

"No, I haven't. I'm a little rusty. I haven't used the library lately."

Now that he thought about it, he hardly ever went to the library, even during his school years. He had never really learned the intricate skills of using catalogues, and indices.

"Shame on you," said the librarian, mockingly. "Well, come along, sir, I'll get you started. Are you interested in scientific publications, or books?"

"Both, I guess."

The librarian flipped through the index quickly and expertly, scribbling on the note paper conveniently at hand with a little stub of yellow pencil. "Let's go to the stacks and I'll show you what books we have."

They walked between the long rows of books, and stopped. "These are the books on DNA." She gestured with her hands where they started and where they ended. "Some are better than others. You can browse through them if you like, but please be careful to put the books back exactly where you got them or they will get lost and we will never be able to find them. If you are in doubt, put them on the table there and I'll put them back where they belong. Okay?"

"Okay."

"While you're looking through the books, I want to check on a couple of magazines for you."

"Thank you very much."

She returned shortly with an old edition of the magazine, Nature.

Burke sat at a table and leafed through the three books he had selected, then flipped open the magazine to a page marked by the librarian. There was a published letter written to Nature from

James Watson and Francis Crick. He read the letter. It was about the double helix. The authors said this about the double helix:

"This structure has novel features which are of considerable biological Interest."

Only later, as Burke read further in books and subsequent publications, did he realize what an understatement that was.

Burke stayed in the library until it closed. He would have loved to take a book or two with him, but he had no library card, and had embarrassed himself quite enough for one day: Maybe later.

CHAPTER 5

GOODBYE SHEILA VANN

B urke shook the sleep from his eyes, as he struggled to understand the voice on the phone. It was the night duty officer at the police station calling. Burke clicked on the lamp beside his bed and glanced at the clock on the night table. It was 2:45 a.m.

"What...murdered...I'm on my way."

"What is it?" Marge asked, groggy with sleep.

Burke dressed hurriedly, his manner agitated, his face drawn. "There's been a murder at the college."

"Murder! Who?

"Dr. Sheila Vann."

When he arrived at the entrance to the Biological Sciences Building where Vann and her associates had their lab, two police cars were there, along with an ambulance. All had their lights flashing. Uniformed police officers stood guard at the entrance into the building, and another was posted upstairs by the door to the lab where Burke had visited with Dr. Vann just hours earlier. Elmo Dempsey was there. The body had been discovered by the night janitor who worked that part of the building starting at around 1:00 a.m. He reported finding the body at precisely 2:10 a.

Dempsey handed Burke a handwritten note with the information on the two men.

Sheila Vann was not attractive anymore. Someone had bashed in her head. She lay crumpled on the flood by her overturned chair, her head haloed by a rusty-red pool of blood. Nearby on the floor, lay a paper punch, a heavy chunk of iron, apparently the murder weapon.

Burke felt sick. He swallowed hard to choke back the urge to vomit. "What do you have, Elmo?" he asked wearily.

"She was struck by a blunt instrument, Boss. Looks like that paper punch over there." Dempsey pointed to the office tool lying on the floor a few feet from the body.

"Has anything been touched?"

"Not a thing. Just the way we found it."

The coroner arrived, and for the better part of an hour, technicians and a police photographer swarmed about the room, performing their various functions. In response to Burke's inquiry, the coroner fixed the time of death at between 6:00 and 8:00 P.M. When everybody finished, the body was removed. Afterward, Burke asked Dempsey to go over the lab and environs: offices, hallway, etc., looking for physical evidence while Burke questioned the janitors, who had been standing-by in another room. He interviewed them in a vacant office, starting with the one who found the body. The man appeared nervous, afraid. Burke did nothing to set his mind at ease. He eyed the man intently while removing his notebook and pen form his inside coat pocket.

"What is your name," He began.

"Ronald Meeker, sir."

"You work for the college?"

Yes, sir."

"For how long?"

"Eight years."

"What time did you come to work last night?"

"I already told the other gentleman all this."

"I want you to tell me, if you don't mind."

"I clocked in at 12:45, and started working a few minutes later down at the other end of the hall, cleaning the offices and empting the trash cans. I got up to the computer lab at 2:10. I know it was that time, cause when I seen her body on the floor, the clock was right there on the wall."

"Did you see anybody from the time you arrived on campus to when you found the body?"

"No I did not see anybody, other than my helper, Glenn Purvis. He showed up about ten minutes after I did."

"When you found Miss Vann in the computer lab, you saw her through the glass door before you entered the room?"

"No, Sir. I didn't see her until I come in and turned on the light switch."

"The light was off in the computer room?"

"Yes, Sir, it was off."

Burke went methodically through a long litany of seemingly routine questions, and when he finished with Meeker, he started all over with Purvis. The stories of the two janitors were in agreement, were plausible, and Burke saw no reason to disbelieve them. Once he had finished with them, he thanked them, and allowed them to go about their business. By that time, dawn was breaking. Word of the murder had been conveyed to the college administration, as well as to Hamilton and Smithers, who converged on the scene a little before dawn, appearing badly shaken. Burke quizzed them together. "I'm glad you are here, gentlemen. I was planning to get with you this morning. I need to ask you a few questions."

"Surely you don't suspect us," said Smithers. His face was all flushed and puffy.

"Of course he doesn't," said Hamilton. "It's necessary police procedure."

"That's correct, nothing personal," said Burke.

"I had a commitment yesterday afternoon," Hamilton began, without being asked a specific question. "A faculty planning session ran late, so I didn't come back to the lab office. You can verify this, of course. At around 7:00 P.M., when the meeting broke up, I checked in with my answering service and received a message that Sheila had tried to reach me. I didn't call back at that time since it was well past normal quitting time. Instead, I intended to call her from home, which I did. I called her home number first, and when she did not answer there, I called the lab. When I got no answer there as well, I dismissed the matter, assuming it could wait until morning, thinking that if it had been urgent, she would have called again."

Smithers stated that he had taken the day off, and that he and his family spent the day with relatives in Chillicothe. "We got home a little after 10:00 P.M. and went straight to bed."

Smithers was still visibly upset, and struggled to hold back tears. "My God, who could have done this horrible thing," he said.

"I was hoping one of you might have some ideas," Burke said.

"Nobody had any reason to harm Sheila," Hamilton said.

Smithers nodded in agreement. "She didn't have any enemies. The very idea is absurd." Tears welled up in his eyes again as he spoke.

"Some drug-crazy hooligan off the street, most likely did it," said Hamilton.

"All right, Gentlemen, thank you, you can go now."

When they departed, Burke got up with Dempsey, and they sealed the two doors to the lab, and posted an officer in the hallway.

※ ※

The entire community was in a state of shock. The college suspended all classes, as Burke, Dempsey, and several other members of the force swarmed over the campus interviewing people, and looking for leads. In the evenings after work, Marge filled Burke in on the gossip and speculation from the town's folks.

"You heard what?" Burke said to her more than once in the ensuing days, as she recounted the latest outrageous or absurd rumor to him.

The forensic technicians hurried through their procedures and evaluations of materials gathered at the crime scene, sensitive to the public's concern. The results were disappointing. No clear prints were found on the murder weapon, and only Vann's, Smithers' and Hamilton's prints were found in the lab. The janitor's prints were found on the outside door knob, as was expected. Beyond that they found nothing.

In the days following the murder, Dempsey conducted intensive background checks on the two custodial workers. They had no records and nothing in their backgrounds aroused suspicion. All items of clothing that they wore on the night of the murder were examined minutely for bloodstains, with negative results. Smithers' alibi checked out. Witnesses placed him and his family in Chillicothe until late in the afternoon and at a gas station along the highway to Stanton as late as 9:30 P.M. According to other attendees, Hamilton had indeed been attending a faculty planning session and hadn't left the meeting until seven in the evening, after which, he reported, he had driven directly home. However, his movements after he left the meeting could not be corroborated by witnesses. Burke made judicious note to follow up on this point, given the fact that the coroner had fixed the time of death at between 6:00 P.M. and 8:00 P.M. Burke considered his planned inquiry into Hamilton's uncertain time period to be a technicality.

Interviews of the members of the college staff, student body and others, such as the woman who was on duty at the telephone answering service used by the lab team, took Burke and his assistants from the Department two weeks. Meanwhile, Dempsey checked the lab's telephone log and the telephone company's records, learning that only a few calls went out from the lab telephones that afternoon. He followed up on all of them. A call had been placed from Sheila's phone to Hamilton's home number at six forty-five, thus narrowing the time of death to between 6:45 and 8:00 p.m.

From Burke's interviews, he identified Sheila's friends and men she had dated. Burke, with Dempsey's assistance, located all of them and interviewed them. All could account for themselves during the critical time from 6:45 to 8:00 p. m.

Burke and Dempsey considered that Vann might have been the victim of a robbery, and they had conducted a thorough inventory of the contents of her purse and person, as well as the contents of the lab and office. Aided by Smithers and Hamilton, they were unable to find anything missing. No motive for the crime nor suspect emerged. All they had to go on was impromptu murder weapon and the puzzling circumstances of the crime, while the only loose end was Dr. Hamilton's lack of an alibi for a few minutes between the time he left his meeting until he arrived home, as he reported, at approximately seven-thirty, and thereafter until Mrs. Hamilton arrived home at approximately 8:00 p.m. *Was there enough time for him to have squeezed in the murder, should he have been so inclined?*

Burke considered it a minor point, but he didn't want to leave it dangling. He drove his car three successive evenings at precisely seven o'clock directly from the location of Doctor Hamilton's faculty meeting place on campus to his home, and determined that, depending upon traffic conditions, the trip could have been made in as little as twelve minutes. Heavier traffic or unhurried driving pushed the trip time to around twenty-five minutes, which was what the doctor had estimated, which still left thirty or so minutes unaccounted for until his mother arrived home.

There was no reason to suspect Hamilton, from all appearances, he and Vann were close friends as well as professional associates. *But why had she tried to call him at his home the night of the murder?*

Burke subsequently questioned Hamilton about this: "Miss Vann called your home at six forty-five the night she was murdered. Do you know why she tried to reach you?"

"No, I don't."

"Did she leave a message on your answering machine?"

"No."

"I take it you hadn't told her about your faculty planning session?"

"No, I had not. She wasn't around when I left the office. Even if she had been, there was no reason why I should have told her. She wasn't my secretary, you know. Besides, I didn't know at the time I left the office that the meeting would run over like it did, and I'm in and out of the lab office all the time, because of my other responsibilities. The nature of our work is such that we only have to come together periodically to review our progress and work on specific problems."

"I see. Had there been other occasions in the course of your work together where she needed to contact you after hours?"

Hamilton thought about it. "No, not that I recall," he said.

"Then, maybe it was something personal."

"Once again, I consider that to be highly unlikely. I'm sorry, I simply have no explanation for it. In fact, I'm as puzzled as you are. By the way, do you know if she tried to call Doctor Smithers?"

"Not according to the phone records. She told me that afternoon that he wasn't in the office. Possibly, she knew he was going out of town."

The two men sat silently looking at each other. Burke realized that he was out of questions as well as ideas. He felt a sudden flush of embarrassment as the eyes of the young doctor gazed into his. He believed that Hamilton was telling him the truth and he didn't want to offend him, so he let it go at that. "Very well, Doctor. Thank you. Let me know if you think of anything that might be helpful to our investigation."

"I certainly will."

Burke got to his feet, turned and left the room, not completely satisfied with respect to Hamilton, but he was at a loss as to what else he could do.

━╋ ╉━

Nothing like the murder of Sheila Vann had ever happened in Stanton. Reporters swarmed over City Hall and the police department. Burke could not ignore them. He tried to be patient and reasonable and deal with them professionally. The murder was the headline story every day for well over a week, until it dwindled to a "still-no-progress reported" type of article. Prominent citizens bombarded the chief with calls to express their alarm, and to ask for progress reports. The chief was beside himself with anxiety and made frequent trips to his credenza to fortify himself with quick shots of bourbon. He stressed the importance over and over to Burke of the need for a quick resolution of the case. "I want an arrest," he said succinctly.

Burke, too, wanted an arrest, and he wanted the motive for the murder to be simple and straightforward, as crimes usually were in Stanton, like robbery, a spurned lover' or a jealous rival. A strange feeling had crept over him as he went forward with his investigation, a disturbing feeling, which he could not shake, and no matter how many times he dismissed it and pushed it from his consciousness, it popped up again. It was the nagging feeling that Vann's murder was a direct result of his having visited with her that afternoon. He knew this was irrational, but he could not help himself. A man either believes something or he doesn't. That lack of belief was why he was not a religious man. He racked his brain trying to think of something he had done or said which might have endangered her. He had told her about the sailor suit, and the brass button with the anchor, that was all. *Could that have triggered something? But what?* It seemed absurd, and yet the feeling persisted.

Over and over, he reviewed the facts of the murder as he knew them. Based upon the, admittedly, limited knowledge he had acquired of her, he found no indication of trouble or conflict. He knew that a murder not solved within the first forty-eight hours or so becomes problematic. The mystical forty-eight hours had long since come and gone, and he had nothing.

The absence of motive or suspect prompted him to mention his growing apprehension that his visit with her at the lab might have somehow triggered her murder. He hesitated, knowing how Newman was, and because of his own uncertainty, but decided to proceed. The chief had seemed puzzled at first by what Burke was saying, as if he didn't understand. Then, as he began to comprehend, he looked at Burke as if Burke were crazy, and then dismissed the notion out of hand: "Just a coincidence, Daniel," he said, firmly and dismissively. "I don't want to hear any more talk like that. Is that clear?"

"All right, sir, but I've run out of ideas."

Newman glared at him. "It's a little early for that, isn't it? What do you know about this girl, really?" he asked. "Was she a party girl? I understand she wasn't married. Did she run around? Hang out in bars?"

"Look, Chief, this woman wasn't a 'girl.' This woman was a scientist, a Ph. D., and a college professor."

"So? Don't college professors take a crap like the rest of us?"

"What are you trying to say?"

"Only that I think maybe you're a little too awed by this gal. Maybe you ought to get out there and dig around some more, find out what she was into. Somebody killed her, and so far, you don't have squat. Stop thinking of her as some goddamn princess."

Burke left the meeting irritated and depressed. He sat at his desk, fuming. He had not found a receptive ear for his concerns.

Instead, he had encountered a scared old man, already looking for a scapegoat. Burke didn't like having his ass chewed out by Newman like that. Newman had never reacted like that before.

"The goddamned old boozer!" he said, as he fidgeted nervously, absentmindedly scratching his belly. Burke could sense that his blood pressure was high. He forced himself to sit calmly in his chair and breathe slowly and deeply through his nose. After a while, he started thinking about Sheila Vann again. *Damn it, maybe Newman, was right! Maybe he did think of her as a princess.* He had only met her once, and yet he could not imagine her being involved in anything smutty. Maybe he was awed by her credentials. Maybe he was a reverse snob. They say people like that don't think much of themselves. Maybe he had fallen in love with her on the spot, at first sight, as they say.

Nevertheless, he wasn't ready to reject his intuition without a fight. He mentioned his suspicion to Marge at the dinner table that evening after the children had left the table, about his visit with Sheila having had something to do with her murder. Marge had a good head on her shoulders. He would test his hypothesis on her. But, she had looked at him funny, also, like he was putting her on, maybe, or was crazy, just like the chief had. All right, maybe he was going nuts. If Marge couldn't see it nobody could. After that, he kept his suspicions to himself. He would do what the Chief wanted to the best of his ability, he would go digging in the muck for Sheila's killer.

Burke got up out of his chair and unlocked the filing cabinet against the wall to the side of his desk where he kept his active or sensitive files, and remover the thick folder on Sheila Vann. He laid it down on the end of the desk, and leafed through the contents until he found what he was after. It was a bust-view photograph of Vann, one which he had acquired in the process of his investigation, and one which he thought most accurately portrayed her. He replaced the folder in the cabinet, relocked it, took his coat from the hangar, and left the building. He got in his car and drove out of the lot, heading toward the west end of town, toward Schilling's Bar and Lounge. He might as well start there. It wouldn't take him too long to canvass the town, to show the picture to every bartender, ask about Vann. That was the first step. That was as far as he had thought. He didn't want to think too deeply about it at the moment. He wanted to just do something, he wanted some action. Right now, though, he felt the need to unburden himself, to talk to someone. Chris was always good for that. He, also, needed to talk things over more with Marge. He often wondered of late, if his stratagem of silence to protect her from what he was experiencing, from what he was feeling inside, was working. Maybe all it did was unduly isolate them from each other, to isolate him from the logical source of support which more and more of late he felt he needed.

Burke didn't park in the garage down the street as he usually did. He took a parking space across the street from the bar, turned off the engine, and sat there for a few minutes, thinking, looking at the three story building which housed Schilling's Bar and Lounge, and remembering. When he first came to Stanton, that building and his friendship with the Schillings, son and father, had been his anchor. Chris and his dad, August Schilling, a widower, had lived on the second floor over the bar. The third floor was used mainly for storage. Mr. Schilling, realizing Burke's status as a young veteran with limited resources, about to embark on an academic career, had offered him a room on the third floor overlooking the Ohio River. Burke had taken it, and he and Chris had fixed it up nicely.

The room had everything one needed, including a private bath and cooking facilities in the form of a stove, sink, and small refrigerator all housed together in a single compact unit that was about the size of a kitchen range. Burke bought a small color TV and a stereo. But what he liked most about the place was a tiny balcony, large enough for a couple of patio chairs, which overlooked the river, and Schilling's' boat dock below. He loved to sit and sip his drink, and watch the lights at night, and the boats and barges on the water, and listen to the sounds of the river. While a student, Burke had taken his women friends up there. The room was still available to him should he wish to use it. He still had the key. But he had not.

He had used this sometime need to be out all night as a ruse in times past, to go to the room, on those occasions when he felt the need to get out of the house, to be alone. There was something liberating about the room, there in the building that housed the bar, perched on the riverbank in a commercial district on the seedier side of town, above where he parked his bass boat. Should things ever get to be too much for him, he could retreat there, in full confidence that nobody on earth could find him. Chris would never tell, even if they put him on the rack and tortured him.

Burke morbid, depressing state of mind continued, as he reflected further on those times, how the two of them had spent a lot of time before and after classes in August Schilling's bar, often making a meal of pickled pigs feet and boiled eggs when they were short of change, and how they had sat for hours at Mr. Schillings private table, when business was light, drinking beer, and listening to the old man's tales of the old country.

August Schilling was a German immigrant, and had hopped off a barge in the late 1920s at the age of eighteen. He made his living peddling fruit and vegetables at a street market in the early days, and somehow managed to acquire the means, over time, to buy the three story building. At the time, it housed a beer joint on the first floor, and rooms and small apartments on the other two floors. As he could afford to, he modernized and expanded the bar and changed the name to Schilling's Bar and Lounge, which, he said, added a touch of class. His was a liberal and accommodating philosophy. He had not objected when his son and his son's friend, Daniel, took their girlfriends to the rooms upstairs, after all, they were both adult men and military veterans. They could enter, if they desired to do so for reasons of privacy, without coming through the bar, by a convenient and clandestine route behind the buildings on the riverside,

Now, as Burke began his investigation into the possible dark side of Sheila Vann, he naturally came back first to talk to his chum, Chris Schilling, who had taken over the bar when his father died in 77, and with whom he still played poker every Thursday night, and saw frequently at lunchtime when he partook of his calorie-rich hot roast beef sandwiches.

Burke sighed, opened the car door, got out, crossed the street, and entered the bar. He sat on a stool at the bar, while his eyes grew accustomed to the subdued light. There were only a couple of other customers there. Schilling, who still worked the bar, along with his hired help, not because of economic necessity, but because he enjoyed it, saw him, and ambled over opposite him. Well, sport, it's not lunch time. What are you doing here?"

"Hello to you, to," he said. How about forking me out two of those pickled eggs, barkeep."

Schilling smirked, walked over to the jar of pickled boiled eggs, and took a large spoon, dipped out two into a dish, walked back and set them down in front of Burke. "Just had to have some pickled eggs, eh?" Schilling said, leaning against the bar,

"No, actually, "Burke said, as he took up an egg and bit into it, "I'm here on an important police investigation."

"That so?"

"Yeah. You know the lady professor that was murdered out at the college? Well, I'm doing a background on her, looking for motive and opportunity for someone to do her in. As a prominent member of the underworld, I naturally came to you. Can you help me out?"

Schilling grew serious as he recollected, then he said, "I recognized her picture in the paper, right away." he said. "She was in here a few times with friends or a date, but never alone, never on the make. She was always a perfect lady. I never heard her mentioned in any negative or derogatory way. Believe me, if she was into anything around this town, I would know about it. Everybody likes to take their shots at the swells out at the college, and the big shots that run the town, you know that better than anybody does."

"Well, keep your eyes and ears open, for me."

"You bet."

⊫⊣⊢⊨

In spite of Schilling's assurances, Burke made the rounds of the other bars and nightspots in town. He didn't learn anything. Apparently Vann seldom visited the bars and dives of the little river town, and kept her love life close to the bosom.

As Chris had said, "She was cleaner than a polished shot glass."

Burke ended the bar hopping phase of his inquiry, and returned to the office. He reviewed Vann's file. She was originally from Cincinnati, had gone to high school there, and had gotten her Bachelor's degree from Xavier University, and her Master's and PhD from Ohio State. She taught pre-med at Stanton College for six years and had been involved with Smithers' NIH grant for three past years. Her record and reputation at the college were immaculate. She was unmarried, but had previously had a live-in boyfriend. After they broke up, she had dated several men, including some on campus. Her parents were dead and she had no siblings.

Burke called the schools in Cincinnati. To a person, they were shocked and dismayed by her death. Everyone had something good to say about her, such as how she was such a nice Catholic girl, or, she was so smart, or, she was a Christian, and so on. Burke knew he was wasting his time. He concluded there was nothing smutty, bizarre, or sinister in Sheila Vann's life, but only in her death—her murder.

Burke is sitting at his desk the following Monday morning, after a weekend on the river fishing and playing with Marge and the kids. He is relaxed, he is sipping his coffee, and he is thinking. He is thinking about the Vann murder.

After the conclusion of the investigations, tests, and interviews, all that remained was Burke's eerily persistent feeling that his visit to Vann had something to do with her death. He had run that idea by both Newman and Marge and each had rebuked him. Well, it didn't matter, he was going with it anyway. He had to consider it.

The only commonality between Burke and Vann had to do with the bones found in Bealer Woods, so, *if her death was related to his visit, it had to be related to the bones somehow. On the other hand, what if his visit had nothing to do with her death, but the test of the bones did. What if the killer worked at the college, heard about the bones, and knew what it meant, and was closely following everything the research team did? Then when Sheila discovers something that the killer didn't want exposed, he is Johnny-on-the-spot, and he kills her to keep her quiet?*

Oh, come on now, he chided himself, isn't that just too far-fetched, really? Hmm, on the other hand, the girl really is dead, isn't she? Yes. And, someone killed her, right? Right? Who did it, then, and why? Was he overlooking something that would make sense of it all?

Newman called him in, at the end of the week. Burke asked Elmo to attend.

"Well, Men," Newman began. "What do we have here, a crime of passion? A robbery? When am I going to see an arrest? I'm getting an awful lot of pressure to solve this case and bring someone to justice. Have you thoroughly checked out all the transients, derelict, and druggies on the west side?"

"I still don't know, Chief, but I don't think it was a robber, or druggies, or anyone off the street."

"Why not?"

"Her purse was in her office next door. It had money and credit cards in it. She was wearing an expensive watch and an emerald ring."

"Well, okay, scratch robbery."

"As far as it being a crime of passion, Elmo and I have checked the alibis of all the men she's dated, and other friends and acquaintances, and they're all clean. They've got airtight alibis. That's not to say there couldn't possibly be someone out there that we've missed. There was no sexual assault involved, and Vann was not a drug user herself, according to the autopsy report."

"What, then?"

"It seems clear to me that the murder was not premeditated. The murderer used an object at hand as the murder weapon, the paper punch, which was convenient there on the table."

"Okay, that makes sense. Go on."

"I believe the murderer was someone she knew. Why? Her position at the computer workstation gave her a view of both doors to the lab, and she would have seen a stranger coming in. It's unlikely someone could have come in unnoticed and attacked her from behind. However, the fact that she was struck from behind, and with an object from the office itself, means that she felt no reason to be concerned for her safety, no reason to suspect that she was in any danger. I believe the decision to kill her was made on the spot because of something that transpired between her and the killer."

"Yeah? Like what?"

"I don't know, but I suspect it had something to do with her work, with what she was doing there at the computer."

"What was she doing at the computer?"

"Since she was killed in the lab rather than in her office, it's reasonable to assume she was working on their research project, as she had been that same afternoon when I visited her. She might even have been working on the tests they did for us for all I know, the tests on the bones, and on Mr. Hanford's blood."

"What? Are we back to that again? I hope you've got something to support that wild imagination of yours this time, Burke. We're police officers, here, not fiction writers."

Newman was irritated, and when he was irritated, he called Burke by his surname. When he was benevolently inclined, he called him Daniel. But he hadn't completely bit his head off, and Burke sensed a tiny opening, a spark of interest in the chief's reaction, so he continued.

"Hear me out chief, okay?"

"Go ahead," Newman said, with a display of impatience.

"There was no sign of a struggle. According to the coroner, the killer struck her from behind and above, while she sat at her workstation. I assume she was either working on the computer terminal itself or with the printouts on the table beside her terminal. Why? Think about it. If you had a visitor in your office, even someone you knew, would you turn your back on that person and ignore him and continue working? Not likely. No, I believe she was showing the murderer something or demonstrating something on the computer much the way she did for me that afternoon."

"Boy, that's some imagination you've got there, Daniel," said Elmo

"Yeah," Newman said. "You're reaching, don't you think, Burke?"

"I don't think so, Chief. Add to all that, the fact that she tried to get up with Hamilton that evening perhaps to tell him something—something she had discovered."

"Discovered? Like what?" Elmo asked"

Burke furrowed his brow and struggled to suppress his growing irritation at their apparent shortsightedness.

"My interviews with people who knew her, consistently brought out one thing about Ms. Vann, she was a cool-headed gal, very professional, and not prone to excitement over nothing. Yet, she telephoned

Hamilton's home number that evening from the lab, something she had never done before, according to him. Now, I know that seems like a very small thing, but it's a departure from her normal behavior. If it had happened at any other time it would be nothing, but it was a short time before she was murdered. That makes it significant. It is just possible that what she wanted to tell him constituted a threat to the murderer, and the murderer did her in because of it."

"Wait a minute," said Chief Newman. "If she had something on someone, something serious enough for that person to kill her, why would she sit there and show it to him, with her back to him, so he can clobber her over the head? Furthermore," said the chief, the volume of his voice rising, obviously warming to his mission of debunking Burke's theory, "what could she possibly have in that damned computer that would—

"Look, I don't know, Chief." Burke spoke through his teeth, struggling against a rising anger. "Do you have a better idea?"

Newman reacted to Burke's uncharacteristic insolence. His face and neck flushed, but he checked himself, perhaps considering that it was not in his interest to lean to hand on this man, who carried more and more of Newman's administrative duties. "Okay, suppose I buy your wild-ass theory for the sake of further discussion," he said. "What does it mean, then, Daniel? What are you telling me? I don't understand what you're driving at! It seems like to me you're suggesting that Hamilton killed the girl."

"I want you to back me up, Chief, so that I can explore this idea of mine. I don't want to stick my neck out here and have it lopped off. The laboratory is still sealed because I haven't released it, and nobody at the college has asked me to. I want to go through the lab again with Hamilton and Smithers, so that I can talk to them, and learn as much as I can about what they're doing there. And I want to get at the contents of that computer. I want to have a search warrant ready to use if necessary. They may object to my having access to the confidential files in that computer. They use real people's real data to test their computer program. I want it cleared by you before I approach them about it, and I want a search warrant ready when I first raise the issue with them."

Newman sighed. "Do you really feel that's necessary, Daniel?" Newman was beginning to soften.

"Chief, as you've pointed out yourself, there's a murderer out there."

Newman looked tired. Burke hadn't really noticed it, but he was a frail, gray, old man, scrunched up in his chair, rolling an un-lit cigar around in his fingers. For a moment, Burke felt sorry for him. It was obvious he wanted this problem to go away. He didn't want the college administration down on him, or the mayor and city council on his back, or the self-important people around town calling him and complaining all the time.

"I think you're nuts, Daniel, frankly," he said. "But go ahead, get your warrant. Then go out there and piss off everybody at the college. But you better have all your duck lined up, boy, before you start charging someone, or even intimating that some important citizen of this community is suspected of murder, and don't blame me if it all comes tumbling down on top of your head—our heads. Mine will get lopped too. Maybe you've never had the mob turn against you, but I have."

"Thanks, Chief. I'll be careful."

Burke and Dempsey make a quick exit. Walking down the hall toward their office, Dempsey said, "Say, Boss, I didn't mean to put down your theory in there, I—

"Don't worry about it Elmo, you did fine."

⌐╫ ╫⌐

Burke did not have to use the search warrant which he carried in his inside coat pocket. He asked Hamilton and Smithers for a meeting at the lab and they agreed, readily and without comment.

In the hallway, though, before they went into the lab Smithers asked, "Have you learned something, Detective? If so, out with it."

Both men appeared nervous. They seemed to have lost their usual cool, superior professional demeanors.

"I assure you, gentlemen," Burke smiled disarmingly, "I'm not trying to be mysterious. I'm going back over some things to further my understanding of them, that's all." Their edginess gave him a strangely comforting feeling, a little shot of confidence. "Let's go into the lab," he said.

He broke the police seal on the door, and they entered. The room had grown musty. They moved about, avoiding the spot where the body had lain.

"I would like for us to take a fresh look at things," Burke said. "First thing, I would like the two of you to reexamine the lab, thoroughly. Look for anything out of the ordinary, anything missing or out of place. I know you did it before, but we were all upset and preoccupied at the time. We possibly might have missed something."

For thirty minutes, Burke sat in a chain in the corner of the room, watching, while the two men examined the contents of the room: the shelves, the filing cabinets, the computer station, and the computer print-outs and reports on the worktable, some of which were splattered with blood, the spots now dry and rust-colored.

"There's nothing out of the ordinary that I can see," said Hamilton, when they had finished. "Have you turned up anything so far in your investigation that you can share with us, Detective?"

"Nothing, I'm afraid."

"Is that it, then? Are we finished?" asked Smithers, appearing puzzled.

"Not quite," said Burke, who was flipping through a note book.

"What are we doing here, then?" asked Hamilton, impatiently. "This is very distasteful to me."

"I would like for the two of you to examine the computer, and explain to me what Ms. Vann was doing when she was murdered."

The two men glanced at each other. Smithers said: "The files in the computer are confidential. The data are about real people. I suppose you know we're charged by law with the responsibility of preserving their confidentiality. There are stiff penalties."

"I understand that, Doctor, but this is a murder investigation. I assure you that I'll be discrete. If there is something you want me to sign, a waiver, I will be happy to do so."

"Oh, I get it," Smithers said. "you're looking for a motive for Sheila's murder. What do you expect to find in the computer?"

"I have no idea," Burke confessed. "If you would feel better about it, I can produce a warrant."

Hamilton said, "I don't think that will be necessary." He looked at Smithers who nodded agreement.

"Thank you," Burke said, pleased that he didn't have to use the search warrant. Warrants, he knew, created adversarial relationships and caused people to be less cooperative.

He had another reason for wanting to work with the two men. He wanted to observe them at close range, under stress, for a dropped word, for anything that didn't fit.

"We don't know precisely what Sheila was doing when she was attacked," said Smithers. "But, I assume she was entering data, or running her reports, all completely routine."

Burked moved across the room to the work table. "What are these papers?"

The two men had already examined the blood-spattered sheets.

"Printouts, miscellaneous reports, nothing unusual."

Burke's thoughts flashed back to the afternoon when he had visited Sheila in the lab. She had been entering data into the computer. He remembered that the data sheets she had were in a brown folder. He looked for the brown folder on the table. It wasn't there. Where was that folder? He shuffled through the sheets, carefully noting the dates. He was looking for sheets with August 23, stamped on them, the day he was there, and the day she was murdered. There were none. He checked the dates on the print-outs. Everything was dated at least a week earlier than August 23."

Strange. He distinctly remembered Sheila saying that she was entering data that had come in during the previous week, which would have been between the 16th and the 23rd. There was nothing among the papers date-stamped during that week.

"Is everything that comes into the lab stamped received and dated?" He asked the men.

"Yes," Smithers answered.

"Does that include these actual test sheets, with the bar code-like markings on them?"

"Yes, everything. What are you getting at, Detective?"

"It's just that when I was here in the afternoon of the day she was murdered she was entering data into the computer from sheets that she said had come in during the previous week. There was a brown folder that contained about a dozen or so of these sheets. I've looked through all the papers here, and there is no brown folder, and there are none of those data sheets with dates after the 16th. Everything I see here is dated at least a week earlier. Where's that brown file, and where are the sheets that were in it?"

Hamilton glanced at Smithers. "What did Sheila do with those sheets after she entered the information into the computer?"

"She kept them permanently. When she finished with them, eventually she put them in the filing cabinets in the storage room. Want to go look for them?"

"Yes, but later," said Burke. "Right now, I'd like for you to start up the computer, please. I'd like to know what's in it, and what she was likely doing last, or when she was attacked."

As Smithers flipped on the main computer switch, he paused and glanced around at Burke. "We don't know that she was working on the computer, but if she was, we can tell which data files she accessed. The computer automatically enters the date and time the files were accessed or updated. It's a fairly simple matter to bring up the file directory and see if any files were updated on the twenty-third."

"Excellent," said Burke.

The computer whirred on, and when the screen lit Smithers entered a password. A menu appeared. He pressed several additional keys as screens appeared and disappeared. He stopped and stared at the screen, his face registering surprise. "I don't understand this," he said.

"What is it?" asked Burke.

"The directory is empty."

"Empty? Are you sure?" Hamilton said as he jumped up from his chair and rushed over to where Smithers sat at the computer console.

"See for yourself." Smithers pointed to the screen, to the empty directory.

"What does that mean?" Burke asked, as he felt his blood pressure jump up a notch.

"I don't know what it means. The data files seem to have been erased, that's all," Smithers repeated. "Sheila never did that, did she? She ran the program once a week, and she routinely backed up the files each time she ran the reports—she was very meticulous about that—but she never erased the files from the computer at that time. I am sure of that."

"You say she always backed up the files?" asked Burke. "How did she do that?"

"On tapes," said Hamilton. "They record very fast. We can check the tapes to see when she backed them up last." He crossed the room to the cabinet. "Here they are," he said, as he retrieved a tray containing four tapes and carried them back across the room. He checked the dates penciled on the tapes. "The last backup date shown here is August 16th."

Burke examined the tapes for himself, noting the dates. They were a week apart. August 16th was indeed the last date shown, and was a week before the murder. "Sheila told me that as soon as she finished entering the data, she was going to run the program again," he said slowly, as if talking to himself. "I remember it very distinctly. She said she would be working late because of that. Why isn't there a backup tape for the 23rd?"

The two scientists looked at Burke, and at each other. Hamilton shrugged. Smithers said, "I don't know. It appears that, for some reason, she didn't run the program after all. Maybe the killer interrupted her and she didn't have time."

"Who else is aware of this backup procedure?" Burke asked.

"Just the three of us, me, Adrian, and Sheila," Hamilton answered, "as far as I know. But backing up the files is a standard operating procedure for computer people. Why do you ask? I don't understand what you're getting at, Detective Burke. Why are you so interested in our research project? Do you really think it has something to do with Sheila's murder? Do you think one of us killed her, Adrian or me?"

"Of course not. I told you before that I don't know that there is anything here at all. But the reality is that Miss Vann was murdered while she sat in that chair," Burke thrust his finger at the chair. "While she worked at this table," he thrust his finger again. "Why? Why here? Why then?"

The two men were silent.

Burke continued, "I don't mean to be offensive, but it's true that I am looking for a motive for murder. I'm wondering if there is anything about the nature of your research work here which might have triggered it."

"Impossible," Hamilton said. "You're barking up the wrong tree."

"Absolutely," Smithers agreed. "The research we're doing here is routine, mundane to the point of boredom. We are not stepping on anybody's toes. There are no other scientists competing with us for honors in this field, nothing like that."

Burke was pensive. He said, "Ever since the murder, I've had this notion that somehow my visit to Miss Vann that afternoon might have been a factor in her murder. I know how far-fetched that must sound to you, but can you see any possible connection your testing of the bones for me might have with this mystery?"

"No. There is no connection between them, none at all."

"I'm sure you're right. It's just that I was here that afternoon talking to her about the tests, and a few hours later she is dead."

"I see," said Hamilton. "You know, Detective, the day she was murdered, I'll bet she encountered a dozen people. What if they all thought they had contributed to her death? Do you suppose the clerk at the convenience store thinks the same thing? What about the teller at the bark?"

"Okay, I get your point," Burke said, but the difference is that I am a law enforcement officer investigating a murder. How about giving me a couple of minutes to get my thoughts together."

What did it mean that the files were erased? Suppose that Sheila, in the process of inputting her data and running her program had discovered something—something that threatened someone, perhaps her murderer...

"Detective Burke?" Smithers interrupted Burke's contemplations.

"Yes, what is it?"

"What do you want us to do now?"

"How long would it take to restore the files from these backup tapes, and run the program again, and produce the report for the 16th? That was the last one she ran, right?"

"Right, said Hamilton. "I don't know, exactly, how long it would take. I'd estimate less than an hour. Sheila handled that end of things. What do you say, Adrian?"

"Not too long, an hour or so."

"By the way," Burke said, "may I have a copy of that last printed report, the one for the 16th?"

"Just a moment, I'll make a copy for you," Smithers said.

Smithers crossed the room to a file cabinet, took out a several-page report, walked out the door and down the hallway. A few moments later he returned and handed the copy to Burke.

"Thanks," Burke said. "Bear with me Gentlemen, all of this will likely come to nothing, as you no doubt believe already, but I want you to restore the data to the computer from the backup tape, run the program for me, and produce the printed report. I'm still looking for the missing data that she was putting into the computer the afternoon of her murder, and it occurred to me that she may have simply forgotten to write the current date, the 23rd, on the backup tape when she finished running the program. Do you understand what I am saying? Does this make sense to you? If she did put the data into the computer, and run her program, like she said she intended to do, then the report dated the 16th and the one we're going to run now won't agree, isn't that correct?"

"That's right," said Smithers. He seemed surprised at Burke's clarity of thought. He glanced at Hamilton, who apparently understood what he was thinking, because he shrugged.

Burke glanced at the clock on the wall, it was 11:57 a.m. They had been at it for nearly two hours. "It nearly noon," Burke said. "I suggest we postpone the running of the program until tomorrow. Is that all right with you? Say, ten in the morning? I have other things to attend to this afternoon, and I'm sure you do as well."

The two men glanced at each other, and both nodded.

"Thank you. I'd like to keep the tapes in my custody overnight if you have no objection."

They agreed. Burke took the tray of backup tapes and the copy of the report, and then locked and resealed the lab. When he arrived at the office, Burke carefully examined the backup tapes. Each had a gummed paper label numbered one through four, with dates penciled on them, indicating the date of last use. When a new date was written, a line was drawn through the old one. Burke took the tray and walked through City Hall to the city's computer room. He saw through the plate glass windows that there were two men working in the room. He tried the door handle. The door was locked. One of the men turned and saw him, and pointed to a sign that said "AUTHORIZED PERSONNEL ONLY". Another sign on the wall inside the room said "THIMK!" which evoked a smile from Burke.

Burke did not know the two men inside, but he had seen them around. He took out his badge, rapped on the door, and held his badge up to the glass. A man came to the door. "What can I do for you, officer?" he said.

"I'm Detective Burke. I'm working on a murder case, and I need some help from you guys, if you could spare me a few minutes."

"What kind of help?"

"I'm not much on computers, and I need to understand more than I do about programs and files, and backing them up on tape.

"Come on in, Detective Burke," the man said. "Have a seat over there at the desk, and we'll be with you in a minute. We're in the middle of something."

Burke did as he was told. While he waited, he looked around the room at the large metal cabinets which housed the computer, with blinking lights, knobs, dials, and tape drives. He noted how cool and comfortable the room was, speculating that the computers had it better than the people in his offices.

Five minutes elapsed before the two men pulled up a couple of chairs, and sat down opposite Burke. "Now, Detective Burke, what is it you want to know?"

"I can't discuss the particulars, but I'm on a case which involves a computer and missing files. My question is this: If you manually input data into a computer from several sources, from standard data sheets, and you run a program using that data, which generates a report, would you erase the data?"

"I wouldn't. If you needed to run the program again you wouldn't have to go back and reinter the data again manually from the original data sheets. That's assuming you retained the original data sheets." The other man nodded agreement.

Burke asked, "If you erase files are they gone forever?"

"That's a good question. Sometimes they can be recovered from the hard drive, sometimes not. It's a pretty iffy process."

"Okay, thanks a lot."

Burke took his knowledge, insights and questions home with him that evening. Marge was in the kitchen cleaning vegetables at the sink. "Hi, sweetheart, he said. He put his arms around her waist and kissed her on her neck. "I know it's a bit unusual for me to make such a request," he said, "but would you listen to me talk through something that has to do with the Vann murder?"

Marge turned to him, the paring knife still in her hand, and a look of surprise on her face. He kissed her, pulled her to him, and gave her a hug, then stepped back and waited for her to answer.

"You want me to help you with your police work? I can't believe it! I What do you want me to do?"

"Just listen, and then give me your opinion."

"Okay, I can do that. Start talking. Is it all right if I scrape my carrots while you talk?"

Burke smiled. "Sure, honey, if you can do it without cutting your finger off."

Burke began by recapping the information about the murder, common knowledge within the community, and then he described his investigation, and told her about his visit to the computer lab. Finally, he reviewed the conversation he had had previously with her, when he had expressed his feeling that his visit to Vann had had something to do with her death."

"Yes," she said, "I thought that was pretty far-fetched at the time. Do you still feel that way?"

"I'm not sure," he said. "That's why I need to talk about it with somebody smart, like you."

Marge smiled, "Watch the flattery, Detective. Go on with your story."

"Okay," Burke began. "I'm thinking now that it wasn't my visit with her that got her killed, it was the bones, the testing of the bones."

Just then, they heard the front door opening, and noise in the hallway. Marge said, "The kids are hers. My goodness, look at the time. Maybe we had better delay this dear, so I can finish dinner. Then we can talk afterwards."

"Okay, I've already worked up an appetite."

The kids rushed in. They had been to a movie with friends.

"Hi, Mom, Dad," Sam exclaimed. "Hey, where's supper?"

"It'll be just a few minutes late, dear, your father and I were talking."

After they washed the dishes, Burke dried them, they settled on the couch in the living room, while the children watched television in the den. Burke resumed where he had left off. "Now, about my visit to Miss Vann, it wouldn't have made any difference whether I visited her or not. I believe she learned something that day, something about the bones, and that is what got her murdered."

"What makes you think she learned whatever it was she learned that day? Couldn't she have learned it earlier?"

"Possibly, but I think not. I believe she would have told me, if it had some bearing on my case, on my investigation. Just assume, for the sake of my theory, that she did discover something that day. How could the murderer have known about her discovery that quickly? Did she tell someone about it? You recall, I told you she had tried to reach Hamilton by phone. Well, suppose by some means she did reach him, and instead of going directly home after his meeting as he said he did, he came to the lab and killed her. But why would she tell him the information? The answer would have to be that Sheila didn't understand what she had found, but the murderer did. Since the killing was with an object at hand, a heavy paper punch, it follows that the murderer only learned the full significance of the information, himself, after he arrived at the lab and spoke with her. Then after the crime, the murderer erased the files on the computer, and took the related papers and the backup tape from the computer. That would mean that the murderer knew computers, and knew what Ms. Vann was doing. Hamilton and Smithers fit that description, maybe the only people who do."

Marge had grown silent in the telling. Any flippancy in her manner was gone. "That's heavy stuff," she said. "Are you saying that Hamilton or Smithers killed Sheila?"

"I'm not saying they did it, I'm saying that it's logical. It looks that way, as hard as that is to believe."

⋙⋘

At ten the following morning, Burke arrived at the computer lab where he found Smithers and Hamilton waiting in the hallway. They went in. Burke carried the backup tapes, which he handed to Smithers, who selected the one dated August 16, and inserted it in the computer. "We'll be here for a while," he said, "might as well get comfortable."

"I have to confess that this case has me baffled," Burke said. "I don't suppose either of you has thought of anything else that might be helpful."

"No, Detective, and believe me, I've thought of little else since this happened," Hamilton said. "I still think it was a random act, some addict off the street looking for money to buy drugs. Things like that happen all the time."

"I feel the same," Smithers said.

"All right, then," Burke said, with resignation, then fell silent to wait until the computer finished.

Hamilton spoke: "I could use some coffee. Anybody else? I'll run to the snack bar."

"Yeah, cream with mine," Burke said.

"How about you, Adrian?"

"I'll take mine black."

"I won't be long."

After Hamilton departed, Burke said, "You have been working with Ms. Vann for a long time. Have you ever known of her having any trouble with anyone here at the college or otherwise?"

"No."

"How about ex-boy friends?"

"No, nothing, you might ask Doctor Hamilton about that, though."

"Why?"

"They dated briefly. He may have more insight into her private life than I do."

"I didn't know they dated. When was that?"

"When he first came back home from St. Joseph's about two years ago. Say, I didn't mean anything by that. I'm not suggesting anything. I assumed you knew about that. Damn, I guess I put my foot in it."

"Hamilton didn't say anything to me about it. I'm sure he attached no importance to it or he would have mentioned it to me."

"Don't tell him I brought it up, please. He may take it the wrong way."

"Okay, I'll try not to. If I need to explore it with him, I'll approach it some other way."

"Thanks, that's a relief."

When Hamilton returned, the three silently sipped the coffee, awaiting the pleasure of the computer. Finally, the printer clattered to life. The three men spread the pages of the report out on the table. Burke took the copy of the old report and did the same. They carefully compared them, page by page.

"They're identical," Smithers said. "Sorry, Detective Burke. It looks like you're indeed barking up the wrong tree, if you expected to find something here."

"Not so fast. Something still isn't right. Like I told you, I saw her entering that new data."

"Detective Burke," Smithers said, "I'm not questioning you, but we don't have any new data. After you left yesterday I spent an hour in the storage room, and did a thorough search of the filing cabinets where we archive the data sheets and the reports, and everything to do with our project, and I found no brown folder and no data sheets dated August 23rd. So if you really did see what you think you did, then Sheila did something else with the folder, or somebody took it."

Burke's confusion and frustration were about to overpower his control. He knew something was not right, but he could not figure out what. Why would she put it someplace else; or why would somebody take it, unless the contents incriminated them?

His body was hot, and he felt damp around the collar, and in his armpits. He hoped his discomfort did not show, he did not want to alienate the men more than they were already. He was struggling mightily to understand matters beyond his level of expertise, with men whose intellects and professional accomplishments he admired.

"Then there's nothing at all unusual here in the lab or in the computer as far as you can tell?"

"Nothing at all," said Hamilton.

"And you, Doctor Smithers, is that your opinion as well?"

"Yes." Smithers answered without hesitation.

"All right," Burke said with a sigh. "Thanks for your help and patience. You can have the lab back, now. I see no reason to hold you up any longer. Just one last thing, I want to hold on to the two copies of the report for now, and the old backup tapes. Can you make out without them?"

"Yes," Smithers said. "Of course. But I'm curious Detective, why do you want to keep those tapes?"

"I can't give you an intelligent answer at the moment," Burke said.

In spite of everything, he had come to believe that one of these two men was Sheila Vann's murderer. The tapes were somehow the key to the question of whether Vann entered new data into the computer. Burke still firmly believed that she had. He had seen he doing it, and she had told him she was doing it. He believed that the murderer took the last backup tape with him after he erased the computer files, and had taken the report and the folder with the data sheets, and whoever took it had to know what they were doing. "I want to keep my options open concerning the question of whether or not Ms. Vann input new data. I consider the reports and the tapes to be evidence in my murder investigation. I'm afraid I can't explain it further at this time. I'll write you out a receipt for these things, and you can have the lab keys back. I won't seal the lab."

CHAPTER 6
REST AND RELAXATION

The next day was Friday, and Burke was tired. He sat at his desk with his feet up, gazing absently out the window at the parking lot and the small city park beyond, where children played—there always seemed to be children playing in the park. He was mulling over where he was in the Vann case. So, Hamilton and Vann had dated. That seemed like more than a casual relationship to him. He wondered why they had broken it off, and why Hamilton had not mentioned it to him, and why Smithers had been so nervous when he had inadvertently let it out. *What did it mean?* He wondered about Hamilton's current love life. Burke made a mental note to check on that. Hamilton was a young, attractive professional man. Why wasn't he married? Why hadn't Burke heard something in the romance department about him? True, the demands of college, then medical school, and then residency were probably brutal and sufficient reason for him to defer marriage, or even serious involvement. That was likely the explanation.

Burke had difficulty maintain his objectivity. He could feel his prejudices creeping in. Even though he admired the accomplished elites in the community, he also envied them, sometimes disliked them, and tended to hold them, to a higher standard in all things.

He didn't cut them much slack. Now, as he considered the possible guilt or innocence of these two young professional men, he admonished himself not to overreact, not to read too much into his intuitions and suspicions, to keep an open mind.

Smithers seemed to have an unassailable alibi, what with his out-of-town trip with his family the day of the murder. How could he have pulled it off? Everything was pointing toward Hamilton.

Burke thought back to the Vann funeral. He had gone, not only to pay his respects, but also to observe those present, look at the guest register, and take note of any suspicious license plates: he knew that murderers sometimes attend the funerals of their victims. Even before the service had begun, he had felt a sickening sense of tragedy. He felt awkward at funerals, but this one was particularly difficult for him, since the responsibility to find the killer of this young woman was his.

He noted that among those in attendance at the funeral were many people he knew, from the town and college. Ripley, Hamilton, and Smithers were there, with family members. He saw people he didn't know. He watched them but observed nothing in their behavior that gave him cause for suspicion. They seemed to know the friends and family of the deceased, indicating that they were not strangers. Nothing helpful to the investigation had come from his attendance at the funeral.

Burke's musings ended abruptly as he came back to the present, to where he sat looking out of his office window at the children in the park. A boy about six or seven tumbled out of one of the swings and landed on his face. Burke leaned forward, his hands tense on the arms of his chair, waiting. The child bounded up and began running about the playground again. Burke sighed, and leaned back once again in his chair.

He had promptly reported to Newman that nothing concrete had come of his examination of the computer. He wasn't about to give him any more half-baked theories. Better to say nothing.

It was worrisome for him as he remembered Newman's attitude toward him at their last meeting. He had made his report as brief as possible. And, while Newman hadn't crowed about it outright, that is, he hadn't said, 'I told you so,' he had coolly recommended that Burke look in more conventional places for Vann's murderer. Elmo hadn't crowed either. In fact, he had seemed sympathetic to Burke, and had said nothing at all about it to him. Burke meant to thank Elmo for that, but Elmo was out of the office, now, and Burke was alone.

The murder of Vann had caused Burke to postpone a planned trip with his family to a lake upstate, to a nice, quiet cabin in the trees. They usually went each year. He yearned to be there now. Summer was gone, there had been frost in the higher elevations, and the leaves were starting to turn into the brilliant showstoppers that they became each fall. *Why not pack up a few things and go for a long weekend before it got too cold?* It was Friday afternoon, and it was only a three-hour drive to the lake. The children would be delighted, and Marge would be stoic but accommodating since the out-of-doors was not her favorite thing. She wouldn't dare say no after he had let her talk him into going to the fall dance at the country club. He scribbled a note and put it on Elmo's telephone, informing him that he intended to leave early, and going out of town for the weekend. He included a telephone number where Elmo could reach him in an emergency.

When he arrived home, Marge was out shopping for groceries. Good, he thought, that would give him time to talk to the kids and prepare a surprise for Marge.

"Say, are you kids ready for a trip to the lake this weekend for some fishing and canoeing?"

"Yeah! Great, Dad. Can I paddle the canoe?" Sam asked enthusiastically.

"You bet, son. How about you, Sis?"

"Neato."

"Neato? May I assume that means yes?"

"Yes, father, you may assume that."

"Great, then go ahead and start packing. We'll surprise mom when she gets home. Don't try to take everything you own; we'll only be there for the weekend."

Sam and Linda ran to their rooms to pack, and Burke did the same. Marge arrived fifteen minutes later, and the children ran out to the driveway to greet her, bouncing and exuberant. They made quick work of unloading and carrying in the groceries. Marge came into the kitchen, where Burke greeted her with a grin. "You think you're pretty smart, don't you, fellow." She said.

"Yeah, I do," he said. "I'll put away the groceries while you get ready."

They pulled out of the drive twenty minutes later and were on their way.

⚔

The lake was small, only a few miles long, a half mile wide at it widest point, with many inlets and bays, which provided favorable conditions for bass, crappie and trout fishing. It was located near Hillsboro, in an area of wooded, rolling hills, and was bordered on two side by a state forest. The access road on the private side, a winding country lane, was barely wide enough to allow vehicles to pass. The cabin was located in a small enclave of widely scattered cabins, among predominantly pine trees which went clear to the high water line, but which, between the cabin and the lake, had been thinned out and with the undergrowth removed, to afford a shady view of the sun-lit lake. The cabin was a simple rustic affair, made of treated rough lumber stained brown, with two small bedrooms, kitchen, bath and great room, which had a wood burning fireplace. Down at the shore, a wooden dock jutted out thirty feet into the water. Beside it was a boathouse containing a small fishing boat and a canoe. Large powerful boats were not permitted on the lake. Both the fishing boat and the canoe were equipped with small outboards, for those who didn't like to paddle.

The cabin belonged to Marge's parents, and had been in the family for years. Burke and Marge had made good and frequent use of it while they were dating, and for a few years after they married. It had been, according to Marge's calculations, the site of the conception of their first child, Linda.

Burke and the kids spent Saturday fishing from their canoe while Marge lounged in a hammock at the cabin, reading a new book by her favorite romance author. Together, he and the children caught several respectable largemouth bass and a string of crappie, although the trout were too small to keep. Sam and Linda cleaned and fried up the catch, which delighted Marge, who made hush puppies, while Burke enjoyed eating them.

A couple of days fishing in the wild can often do wonders to elevate one's spirit and clear away the accumulated mental debris, and by Sunday morning, even Marge, began to thaw out a bit. After breakfast, she and Burke took a long walk along the shore, while the children washed the dishes and prepared for another day of fishing.

"Let the kids go fishing," Marge suggested, "and you and I can spend some time alone in the cabin."

"Last night wasn't enough for you?"

"It's hard to relax with the children so close by, with Linda in the room next door, and Sam on the fold-out in the living room."

"Okay, the kid are old hands at it, so they can paddle the canoe as long as they stay close by. I don't want them using the motor."

"Good. Tell them to wear their flotation gear."

When they returned from their walk, Sam and Linda were all set to go.

"Would you kids like to go out by yourselves in the canoe, and let your daddy and me take it easy?"

"Yes," they both said.

"Okay, bring your things along, and let's go down and check out the canoe."

When he returned to the cabin he and Marge had a leisurely shower together, then made love, like a couple of naughty teenagers, like they had in the old days, in broad daylight, with the bedroom window open, and brisk, fresh, pine-scented air wafting through.

Sam and Linda returned midafternoon with a nice catch, which they cleaned and prepared. "Mom and Dad, you deserve to take it easy. We'll prepare the evening meal," Linda said.

Burke called back to the station for one more day on the lake. Monday, the four of them went out in the larger boat, and Marge actually fished, baited her hook and everything. Everybody laughed and had a good time

⭑⭑⭑

Burke returned to the police station on Tuesday considerably refreshed. Elmo said that Hamilton had called for him on Friday after he had left.

"What did he want?"

"Said he had something to tell him, and would call again later."

"Did it sound urgent?"

"No. I didn't probe him, and he didn't volunteer to tell me. I figured it was your business. I got his number anyway. It's there in your basket."

"Okay, thanks, anything else going on?"

"Traffic accident on the bypass at Tyson. Minor injuries. Nobody local involved."

"That's a bad intersection. We need a light there. The council knows about it, but doesn't seem to want to do anything about it."

"Budget problems, I imagine."

Elmo returned to sipping his coffee, scanning the financial pages, and scribbling on a note pad. Burke checked his in-basket.

He found a few routine interoffice memos of no particular interest. He wheeled his chair around to the window. Dark clouds were moving in low to the ground, and the wind was kicking up. The playground was empty of children. He couldn't believe it, there were always kids in the park. But, the empty swings swung ghost-like in the wind.

"Looks like it might rain," he said.

"We could use some rain," Elmo said.

Burke continued to gaze out the windows, remembering the big bass he had caught. That sucker put up a good fight. They were lucky to have gotten the trip in when they did. Soon the weather would change in earnest. He didn't look forward to the winter. He didn't like snow. If he never had to go through another icy, freezing, accident-prone winter, it would be too soon for him. He turned the chair back around to the desk and reluctantly turned his thoughts once more to the Vann case.

Dempsey had been handling the office routine and Burke had been concentrating on the case. But Burke had been thinking that he needed a sounding board to test his ideas. Newman was of no use to him. Burke simply didn't go to him anymore if he could get around it. Why not involve Elmo more? Confide in him. What could it hurt? Elmo seemed to be playing straight with him these days. Yes, that's what he would do. He would invite Elmo out to lunch at the Steakhouse out on the highway and see what that got him.

"What are you doing for lunch today, Elmo?"

"Me? Nothing special, why?"

"I thought we might have lunch together at the Steakhouse, on me, of course. That is, if you don't have any other plans."

Dempsey looked at him suspiciously. Their overt relationship could normally be described as polite, that's about all you could say about it. They were both political appointees in government positions, from different political factions. There had never been even the slightest social component to their relationship.

"Well, what about it?" Burke asked, when time had elapsed and Dempsey hadn't yet answered.

"Sure thing, thanks. What's the occasion?"

"No occasion. We can talk about the Vann case over lunch. Eleven okay with you?"

"Sure."

An hour later, since Hamilton hadn't called again, Burke picked up the phone and dialed his number. The phone rang five times, and then clicked a couple of times preparatory to the recorded voice. Burke hung up. He didn't want to hear that syrupy recorded message. He would try again after lunch. He busied himself with the paperwork in the inbox until eleven.

◄┼►

At the Steakhouse, Dempsey sliced into his small, greasy, rib-eye steak and listened, while Burke talked. He was still waiting for his deluxe cheeseburger.

"Elmo, "Burke said, "I've told you about what they're doing over at the college, about the DNA business, which you know more about then me, but I don't believe I told you about the NIH grant they're working under."

"No, I guess not. What's a NIH grant?"

Burke's cheeseburger arrived, so he took a big bite of the burger, and between chews he gives Elmo a brief explanation: "They're developing a computer program to analyze DNA data. To test the program, they use real data from real people from all over the country. That's why they were able to help us with the bones, they were geared up to do that stuff already."

"What is it for?"

"I don't know, all kinds of purposes, medical, for example, but the one of interest to us is finding people related to each other, and determining how they are related. We got them to test the bones and Mister Hanford's blood to see if they are related to each other."

"What if Sheila or one of the others put the DNA from the bones, or from Hanford, or both, in with her test samples from around the country, and when she ran the program, she discovered somebody else related to them, somebody she knew?"

Dempsey sliced off a chunk of steak and chewed thoughtfully as Burke waited for him to respond.

"You mean somebody from Stanton?" Dempsey asked.

"Not necessarily, but could be."

"Let me see if I've got this straight. The computer program tells them the bones are related to someone in Stanton."

"It doesn't have to be someone in Stanton, just someone she knows." Burke said.

"You are saying that maybe Sheila took the tests they ran for you on the bones, and she put that info in the computer with the data for that computer program of hers and when she ran the program, she identified someone, someone she knew who was related to the bones." Dempsey said, with his first show of interest.

"Right!" Burke spoke so loudly and exuberantly that he startled Dempsey, who sat with his mouth open for five seconds staring at him. "That's what I believe happened," Burke said, more quietly, glancing about to see if anyone had noticed his exuberance.

"I see what you are getting at." Dempsey said. He thought some more, then said, "So she discovers this, and she tries to get up with Smithers, who is the boss of the operation, to tell him what she's discovered, but she learns that he's off for the day. Then she tries to get up with Hamilton, but she can't get up with him either, so she tells someone else and that someone kills her."

Dempsey stopped talking, and Burke waited for him to render his opinion.

"No, you see, it breaks down right there, Boss. What are the odds that the person threatened by this information is going to be right there on the spot? That's just impossible. And why would she tell the actual person she identified. She wouldn't do that. That would be stupid. Because anyone would suspect that person as possibly being the one who put the cleaver in the forehead of the adult skull."

"You would think that would be the case," said Burke. "You would think she would not do that, but that's exactly what it looks to me like she did do."

Dempsey shook his head. "No, she would have talked it over with one of her buddies first, one of the other two scientists, Hamilton or Smithers."

"Right, Elmo," said Burke. "I agree with you. That is precisely what she did. She did find one of these guys, Hamilton or Smithers, and whichever one she got up with killed her."

"Oh, come on. Be serious. It would have to be someone else she told about it," Elmo said. "You don't know who all she might have talked to. A whole bunch of people could suddenly become suspects if she told them what she was excited about."

"Well, you're right, but suppose—

"Suppose this, and suppose that," said Elmo. "That is the most incredible theory I ever heard in my life, Boss. See, you got to do too damn much supposing. It just breaks down there."

Burke sighed, and looked sadly at Dempsey. "It does seem that way, doesn't it?" he said. "But, what it might means is that our reasoning got off track at some point. Maybe it's just a question of going back over it and finding out where we got off track, don't you see? Put aside your doubts for now and let's go on with our theory. Let's say, for the sake of argument, that Sheila did indeed identify someone in Stanton who was related to the child and the man with the gash in his forehead."

Once more Dempsey thought while he chewed. Finally, he said, "Okay, the first thing that comes to my mind is that the person that's related to the skeletons was also the one who killed them. And that person then killed Sheila to keep her from exposing him."

"That's right Elmo. That certainly would be the first thing that pops into someone's head. The only thing wrong with our theory, though is that there is nobody unaccounted for here in Stanton, or anywhere around going back forty years," Burke said, now seeming to argue against himself.

"Obviously the victims were from out of town," Elmo said impatiently. "Listen, this is beginning to give me a headache, and I haven't had my desert, yet. You know what I really believe, is that some lowlife on drugs saw a light in her window and figured there was somebody there he could rob for money to buy drugs."

Burke sighed again. "That's what everybody seems to think. Let's order our desert."

Burke suddenly realized that he had been getting more and more intense. He glanced around to see if people were watching. No one seemed to be. Still, it was time to give it a break. He was pleased at Dempsey's comprehension of his theory, wild-ass or not. "I'm thinking about that apple pie, Elmo," he said. "I like it warmed up with a scoop of vanilla ice cream."

"Sounds like a winner to me," Dempsey agreed.

Burke felt better after their talk. Dempsey surprised him by how quickly he had grasped his theory even if he didn't go along with it. During the apple pie and ice cream Dempsey had called Burke Sherlock Holmes, and he had replied, "I guess that makes you Dr. Watson." The idea amused Burke. *We may have some serious bonding possibilities here*, he thought.

"Listen, Elmo," Burke said, as they drove back to the office. "Keep what we discussed to yourself. Newman would not be happy if he knew I was talking to you about this. He thinks it is a nutty idea and he told me to lay off it, remember."

"Yeah, he sure did."

They drove back to the office without further conversation. Burke was curious to know if Hamilton had called again. He found a note on his desk when they got back to the station. There had, indeed, been another call from Hamilton. Burke dialed the number and received a busy signal. "Damn!" he said. "I hate this telephone tag." Fifteen minutes later, Burke dialed Hamilton's number once more. Hamilton didn't answer. This time, he left a message on the infernal answering machine.

Dempsey got up and left the room while Burke was on the phone, and he was gone for about forty minutes. When he came back, Burke thought he was acting a little strange, because he didn't even look Burke's way, but took his seat and put his nose into some papers, like he was terribly busy. Burke was curious, and considered asking him where he had been, but before he could decide his phone rang. It was Hamilton.

"Sorry I missed you earlier," he said."

"No problem, what's on your mind?" Burke replied.

"I wanted to tell you about a visit I had last Wednesday evening. You remember Mrs. Halper, Mr. Hanford's housekeeper? Around seven in the evening, I was in my office catching up on some paperwork. I looked up and there she was, standing in the doorway. She seemed disturbed about something, so I asked her to come in. She sat down, and I got her a glass of water. Then she just sat there, staring at me and looking scared, fumbling with a handkerchief in her hands, babbling about how it was too late now, and things could not be rectified, and about how Mr. Hanford could not endure it. I tried to get her to calm down and make some sense. One thing I understood clearly, she said for me to tell you to call off your investigation before there was another tragedy."

Burke perked up. "Really? That's a strange thing for her to say. She didn't call or anything beforehand, while you were out maybe? Did you check your messages?"

"No, there was no message. She popped in on me, totally unexpected."

"What do you think she meant by, it being too late, and Mr. Hanford couldn't endure it?"

"My initial reaction was that she was worried about Hanford's health, perhaps he had taken a turn for the worst."

"Why do you suppose she came to you, to give me a message? Why didn't she come to me?"

"I have no idea."

"Why didn't you call me right away? That was almost a week ago."

"Well, I did call Friday. I understand you've been gone since Friday. I suppose I should have tried to locate you Wednesday night or Thursday morning, but frankly, Detective, with everything that's going on in my life right now, I suppose I didn't attach much importance to it at the time. I just thought—I'm not sure what I thought."

"You say you attached no importance to it initially, but now you do. What changed your mind?"

"I got to thinking about it, and discussing it with Mother, and she suggested I should tell you right away."

"Did you get the impression that Mrs. Halper was threatening you?"

"No, not at all."

"Threatening someone else?" Burke added.

"No. I took it more as, uh, a premonition, an expression of concern on her part. But the more I thought about it later, it did begin to seem threatening."

"Did you come away with the impression that she had something to do with the death of Ms. Vann?"

"No, I really didn't."

"Did anyone else see or talk with her?"

"Not to my knowledge."

"Okay, Doctor. Thank you very much for letting me know. I'll look into the matter. I'll let you know if anything comes of it."

Burke felt a shiver pass over him as he experienced a moment of foreboding. A premonition of evil, which, even though he always said he was not superstitious, occasionally slipped up on him. What a strange thing for Hamilton to say, that he didn't attach significance to it, and that his mother suggested that he inform me. Very strange. *What kind of man is this, anyhow? It's damned obvious that he should have informed me. What am I to make of this fellow?*

Burke recalled that he had seen Hamilton and his mother at the Vann's funeral, walking into the chapel. He had nodded to them, and they had reciprocated. Something about Hamilton's demeanor had reminded him of a little boy tagging along after Mother. It was all very strange. At the time, Burke had attributed his demeanor to grief. The more he interacted with Hamilton, and the deeper he got into the Vann affair, the stranger Hamilton seemed to him.

"What was that all about?" Dempsey asked when Burke hung up the phone.

"That was Doctor Hamilton, said he had a visit from Hanfords housekeeper last Wednesday evening. Said she was upset, and asked him to give me a message to drop my investigation before there was another tragedy."

"What?"

"Yeah, that's what I thought, too. Hamilton didn't think it was important enough to track me down and tell me about it. What do you make of it, Elmo?"

"You got me. Maybe the old man is sick? Maybe all the excitement is getting to him, and the housekeeper is trying to protect him."

"I'm going to call his home, and check up on him."

Burke found the Hanford number and dialed. He waited a long time, but did not hear the phone ring. Finally, he heard several clicks and a recorded voice announced that the phone was out of order.

"That's odd."

"What?"

"The phone is out of order."

"Out of order?"

"Yeah. I got a recording. I have a feeling something is wrong. I'm going to drive up there, Elmo, and see what the hell is going on. I'd like you to come along."

"All right."

"Let's go, then." Burke tossed him his keys. "You drive."

Elmo drove fast and they arrived in Brockton at 3:30 p.m. Burke directed him out route 37 to the outskirts of the town to the Hanford residence. As they made the turn-off into the drive leading to the house, Burke sensed that something was indeed amiss. He gestured toward the shrubbery bordering the drive. Some of it was broken and disheveled. Debris littered the crushed stone roadway. "Something has happened, alright," he muttered. As they rounded the first curve in the s-shaped drive, they confronted a barricade. Yellow tape stated in bold lettering, "Police Line. Do not cross."

They exited the car, ducked under the tape, and walked around the second bend in the drive until the house came into view. It was a burned-out shell.

A uniformed police officer approached them from the direction of the house. "Hey! What are you fellows doing here? Didn't you see that police line?"

Burke pulled out his badge and held it up to the officer. "I'm Chief Detective Burke of the Stanton Police Department. This is Detective Dempsey. What's happened here?"

The officer eyed them suspiciously, and looked first at the ID, then at Burke, then at Dempsey. Satisfied they were who they said they were, he said rather sourly, "As you can see, there's been a fire."

"Anybody hurt?" asked Burke, ignoring the sarcasm.

"One of the occupants of the house is dead, burned to a cinder. The other is in critical condition."

"Who's dead?" Burke asked, a sick feeling rising in his stomach.

"An old lady, the housekeeper. The man who lived here is at City Hospital. Apparently, the housekeeper was asleep upstairs when the fire broke out. Mr. Hanford slept downstairs in the rear of the house. The firefighters found him out in the yard, delirious and nearly dead. He inhaled some smoke. Apparently he's pretty banged up, too."

"Do you know how the fire started?"

"Not yet, the arson boys are still investigation." He nodded in the direction of the house. Burke could see men working among the charred ruins.

"When did the fire start?"

"The report came in early Sunday morning, sometime around two. Say, Detective, you mind telling me what your interest is in this? You're pretty far from home."

"We've been working on a missing person's case that involved the Hanford family. I'd like to have a word with the officer in charge of the arson squad, if I may."

The officer hesitated. "Wait here," he said, "I'll see if it's okay with him."

They watched the officer speak to another man, and then he wheels around and returns. "That's Sergeant Lawson there, Arson Supervisor. You can go on up."

"Thank you," Burke said.

They walked on to where Lawson stood, beside the burned-shell. The devastation was total, and shocking. Nothing remained of the house and garage, except ash covered foundation, and charred and partially melted metal fixtures and appliances strewn about

"Detective Burk, is it?" Lawson asked.

"Yes, and this is Detective Dempsey. Sorry to disturb you. Have you determined the cause of the fire?"

"Not yet. We won't finish up here till tomorrow some time, I imagine. Then we still have laboratory work to do."

"I would certainly appreciate it if you could provide me with a copy of your report. I don't know that it has any bearing at all on our investigation, but it very well might." Burke said.

"Officer Brodsky said you were investigating a missing person involving the Hanford family, would that be his long-lost son?"

"Yes. Are you familiar with that case?"

"Oh, yes. Everyone in these parts of the country is familiar with that situation."

"Do you have an opinion of it?" Burke asked.

"Oh, I don't know, I suppose I regard it as a hopeless situation. Unless you've come up with something new that I don't know about, I would think you're wasting your time."

"I'm not at liberty to discuss the case, and I would appreciate it if you would keep our involvement confidential. Now, about that arson report ..."

"Sure, I'll send you a copy. Do you have a card?"

Burke took a business card from his wallet and handed it to Lawson." Thanks for your help," he said, "and good luck here."

"Thanks," Lawson said, as Burk and Elmo turned and walked toward their car.

Driving back toward town, Burke said, "I wonder why Markowitz, didn't call us about this. Take a right at the next light. I want to go by his office."

The door to Markowitz's office was locked. A note taped to the inside of the glass door said that Markowitz was on vacation and gave a date when the office would reopen. Burke got behind the wheel and swung the car in the direction of Brockton City Hospital. In the lobby, he showed his identification to the girl at the reception desk. "Police officer, Miss. I'd like to see Mister Hanford."

"I'm sorry, sir, Mister Hanford is in intensive care. No one is allowed to see him."

"Could I speak to the attending physician, please?"

"One moment. I'll page him for you."

The intercom echoed through the corridor: "Doctor Stewart, please call the front desk, Dr. Stewart."

Shortly, the receptionist's phone rang. She answered it, and then said to Burke, "He'll be right with you."

Doctor Stewart said that Mr. Hanford was heavily sedated and on oxygen. "He was barely conscious and suffering from burns and smoke inhalation as well as contusions and abrasions."

"How long before I can interview him, do you think?"

"I don't know, perhaps days, perhaps never. He may not survive."

On the way out of the hospital, Burke found a pay phone off the lobby and placed a call to the Brockton Police Department. He talked for five minutes, gesturing emphatically once or twice. Then he hung up and rejoined Elmo in the reception area.

"What was that all about?" asked Elmo.

"I called the Brockton Chief of Police. I suggested to him that Mr. Hanford's life might be in danger, and not just from his injuries. I gave him a thumbnail sketch of what's been going on involving Mr. Hanford. He agreed to put a guard on his room for a couple of days, at least until the arson investigation is concluded."

"Isn't that sticking your neck out pretty far?"

"Maybe."

During the return trip, Dempsey was again driving. Burke slouched somberly and pensively in his seat, hardly responding to Dempsey's occasional comments. His lids hooded his eyes, as if he were about to doze off, but his mind was working overtime. He was confused, puzzled, and saturated with a sense of the bizarre.

Notwithstanding his "theory of the crime," and what he had just told the Brockton police, and, almost against his will, a new scenario began forming in his mind. A housekeeper in a wealthy household, seething with jealousy and hatred for the mistress of the house, perhaps in love with the mistress' husband, wreaks her terrible vengeance upon the family, destroying it, over decades. What hatred, what pure hatred! Was that the role Mrs. Halper had played in the Hanford household over the years? Had she abducted and killed the child, and yet stayed there in the house, contributing her venom in a thousand subtle ways, to eventually destroy first the wife, then, the husband?

Burke shook himself out of his morbid speculations and glanced at Dempsey, who was watching him out of the corner of his eye as he drove. "You all right, Boss?"

"Oh, I'm anything but all right, Elmo," he mumbled.

Dempsey turned back to his driving, clearly startled by the expression on Burke's face.

"Mrs. Halper did it," Burke whispered, barely audibly. "She set the fire. She meant to kill herself and Mr. Hanford, to end the Hanford family, to obliterate it for all time. Here's how I believe it happened: She became alarmed when she read in our newspaper that the bones of the child were unearthed. She became even more alarmed when we showed up to take blood from Hanford. I suspect she was an ignorant woman, and became fearful that the DNA tests would implicate her in the murder of the infant. She struck out blindly at those performing the tests. She must have been stalking them, and killed Sheila during a moment of sheer madness. Then she visited Hamilton, and pleaded with him to persuade me to stop the investigation."

"What? Are you serious?"

"Dead serious. How could I have been so blind? Why didn't I see the signs?"

"What kind of nonsense have you pulled out of your hat, Boss?" Dempsey said, a look of concern on his face.

"That what you think, Elmo?"

"What do you expect me to think? I'm wondering if you have gone nuts or something. Oh, I get it. You're pulling my leg, right? Very funny."

But Burke wasn't laughing. He wasn't smiling. His glazed eyes stared on into space. The car rounded a curve.

"There's a truck stop coming up," Dempsey said. "How about let's pull over and get us some hot coffee."

"Okay."

Darkness was falling. The lights of the truck stop were illuminated. Dempsey pulled into the big, graveled lot and parked the car, and they walked inside and found a booth by the window. Outside the window, the big diesel rigs maneuvered in and out underneath the tall, neon-lit overhangs of the fueling bays in a steady continuous ritual, like the choreographed dance of behemoths. Inside, drivers with potbellies hanging over their denim jeans and billed caps over uncut hair, hunkered down on the counter stools cupping their coffee mugs, or shoveling in ham and eggs under a sign that said, "Breakfast Anytime." Others wandered in and out of the sprawling building where showers and cots were available for rent by the hour or by the day, and where there was a surprising array of merchandise and amenities available to purchase.

"Order me some coffee, Elmo. I'm going to the restroom to throw some cold water in my face."

"Right, Boss."

They sat quietly, sipping the hot coffee, and watching the continuous motion, inside and outside the window, and the industry of the waitresses and service personnel. Presently, Burke said, "Well, let's get back on the road."

The rest of the drive was uneventful. Burke leaned back against the headrest with his eyes closed listening to quite jazz music on the radio. They pulled into the city hall parking lot. Burke elected not to go inside. Dempsey got out of the car and Burke took the wheel and drove home. After a cold supper, he told Marge he was tired and went directly to bed, where he tossed, turned, agonized, and occasionally dozed. At breakfast, Marge commented: "You have bags under your eyes, dear. Didn't you sleep well?"

"No."

"What's wrong? Are you sick?"

"No, I'm not sick. There's been another murder."

"What! Who is it this time?"

"Hanford's house in Brockton burned down. His house keeper was killed in the fire and Hanford is in intensive care. He may not survive. That's why I was late. Dempsey and I drove up yesterday afternoon."

"My God!" She exclaimed. No wonder you didn't sleep. But, do you mean that someone deliberately burned down his house?"

"Yes, but I don't know that for certain. The arson squad hasn't completed its investigation."

Burke finished breakfast. Marge didn't press him for further details. He got up, kissed her on the cheek, and said, "I'll see you tonight, hon."

He got to the station early and got started typed a report for Newman. He noticed that when Dempsey came in, he seemed fidgety and uncomfortable, like he wanted to talk, but Burke put him off while he finished the report. He wanted to brief Newman as quickly as possible and get that bit of unpleasantness behind him. When he finished the report, he dialed Newman's number. His secretary answered, and said Newman wasn't in yet.

"Give me a ring when he comes in, please." Burke said.

"Nine o'clock came, and he still hadn't arrived. While he waited, Burke gave Hamilton a call to tell him what had happened, since his report of Harper's visit had prompted the trip to Brockton.

When he told him the house had burned down, and Halper had died in the fire, Hamilton gasped audibly, and seemed by his voice and manner to be genuinely distressed.

"What about Mr. Hanford?" he asked.

"He's in intensive care. He may not survive."

"Do they know the cause of the fire?"

"Not yet. There's an investigation underway."

As they talked, Burke listened to the intonation of Hamilton's voice. He sounded sincere, but very intense—abnormally so. Burke sensed that something wasn't right. Hamilton's reaction was *too* alarmed, *too* disconcerted, which was a strange reaction from a medical doctor, accustomed to death and suffering, especially so since the situation at hand concerned people he had met only once or twice.

After he hung up, Burke called Elmo over.

"I just got off the phone with Hamilton."

"Yeah, I heard. How did he take it?"

"Not very well. He seemed excessively upset."

"What do you mean by that?"

"I don't know what to tell you except that he seemed to be disproportionately disturbed, like he was taking it personal."

Dempsey studied Burke's face for a moment. "Are you okay, Boss?" he said. "You don't look too good this morning."

"Yesterday was a rough day."

"I know, I was with you, remember?"

Chief Newman came in about ten-thirty. Burke carried his typed-up report, and he and Dempsey went in to brief him on what had happened the previous day. The Chief read through the report quickly, and said, "Son-of-a-bitch! What next?"

"There's a chance that the fire was deliberately set, "Burke said. "They were conducting an arson investigation while Elmo and I were there, said they would send us a copy of the report. If arson is found, my bet is on Mrs. Halper."

"Mrs. Halper? Who is this Mrs. Halper, again?"

"The housekeeper, Clarence Hanford's housekeeper—the old woman who burned up in the fire."

"Oh, yes. What are you saying? That you think she set it? Why do you think she set it?"

Burke glanced over and saw Elmo looking at him. He looked tense, as if he was straining to keep from saying something. Burke figured he was trying to warn him not to bring up the fantastic theory Burke had given him the night before on the drive back from Brockton. Burke had better sense than that. "She was a queer duck, Chief, right from the get-go. It's just a feeling I have. I don't have anything to back it up."

"Well, what else is new?" Newman grumbled. "So, how does this tie in with the Vann case, if at all?"

"I don't know. Maybe it does, maybe it doesn't. Maybe Halper killed her, too. Maybe Halper was nuts. I'm not prepared to draw any conclusion at this time. I'm only hoping the paper doesn't get wind of this and try to make some connection. I suggest we keep the fire and everything to do with the Hanford matter under our hats for now."

"I agree," Newman said. "You got anything to say, Elmo."

"No, Chief."

"All right, then, that's the way we'll play it."

As they left the Newman's office and walked down the hall, Dempsey said, "Newman seemed to take it very well, didn't he?"

"Yeah, he just wants it all to go away."

"What you said about Halper maybe killing Vann, Daniel—"

"I know what you're going to say," Burke interrupted, "I'm still struggling to work my way through all this. Sometimes, when I'm tired, I might tend to get a little overwhelmed."

They were silent for a few moments, as Burke realized he had inadvertently shared an intimate moment with his subordinate. He had displayed weakness. Back in Vietnam that could get a man killed. Dempsey had not exploited it, at least not yet.

"Seems like things are getting worse and worse," Dempsey said. "Complication added to complication and nothing getting resolved."

"It does seem that way."

"I been thinking, Boss, that if we could only identify the bones, everything else would start to fall into place. If it turned out the bones had no connection with the Hanford-Halper situation, we would know that we have two separate matters on our hands, if not three, and we could stop trying to jumble them all up together."

"Don't you think what Mrs. Halper did, coming to see Hamilton, saying what she said, ties them together?"

"Not necessarily. The old lady could have been talking about searching for Hanford's kid, stirring him up, getting him all excited about that. Maybe that's all she was concerned about, not about Vann or old bones."

"I see where you're coming from. I don't know, Elmo," Burke said wearily. "You may be right. How do you propose we go about identifying the bones? What do you want to do that we haven't tried already?"

"I don't know. Try harder, maybe. Focus."

Burke sighed, "I'm ready to try anything at this point."

CHAPTER 7
CHAOS AND CONFUSION

A few days later, Burke and Dempsey were in the office when the clerk came by with the mail. Burke looked through it "Here's something from the Brockton Police Department. Must be the arson report." He tore it open and read it. "Damn! The cause is indeterminate."

"That's too bad."

"Yeah. You know, I was half hoping they would prove arson—I wanted them to find evidence that Halper did it."

Dempsey didn't answer. It was just as well. Burke felt a tinge of shame. His mind was all cluttered up with the wreckage of his initial theory of the crime. To that, he added this new, crazy, jumbled-up notion that Halper was the villain in the affair. If she did set the fire and if she did kill Vann, he saw no way to prove it. What good was it then? There would never be closure. Maybe the chief had been right all along. Maybe there was no connection between any of it. Maybe they were all coincidences, random occurrences, to which his untrained mind attributed cause-and-effect relationships that didn't exist.

The idea that the old Newman might be right galled him. He was not going to condemn himself for using his imagination. He believed that a good imagination was essential to being a good detective. The only trouble was, that detectives eventually have to get evidence and prove things. He had been able to prove nothing. There was one fact, though, which he held on to, and that was the fact that Sheila had been loading data into the computer that afternoon when he visited her. Somehow, he believed that was the key to the riddle.

He walked over to the filing cabinet where Elmo kept the evidence in the Vann case. It was locked, as it should have been. He and Elmo each had keys. Burke took his key and unlocked the cabinet. He leafed through the materials looking for the reports from the computer runs of August 16th. He found the reports, and he was about to shut the drawer when he stopped and again scanned the contents of the drawer. Then he opened the second drawer and examined it, then the third. He closed the drawers, locked the cabinet, and took the reports back to his desk.

Dempsey came in and sat down at his desk.

"Elmo?"

"Yeah, Boss."

"Where did we put the backup tapes from the Vann case?"

"In the top filing cabinet drawer. You want them?"

"Yes, please."

"You bet."

Dempsey went to the filing cabinet, took his keys from his pocket, and opened the drawer. Burke watched him carefully. Dempsey looked puzzled. He searched through the contents of the drawer, then closed it and opened the second drawer. He repeated the process for the third.

"They're not here."

"Not there?"

"No."

"Well, where are they?"

"I don't know."

Burke walked over to him. "You didn't have occasion to take them out and put them somewhere else, like the evidence room?"

"No." Elmo said softly.

"I haven't touched them either, since you put them in there, in the tray," said Burke. "I saw you put the tray in that top drawer, myself."

"That's right, I did. So what happened to it?"

"Obviously, someone has taken it," said Burke.

Dempsey leaned over close to the file drawer and examined the lock and drawer minutely. "I don't see any jimmy marks."

Burke inspected the locking mechanism and verified that it was unmarked and in good working order. "You and I have keys. The only other key is in the safe in Newman's office."

"That's the way it's supposed to be. Want to check with the chief?"

"No, not just yet, Elmo. I've got to think this through."

"Boss, I hope you don't think that I—"

"No, Elmo, I don't. Don't worry about it, and keep this to yourself for now. I don't want whoever took it to know that we know about it. I'll talk to the chief later, but I have a notion that we've seen the last of that tray of backup tapes. And you know what, Elmo?"

"No, what?"

"I don't believe I can blame this on Mrs. Halper."

With the disappearance of the tapes, Burke paranoia really kicked in, and his imagination went into overdrive. He appeared agitated and somewhat overwrought, and, at home that evening, Marge inquired as to what was ailing him. "You won't believe it, hon," he said to her, and against his better judgment, he told her about the findings in the arson report and the disappearance of the backup tapes.

"Oh, dear, what next!" she exclaimed. "When is this madness going to end? What does it mean, Daniel?"

156

"I just don't know."

"Daniel, don't let it get you down. It's not worth it. I can see how it is affecting you."

"I won't deny that."

"You've got to back off a little. You could have a heart attack."

"Whoa, settle down, darling, take it easy. I 'm okay, but I'm glad I told you."

⊷⊰⊱⊷

At work the following morning he created a list of people who could have any reason to take the tapes, and eventually he narrowed the list, once again, to Smithers and Hamilton. He could not figure out how they could have gotten access to the filing cabinet unless someone inside City Hall aided them. The thief would not necessarily need a key. Practically anybody in the know could pick the lock on a standard filing cabinet. Any cop could do it, the question was, why? Why would someone on the inside of the department aid a murder suspect? The whole thing threw Burke for a loop. For the first time he felt a tinge of fear.

Burke held back for the next few days, remembering Margie's admonition, and deciding not to mention the missing tapes to anyone, but to keep his eyes and ears open. Dempsey agreed to cooperate, and Burke agreed with the suggestion that they should concentrate on identifying the bones. He gave Dempsey a free hand to finish any research remaining at the newspaper office and the library archives. Burke got the name of a trade association of clothing manufacturers, and wrote the association a letter asking for help in tracking down the manufacturer of the child's playsuit and the other cloth fragments found with the skeletal remains. He made a blow-up of the brass button, and the picture of the child wearing the playsuit, with his face blanked out, and sent them with the letter. Dempsey drove to

Columbus to access the library and newspaper archives there, to research the old editions of the major state-wide newspaper, the State Journal

Dempsey made several overnight trips. He turned up some missing person stories from newspaper archives, a few kidnapping stories and murders, but most of them did not match the ages or circumstances of the bones and Dempsey ruled them out on the spot. Only three of the stories he found in the archived seemed to have even the remotest possible relevance to the bones. They involved people who had disappeared without a trace, including three men, one with a young male child. When Dempsey got back to the office, he gave Burke a rundown on the three cases:

"One article," Dempsey began, reading from his notes, which he had not yet had typed, "which appeared in the June 17, 1961, State Journal, concerned an occurrence in Springville, about 100 miles northwest of Stanton. The headline was, Local Man declared legally dead. The article read: 'Superior Court ruled today on the motion of attorneys representing Mrs. Francis Keaton, declaring her husband, Walter Keaton, to be legally dead. Mr. Keaton allegedly left his home on the morning in April 4, 1954, and failed to return. The following day his wife reported his absence to the police. The authorities investigated the matter thoroughly, and discovered no evidence of foul play. Neighbors stated that a stormy relationship existed between the couple, and the speculation was that he had taken off for parts unknown. Seven years having elapsed, the court declared Mr. Keaton legally dead. Mrs. Keaton, a nurse at Springville General Hospital, declined our request for an interviewed following the ruling.

"The second article involved a fire that occurred in Brockton, the hometown of Mr. Hanford, in April 1954. The victims were Barton and Wilma Layton, and their four-year-old son, Barton, Jr. The fire burned with great intensity, and the authorities recovered no bodies, leading to speculation that the alleged victims had not been present in the fire at all. The cause of the fire was chemical in nature, which the Police ruled as arson.

"The third case involved a single man, one Fred Burch, who failed to show up for work one morning in October 1954, at the dry-cleaning establishment where he worked in the town of Bentonville, which was sixty miles north of Brockton. His employer called his residence and was unable to reach Mr. Burch. He made inquiries of his landlady, and then notified the police. The furnished room Burch rented was searched, and found in order. It and contained a full complement of clothing, toiletries and other personal effects, but no clues as to his whereabouts were found. They were never able to locate Mr. Burch."

"Good job, Elmo. Follow up on these cases—see what else you can find out about these people. Have you worked out your methodology yet?"

"Yeah, everything is under control. I'm going to do a lot of calling, and I may need to do a little more traveling, too."

Dempsey set up files on the three cases and began digging for additional information. He called the State Journal again seeking any follow-up stories on the three articles, and called the police departments in the towns where the three incidences had occurred to gain access to any official police files of the cases, but because of expected delays, he decided to drive to the towns and examine the files directly.

He called the National Registry of Nurses for the address of Mrs. Francis Keaton. He wrote letters to people mentioned in the articles. He wrote to The Insurance Underwriter's Clearing House to find out about any life insurance policies issued on the missing people.

With the disappearance of the back-up tapes and a few days of rest and introspection, Burke lost his enthusiasm for the "Halper as arch villain" theory. Maybe she did cause the fire, but he had no way to know that, or to prove it. He decided to give her the benefit of the doubt on that score, since he no longer suspected her of murdering Sheila. However, her behavior, as reported by Hamilton, remained troubling to him, if it actually occurred. He was back with Hamilton as his main suspect in the Vann murder. He was prepared to accept the idea that he had three separate, unrelated mysteries on his hands, until such time, if ever, that he could demonstrate a connection between them. With Dempsey fully engaged in the effort to identify the bones, Burke was free once more to focus his attention on the Vann case.

If Newman knew what he and Dempsey were doing, he was quiet about it, and while he was quiet, Burke needed to apply a little pressure on Hamilton, to see how he reacted. He called the doctor and made an appointment to meet with him in his office concerning "a few loose ends." He arrived at Hamilton's office and accepted a chair opposite his desk. Hamilton's appearance startled him. His skin had a sickly pallor, his eyes looked tired, and were red, with dark splotches underneath. He looked as if he hadn't slept for days, and perhaps had neglected his personal grooming.

"Loose ends you say, Detective?" Hamilton's voice was edgy, unfriendly.

"Yes, uh...thank for seeing me, Doctor, on short notice like this."

"No problem," he said, but Burke suspected otherwise.

"Excuse me, Doctor Hamilton, are you ill? I can come another time if you like."

"No, no, I'm tired, that's all. I've been working hard at the hospital. I appreciate your concern."

Hamilton's voice lacked sincerity, but Burke smiled and continued. "First I want to go over again with you where you were at the time of Miss Vann's—uh, death."

"Why? I've already told you that I attended a faculty meeting and afterwards went directly home. I assume you've verified that?"

The abruptness of Hamilton's challenge startled Burke momentarily, but he quickly recovered. "Yes but in the interest of thoroughness—you said you left the meeting at seven and drove directly home, and that you were there alone until your mother came home from her meeting around eight."

"That's right."

"I drove from your meeting place to your home several times on different days," Burke said cautiously. "My best time for the trip was twelve minutes and my worst time was twenty-five minutes. The latter was when I took my time and missed a few lights. Even using the worst case, that leaves you with sufficient time to have swung by the lab and killed Sheila."

Hamilton half rose from chair. His face was flushed and distorted. "You think I killed Sheila. That's absurd! Why, I—I cared for Sheila a great deal."

"No, Doctor, please. I'm sorry, that question didn't come out quite right. I merely meant to emphasize the time, not level an accusation against you. There is just this little discrepancy in your alibi that I need to clear up." Burke waited for Hamilton to settle down again, and then he continued. "Was traffic particularly heavy that evening, Doctor? Was there a road accident? A traffic light out? Anything to account for that extra time?"

Hamilton fidgeted in his chair, clearly not happy. "No," he said. There was nothing unusual that I recall. Maybe I got home earlier—or later. I don't know, I wasn't thinking about it at the time."

"Okay, let's put that aside and go on, just a couple of other points. You said just now that you cared a great deal for Sheila. How do you mean that?"

"How do I mean it? I don't understand the question. She was a wonderful woman, a friend, a brilliant teacher and scientist with a bright future. Her death was a great tragedy, and a great loss to me personally. What did you think I meant?"

"I thought you might have meant to include, romantically, as well. I understand that the two of you dated."

"We went out a few times when I first returned to Stanton. It wasn't serious. We were colleagues."

"Well, I only wondered why you never mentioned that to me, that you had dated, I mean."

"I didn't mention it? Then how did you know?" He was practically on his feet again.

"I'm sure it came up quite innocently during the course of my investigation. So you had no reason to conceal that fact from the police."

"Of course not. Not at all."

Because of Hamilton's demeanor, and his agitated state, Burke thought it advisable to proceed more cautiously with him, not to press him too far. Something was obviously already pressing on him hard. It was amazing to Burke how this man had changed in the brief time since he had seen him last.

"All right, Doctor Hamilton, I won't keep you much longer. I know how busy you are, and I certainly apologize if my questions are causing you discomfort. The other thing I am curious about …" Burke paused, seemingly deep in thought, and then continued. "You see, Doctor, I'm a man who is suspicious of coincidence. Maybe it goes back to my poker playing days in the Marine Corps. I believe in odds, and probabilities, and cause and effect. That's really, more or less, the main reason why I'm here."

"I'm sorry, you've lost me. What are you driving at?"

"It's the visit you had from Mrs. Halper, and her death shortly thereafter in the fire, and the fact that you didn't tell me about her visit right away. Do you realize that when you finally told me, she was already dead? Ironic, isn't it, how things happen sometimes. I'm particularly puzzled by that, because, I'm sorry, it simply doesn't make any sense to me. According to you, she asked you to convey a message to me—that I should call off my investigation before another tragedy occurred. It strikes me, Doctor, that her visit, and her general bearing as you described it to me, should have triggered an immediate response on your part. It should have set off an alarm bell. Yet you told me, when you finally got around to letting me in on it, that you attached no particular significance to her visit at the time, and only bothered to tell me about it later because your mother suggested it to you. Frankly, Doctor, that strikes me as extraordinary. Beyond that, one has to wonder why the woman came to you in the first place, and not to me. After all, I believe it's true that you only met her the one time previously, when we went there for the blood sample."

Hamilton didn't answer. The blood seemed to drain from his face. He was pensive, not moving, simply staring into Burke's eyes, a forlorn expression on his face. Burke waited him out.

Finally, Hamilton spoke. "I see why you're here, Detective. Are you going to arrest me for Sheila's murder? How about the fire at the Hanford house? That, too?"

"I'm not here to arrest you, Doctor Hamilton, I'm only here for answers, if you have any. I don't have sufficient evidence to arrest you—not yet."

"I have no better answers for you than I've already given."

"Well then, I suppose our business is completed for now. Thanks, as always, for your cooperation."

Burke rose from the chair and walked to the door. Hamilton remained seated without speaking, gazing at his clasped hands on the desk in front of him.

As Burke walked down the hallway toward the exit he said to himself, "I guess we know where we stand now, Doctor."

—=++=—

The following morning, Newman called Burke into his office. Newman's face was pale and drawn—a grim mask. He spoke slowly, sternly, without preamble. "I've warned you before, Burke, now for the last time, you've got to get off this insane obsession of yours about Doctor Hamilton. People are calling your motives into question. You and I both know that I didn't want you here in the position you hold, but here you are, that's politics."

"Wait a minute, what people are calling what motives into question? What does that mean?"

"Important people, goddamn it! It means you have an agenda. You have a problem with doctors, professional people. It's common knowledge you have an attitude." Newman paused for a moment as if gathering his thoughts, as if reconciling himself, once again, to having the protégé of his arch political enemy hovering at his breast. "Since you've been here," he continued, "I've bent over backwards to be fair with you, to keep the politics swirling about us all the time from interfering with you executing your duties. Do you know why?"

"No," Burke said, his voice edgy. He was beginning to get really pissed off. "Why don't you tell me?"

"Because I know there isn't a political bone in your body. I know that you only want to earn a living and support your family. I know that since you've been here working for me you have kept your nose clean politically. I've appreciated that."

"Well, Chief, I won't say I'm not surprised to hear you say that, because I am surprised. You're exactly right, though, I don't give a damn about your local political crap, or my father-in-law's either, for that matter. I'd tell you to take this whole thing and stuff if it wasn't for my kids. Right now I'm trying to do my job and maintain some semblance of my self-respect, which is shaky right now."

Newman absorbed the tirade with surprising grace. "I can understand that, Daniel, that's why I'm trying to help you. I'm telling you that you are all wet on this thing of yours about Hamilton. Hamilton is a good kid, and he's a damn good doctor from everything I hear, and I hear a great deal. You've got to get this out of your head, or I won't be able to protect you, and Belden, your father-in-law, won't either. Believe me, there are people telling me this. What you have to understand is that you're messing around in something beyond your pay grade—maybe beyond your understanding. I suppose, frankly, that's because you're a product of the lower classes, and from the big city. You don't understand about families in a small town like this that go back into the shadows of history. These people are not like you and me—yes, I include myself in that—these people are not just prominent citizens, these people are super-citizens, they got more rights than you and me."

Newman trailed off into a troubled silence, staring off across the room, as if he were alone with his thoughts, with Burke momentarily forgotten.

"That's funny, Chief, you describing a new, higher level of citizenship?"

"There's nothing new about it, Daniel, the only thing that's new is that you are about to become aware of it, in very unpleasant ways, if you don't listen to me and stay away from Hamilton?"

Burke didn't respond. He didn't know what to say. It was obvious someone was pressuring Newman—someone powerful enough to give Newman the willies.

"All right, Chief, I hear you. I'll do my best to cool down the heat. That's the best I can do. But, frankly, I'm not really doing anything to the man. Personally, I like him. I've only asked him relevant questions in a murder investigation."

"It's up to you, Daniel, just keep that lovely family of yours in mind, and try to do what's best for them. These people can ruin a man."

"What people?" He asked. "Be specific, tell me who I'm up against."

"Talk to Belden."

"All right, Chief. Is that all?"

"Yeah, that's all, Daniel."

Once again, Burke found himself walking down the hall, his ass stinging, his emotions on a roller coaster ride, from anger to fear to anger again. He walked out of the main entrance of City Hall, and down Main Street, the two blocks to the law offices of Samuel Belden. He had not been there in six years.

Belden's law office was on the third floor of a three-story building that he owned. The receptionist announced him, and shortly, Belden came out of his private office with a surprised expression. "Daniel! Is something wrong? Marge and the kids—

"They're fine. I'm here on my own."

Belden showed him into his large corner office, which had two large windows overlooking a portion of the town and a patch of the Ohio River. The room was a study in highly-polished wood and maroon leather. Belden motioned him to a chair near one of the windows and sat opposite him. "It's been a long time since you've been to my office," he said.

"Yes, it has."

"Get you anything?"

"No, thanks."

"What's happened, Daniel? What can I do for you?"

Without preamble, Burke began. "It's this case I'm on—the murder of Sheila Vann, out at the college. I think I know who did it."

Belden leaned forward in his chair. "Who?"

"Mark Hamilton."

Belden's eyes got big. "Doctor Mark Hamilton? Doris Hamilton's kid?"

"Yeah."

"Whee! Are you sure?"

"No, I'm not sure at all. If I was sure, it would be easy. I strongly suspect him. Let me say it that way."

"And?"

"I've been warned off him at the risk of losing my job."

"By whom?"

"Chief Newman."

"Why that old bastard!"

"I get the impression it is not him talking, it's someone else. Someone has put the bug in his ear. He's warning me off, maybe even to save my job for all I know, rather than to get rid of me."

"You may be right about that." Belden said, thoughtful. "In his day he was a formidable opponent, but now he's a sick, old man. I hear his liver is about to give out on him. I wouldn't want you to repeat that. Tell me what he said. No, wait, tell me what you have on Hamilton, first."

For thirty minutes, Burke talked, explained where he was in his thinking about the murder of Sheila Vann, and that Hamilton was his prime and only suspect. He threw caution to the wind and went through his theory on how her murder might tie in with the bones, and with Mr. Hanford's missing son."

"That's quite a story, Daniel, but I can see where you're coming from."

"I'm happy to hear that. So far, the few people I've mentioned it to, think I'm nuts."

"It's not that they don't understand you, it's that they don't want to understand you. Most people around here know the score. There are people in this town who think they're above the law, and they look out for their own kind. People are afraid to take them on, or even appear to be taking them on. That kind of mentality leads to a lot of self-deception." Belden paused thoughtfully then continued. "Young Hamilton was a sports hero in high school. The bigwigs adopted him into the fold—greatness by association. Doris is a formidable personality in her own right, came from an old established family herself, although they're mostly all dead and gone now, or moved away. Between the two of them, they have a lot of friends and allies in this town."

"What do you think I ought to do? I have Marge and the kids to think about. That's why I came to you. Otherwise, I would not have bothered you."

"I'm glad you did, and it's no bother. You've never asked my advice before. I know what you think of me, and I'm wondering why you decided to come to me now. It must have been hard for you."

"I—I don't know exactly. Probably because I have no one else to turn to in a situation like this. Besides, you got me the job with the city, and for that and other reasons, I figure you have a legitimate interest in whether I keep it or not."

"Look, Daniel, if you want to know the truth, I didn't do any more for you than I've done for a dozen other young people over the years. A man has a family, he needs a job. Sometimes they come to me—that is one of the burdens of being in politics. I do what I can for them, if I think they're worth the trouble. Of course, in your case, even though you didn't come to me, I felt that impulse a bit stronger, since you married my only daughter. I interceded on your behalf without your knowledge, because I suspected you would have resented it had you known, and maybe even declined the job."

"I understand. I never properly thanked you for that. Thank you. Now, I guess what I want from you is to tell me who I'm up against. After that, I'll make my own decision, and be solely responsible for it."

"Does that mean you intend to press on with your investigation?"

"Yes. I intend to take it wherever it leads."

"You don't know how glad I am to hear you say that. Then I'll do what I can to help you, but I can't guarantee it will end to your liking.

"That's good enough for me."

"The money interests run this town, like any other.," Belden said, leaning back in his chair, assuming a didactic pose. "It's always the same, the presidents of our two banks, and a few other wealthy individuals usually have their way. Money always translates into power, you know. The school board has a lot of influence because of the jobs they control, and the budget. Those boys can make or break a merchant just by changing the brand of toilet paper they use in a school or two. Usually the banks are the oldest money. Occasionally one sells out to a national chain, and the sellers move to Europe or somewhere, but largely, they hang around, generation after generation. You know who they are, you've been around here ten, twelve years. As to what I advise you to do, I advise you to keep as low-key as possible and still do your job. Don't do anything to antagonize Chief Newman. In the meantime, I'll check around and try to find out who specifically, besides Doris and the doctor himself, is pressuring Newman"

"What about you? Everyone know you're a power around here."

"Me? Some people consider me one of those people I just described to you. Modesty prevents me from tooting my own horn. Let me just say that I know where the bodies are buried. That's what will save your job if the going gets rough. Don't worry about it, they'll have to go over me to get to you. You just do your job responsibly."

Burke felt a surge of emotion. His eyes actually felt like they were watering up. "How can I thank you, Sam."

"Take good care or my daughter and my grandkids. Oh, and one other thing, the price of my advice is a game of golf sometime, soon."

"I'm not a very good golfer."

"That's my price, take it or leave it. Seriously, it's a well-known fact that you and I have not been on such good terms. It won't hurt for you to be seen with me now and again."

"Okay, whenever you say."

"Wonderful."

CHAPTER 8
MORE MURDER

Wednesday afternoon the week following his meeting with Hamilton, a call came in to Burke from Professor Ripley. After a brief exchange, Burke put down the receiver and mumbled, "I wonder what's on his mind?" Then he said, "Say, Elmo, that was Ripley. He wants me to come to his office. Says he needs to talk to me about something important. He wouldn't say what it was. I'm going over there right now and see what's going on."

"Oh, boy, sounds like more trouble."

"I'll find out shortly."

Burke rushed out and drove to the college. Ripley's secretary was not at her desk. Burke rapped gently on the inner door.

"Come in," a voice called.

Burke opened the door. Ripley was not alone. Two other men sat in two of the five chairs arranged in a semicircle in front of his desk. One was Smithers, the other man Burke didn't recognize.

"Come in, Detective Burke. You know Professor Smithers, and this is Mister Holmes, the head of security for the college."

The two men stood, and shook hands with Burke, and then everyone took their seats. Burke waited for Ripley to speak. He appeared uncharacteristically solemn.

"I'm afraid we have another potentially troubling situation here at the college, Detective. Burke. It seems Doctor Hamilton has disappeared."

"Disappeared?"

"Yes. He hasn't been seen since late last Saturday night. One of Mr. Holmes' security people had an encounter with him then, at about midnight. He was on campus apparently drunk and ran his car into a tree. It only put a dent in the fender. When the security guard approached him, he became belligerent and abusive, and then drove away. The guard said Hamilton was a mess: unshaven, rumpled, and wild-eyed."

"That hard to believe," Burke said, then recalled how Hamilton looked the last time he had seen him.

"Nobody has seen him since," Ripley continued. "We don't know where he is. Those of us who know him know how utterly out of character this is. We're afraid he may be having a nervous breakdown, perhaps triggered by Vann's murder. We thought we should bring you in on it and hope you'll treat it confidentially for now."

Burke didn't know what to say to that. His first thought was to wonder why they had not gone to Chief Newman instead of him. He said nothing, only nodded to Ripley. His thoughts focused on Hamilton. He had intended to put pressure on Hamilton, but he hadn't anticipated anything like this. He felt a pang of remorse. He actually liked the young doctor and hoped nothing had happened to him. It's easy to forget sometimes that people are innocent until proven guilty.

"What does his mother say?" Burke asked, emerging from his introspective moment.

"Doris is beside herself. She has no idea where he is. She confirmed that he has been troubled lately, and she doesn't know why, either."

Oh, but she does know, Burke thought, she knows that I suspect him of murder.

Burke turned to Smithers, who had remained quiet until now. "How has he been at work lately, since the murder?"

"It's the strangest thing. In the last few weeks I've watched him unravel a little at a time. I tried to talk to him a couple of times, but he pushed me away. I don't know what's going on with him."

"Even if he is reacting to Miss Vann's murder, don't you think his reaction is extremely odd?" Burke said "Him being a professional man, and all?"

"Yes, I do find it odd," Smithers said. "After all, we all worked together. I cared for Sheila as much as anybody did. I have no explanation for Mark's slide off the deep end like this."

"I'm not suggesting it," said Burke. "But have any of you considered the possibility that Dr. Hamilton may have had something to do with Miss Vann's death, that maybe he killed her?"

This time no one spoke.

"You asked me if I would keep this confidential for now. Well, I'm prepared to do so for a reasonable time while we try to find Hamilton and get to the bottom of this. If I'm willing to do that, I expect you to level with me. Have any of you considered the possibility that Dr. Hamilton killed Miss Vann?"

"I admit that the idea flitted across my mind briefly," Smithers said. "But, I immediately dismissed it as absurd. I know this man, and he would not do such a thing. Besides, what possible reason could he have to kill her?"

"Since we're confessing here in confidence, I'll admit that I briefly entertained the notion," Ripley said. Everybody looked at Holmes, the head of campus security. "I don't know him," Holmes said. "I never even met him. I have no reason to suspect him of anything, other than driving drunk on campus, and colliding with a tree, and mouthing off to my guard."

"How about you, Detective, do you have such a suspicion?" Ripley asked.

"It has crossed my mind more than once, but like Dr. Smithers, I haven't come up with a motive."

"Is that the official police position, or is that your position?" Smithers asked.

"There is no official police position, yet. I'm the investigating officer, and I look at evidence. I try not to have personal opinions until I complete my investigation, although I don't always succeed. Under the circumstances, I think you should know how I feel about it at this moment.

"I know I said I suspected him once, briefly," Smithers said, forcefully, "but I don't believe it. I simply refuse to believe it,. Something else is bothering him."

"I feel the same way," said Ripley."

"Okay, Gentlemen, we're really all together on that," Burke stated. "We each, at one time or another, considered that he might have killed her, but we really don't believe it. Even that is a little odd, don't you think?"

Holmes seemed to feel the need to reiterate his position. "I have no basis for an opinion, one way or the other. All I know is that the young woman is dead, and somebody killed her."

"Then what should we do about Hamilton," asked Ripley. "We need to find him. He may be in trouble."

"We don't know that anything has happened to him," Burke said. "All we know is that he appears to have been inordinately affected by Vann's death, but even there, we're making assumptions. We know he's upset and seems to be acting irrationally. However, maybe he has simply gone away for a while to be alone, to work through whatever is bothering him. We can check around quietly for a few days, and wait and see if he turns up. If he doesn't, then he must be reported missing, officially. That's the best I can offer you, and that's assuming that Mrs. Hamilton goes along with it."

"I feel certain she will," said Ripley. "I'll speak to her about it immediately. It would be a shame to ruin a young doctor's career if there's any way around it."

"I agree," Burke said. "Keep me advised if anything turns up, and I'll do the same."

"Thank you, Detective Burke, for your cooperation."

As Burke walked down the hall toward the exit, he heard his name called. He turned and saw Smithers approaching. Burke waited for Smithers, who came up to him and said, "I didn't want to say anything in front of the others, but there is something I think you should know."

"What's that?"

"I was working late last week, and I passed the lab and saw Mark in there running the computer. I was curious, so I entered the lab and spoke to him. He seemed edgy. I asked him what he was doing, and he put me off, said it was nothing important, just routine, but that he needed to attend to it, and he would talk to me later."

"Shuffled you right out of the room, huh?"

"Yes, that's it exactly. I thought he was acting peculiar, but I didn't want to make an issue of it, so I left. I saw something in the lab that didn't register at the time, but that kept bothering me. Then it came to me."

"What was it?"

"There was a tape lying by the computer. It looked just like one of the backup tapes. But you took the tapes with you, so it couldn't be one of those."

"That would seem to be so," Burke answered less than directly. He wanted to see where Smithers was going. "You haven't gotten around to making any new backup tapes?"

"No, we haven't. We haven't done anything in there since... I was naturally curious as to where the tape came from. I wanted to ask him about it later, but I chickened out and didn't"

"I see. So you think he found another tape, is that it? The mysterious backup tape that the two of you concluded never existed, since you concluded that Miss Vann never ran the program, and therefore made no backup tape?"

"Okay. I deserve that. But, it occurred to me that he either had another tape all along, or he found it later, and he was running it to see what was on it. This was when the thought flickered through my mind that maybe he killed Sheila."

"This could be very important," Burke said. "Is there a possibility that he left that tape in the lab?"

"I doubt it, but anything's possible."

"Could we search the lab right now?"

"Sure, let's go."

The two men hurried along the hallways to the computer lab. They searched through everything, thoroughly, until they were satisfied that the tape wasn't in the room.

"Do you have access to Hamilton's office?" Burke asked.

"Yes, I have a master key."

"You'll have to invite me in, or I'll have to go get a search warrant."

"Consider yourself invited."

Smithers inserted the master key and unlocked the door to Hamilton's office. They searched through the credenza, the shelves, and the desk. The large file drawer in the desk was locked. "Can you get in this drawer?" Burke asked.

Smithers hurried out to the lab and returned with a large screwdriver. He inserted it in the slit between the drawer and the frame of the desk and pried. The wood bowed and the drawer sprung open. Inside was a tray with four backup tapes. One tape lay on top of the other three, as if it had special significance. Burke recognized them as the tapes heisted from his filing cabinet at Police Headquarters. The one on top had the oldest date, March 8, 1983.

Smithers looked puzzled. "I don't get it. This looks like the tray you took with you." He examined the tray and the tapes. "It is. How is that possible?"

Burke didn't answer. It was at that moment that he knew beyond any doubt that Smithers was innocent of the death of Sheila Vann. "Let's make sure they're the same tapes. Let's load one on the computer—the one on top."

"But---?"

"What got Sheila killed may be on one of these tapes. If it is, it means that Hamilton may have killed her for it."

Smithers' eyes got large and his cheeks paled.

"Can we run this tape now?" Burke asked coldly.

"Yes. Let's do it,"

They returned to the lab and Smithers started up the computer and inserted the tape.

"Wait!" Burke said. "Let me see the tape again." He remembered something the two programmers at City Hall had told him about backing up files. Computer people use several tapes and rotate them so that even if a tape is lost or destroyed, only one backup cycle is lost. It is a numbers game. Smithers removed the tape from the computer and handed it to Burke. He checked the label. "This is tape number one in the sequence of four, the one with the oldest date. Do you know what that means?"

"Of course!" exclaimed Smithers. She started over with tape number one, but she didn't write the new date on it"

"Let's run the tape and see if we have guessed right."

"If she did run the program that day, and backed it up, then she used this tape to do it.

"That's a big 'if.' Let's find out."

What seemed like an interminable time later, the program finished and the report printed out. They studied the five pages of the report.

"I can already tell you that this report is different from the one we looked at last time," Smithers remarked. "That means that you were right all along, Burke. She did enter additional data. She did run the program, and she did back it up. The only thing she didn't do was write the new date on the tape."

Smithers continued leafing through the five pages of the report. On the fifth sheet, he said: "Hello! What's this?"

"What do you have?"

"There are three matching pairs. That's peculiar," Smithers said.

"What's peculiar? Come on, man, explain it to me."

"Sheila always included in her database two sets of data from known, closely related individuals as a control, as a verification that the program is functioning properly. That accounts for one of these matching pairs, but not for the other two."

Burke's excitement was growing. He sensed where this was going. "Can you determine who the other people are?"

"Yes, but it's a tedious process. It was seldom necessary, but when it was Sheila always handled it."

"But you know how?"

"Yes, I know how. I'll have to go back to original data sheets like those I showed you at our meeting here the other day, and then trace them back to their donors. Information is encoded on the data sheets, which we can cross-reference to identify the persons who contributed the samples. If we didn't have that capability, the data would be useless. That is why these files have confidential classifications."

"I understand. But this could be what we're looking for, Doctor. Don't quit now."

"Okay, I'll have a go at it. It will take me a while to locate and decipher Sheila's records. This part of our system is not computerized yet."

All right, I'll stay out of your way. Where is the nearest men's room?"

When Burke returned, Smithers was hard at it. He was flipping through some sort of ledger, and had data sheets spread out all over the table; he seemed to have found his groove. Burke sat in a desk chair, rocking gently back and forth, tapping his fingers on the armrest, unable to relax. He sat back in the chair and thought about that big trout up at the lake that he hadn't caught yet. He pictured the canoe gliding effortlessly along, to where the stream runs into the lake. That was where he had his best luck catching trout. He pictured himself tossing the fly, rather expertly he imagined, right up to the edge of the ripples where the water flowed over the stones. He felt the trout hit the fly."

"I've got it!" Smithers shouted. "I've got both of them. You're not going to believe this!"

"Tell me," said Burke, as the imaginary trout flopped off the hook and swam away.

"The first matching pair was the control, like I said."

"And the second?"

The second was the father and son skeletons. But the third …"

"Yes! Yes!"

"It's Mark Hamilton and Clarence Hanford."

"What?"

"You heard me right, Hamilton and Hanford."

"Wait a minute, explain this to me. You're saying that Hamilton and Hanford are a matching pair?"

"That's what I'm saying. They are a very high probability match, above the 95 percentile, meaning they're closely-related."

Burke was struck dumb for a moment, then he found his voice again. "I'm thoroughly confused. First of all, I don't understand why Hamilton's DNA profile was in this database, and I don't understand why Hanford's DNA profile was in the database, either—or the skeletons. What's going on here? It was my understanding that the tests for me were totally separate from your research project, and that the data used in the research project was real data that came from other places, hospitals and clinics from around the country. Can you explain this to me?"

Smithers seemed to be collecting his thoughts. "When we first started the project, we all ran DNA analysis on ourselves and included them in the database. We also did tests on volunteers from the hospital and the college, that's why Hamilton's is in there. Mine and Sheila's are in it as well. But why Sheila added Hanford's I don't know. And why she added the two skeletons, I don't know. But that appears to be what happened. Maybe it was inadvertent. Possibly, she entered them by mistake, the sheet got mixed in with the others. On the other hand, she may have put them in on purpose. I have no way of knowing."

"Are you sure of your interpretation? Is there any possibility you are mistaken?"

"I'm afraid not. The data and the results are there in black and white for anybody to see and to verify if they know how, and want to go to the time and trouble to do it. But I'll go over it again if you like, just to be sure there is no mistake."

This is fantastic, was all Burke could think—he kept repeating it over and over in his mind.

"Is it possible that Mark is Hanford's missing son?" Smithers said, breaking the silence, his eyes large and incredulous.

"You tell me, you're the brains of this outfit. It doesn't necessarily mean they are father and son, does it? Couldn't they be uncle and nephew, or cousins?

"I don't think so. The degree of DNA similarities is too high, above the 95th percentile. I think it is too high for them to be anything but father and son."

"If that's the case, that could easily account for Hamilton's mental state, and possibly gives him a motive for murder. If Sheila stumbled across this startling information, and foolishly gave it to Hamilton, she got her brains smashed in for her trouble."

"That's an assumption on your part. You don't know that for a fact," said Smithers angrily. "I don't believe it for a minute."

"Don't you? Sheila is dead, isn't she? Did somebody murder her right here in the lab, or was that my imagination?"

Smithers fell into a pouting silence. He had no comeback for that. Burke waited. Then Smithers said, "If you're right about this there's no telling what Mark might do in his frame of mind. Can you imagine the shock of learning that about yourself? I'm assuming he didn't know. He has to have a thousand question that are driving him crazy."

"Yes, I imagine," Burke said thoughtfully. "As difficult as this is going to be for you, I must have your solemn word that you won't breathe a word of this to anyone, what we have discovered here tonight, until I notify you otherwise. We must keep this from everybody, and I mean everybody: the men we met with today, your family, his mother, his friends, everybody. Do I have your word on that?"

"Yes, I know how important this is. You think Mark really killed Sheila?"

"I'm not sure of anything, but it looks that way."

"Think of all the implications, the scandal," Smithers said, introspectively. "He might have done it to protect his mother. You're aware of the implications for her: an illicit affair, adultery—she is a proud woman. He may have felt that having this become public would destroy her. It's all quite confusing."

Sweat stood in little beads on Smithers' forehead, and his eyes had a wild, distant look. "I just don't get it," he said. "It seems impossible."

Burke ignored him and continued talking and planning. "I need to take the report and the tape with me, and those two data sheets. "I need a statement from you as to what transpired here, Professor Smithers, will you come to the station with me right now, so I can have a secretary take a statement from you? This is very important. I'll have her type it and you sign it, right on the spot. I'll have to swear her to secrecy, too."

"Okay. Let me close down the computer. I suppose you want to seal the lab again."

"Yes."

"Listen, about the tapes, I don't understand how they came to be in Hamilton's possession."

"Someone stole them out of our filing cabinet at police headquarters."

"Mark?"

"I don't know who did it."

Burke mind was racing while Smithers closed down the computer. He was thinking that he knew something important that Smithers didn't know. Smithers didn't know about the fire in Brockton. Smithers didn't know about Halper and that she had died in the fire, and that Hanford was in intensive care.

And what about the bones? Burke always came back to that. How do they fit in? Who were those people? Then there is that brass button, the brass button with the anchor? *Hamilton would know the answers. He had to find Hamilton.*

Smithers finished up and he and Burke hurried out of the building together. "Where did you park?" Smithers asked.

"Over this way."

"Me, too."

"You follow me to the police station," Burke said. "We'll park in the lot behind City Hall."

Burke heard a noise, a couple of pops. "What was that?" he said, and turned toward Smithers. He saw a red stain appear on Smithers' shirt, right over his heart, and saw Smithers crumple to the ground like a wet towel, but he didn't hear the next two shots, the one that put a hole through his outer ear, nor the one which creased his skull and knocked him unconscious.

CHAPTER 9

BETTER THAN A HOLE
IN THE HEAD

Burke regained partial consciousness to excruciating pain. He didn't wake up so much as he became aware, in a limited sense, of undulations in a milky haze. He felt the touch of hands upon him, but could not interpret the sensory input. Then wispy, ghostly forms began to solidify, and amid the roaring in his ears, he could make out a word here and there. He slipped into and out of consciousness until he eventually became aware that someone was sitting in a chair beside his bed, holding his hand. Then, he became aware of people moving him about, adjusting things, draining fluids into and out of him. For days the pain persisted, his vision remained blurred, the roar of a waterfall continued in his ears. Then there was a woman beside his bed. Then there was a woman and children beside his bed. Doctors examined him, got close and made noises with their mouths. Another man who was his doctor examined him, and said words, which he began to understand.

Then, one day he opened his eyes and stirred about in the bed. This brought him immediate attention, and people were leaning down to him, right in his face, saying, "Daniel, can you hear me?" Nurses stuck thermometers in him and took his blood pressure. The doctor, nurses and technicians looked into his eye slits, and called his name. "Mister Burke, can you hear me?" They massaged his limbs, and moved him this way and that.

"He's moving," one of them said, and Burke breathed a sigh of relief.

"I think he can hear us," another said breathlessly.

Where previously, he had not been able to move a muscle, now, he was relieved to hear that he had moved, and realized then that he had been completely paralyzed. As soon as he got enough presence of mind about him, he became terrified. He experienced the most profound fear he had ever experienced, like being immobilized in something solid, ice perhaps, although he had no sensation of freezing.

The next thing he knew, he woke up one morning, and wanted a drink of water very badly. He reached out to the table beside the bed and tried to grasp the handle of the pitcher to pour himself a glass. His grip was unsteady and the pitcher tumbled to the floor with a clatter. Moments later, a nurse entered. She spoke excitedly, "Mister Burke! You're back with us, are you?"

"Give me some water, please," he said.

Burke did not remember anything; he didn't recognize anybody. The doctor told him he had been shot, that his skull was fractured. He was on pain medication constantly, dripping intravenously through a tube into his arm. He was lucky to be alive, the doctor said.

But Poor Smithers, he was to learn later, had not been so fortunate. He had taken two shots to the heart, and had died instantly. The bullets had struck very close together—a tight pattern—reflecting expertise on the part of the shooter.

Bits and pieces of his memory came back to him, and he began to recognize members of his family, first his wife then his children, then Elmo, who came to visit often. Finally, they let him go home. Marge fixed up the den for him.

A few days later Elmo came to see him, and found him standing beside the bed, with the aid of a walker, with the family close around him.

"Doctor wants me out of the bed and moving around," he said."

"That's great news, Boss. How's your memory? Are things coming back to you okay?"

"I thinks so, Elmo, I am recognizing people, remembering their names."

How about what happened that night?"

"Not a thing, only what people tell me.

"Well, don't worry about it, it will all come back to you."

"It's the weirdest feeling Elmo, you can't imagine how strange it feels to know someone shot you, shot us, me and Smithers— wanted to kill us! Did kill him, and I don't remember a damned thing about it."

"Yeah, has to be rough. The doctor says your short-term memory was damaged by the skull fracture."

The exertion of standing, even with the walker, sapped his strength. Burke toppled back into bed, and drew the sheet over his legs.

"Well, I better be going, Boss. Hang in there."

"I will, Elmo. Thanks for coming by."

⊯ ⊯

Burke improved quickly, with exercise and good food, and plenty of attention by family and friends. The skull fracture was healing nicely, the pain had eased, and all that remained was his impaired memory. Elmo decided that what he needed to jog the memory was total emersion, so he drove Burke around town, and they stopped in the office very briefly, they talked shop, Elmo recited everything

184

about the bones and the Vann case until Burke might have been hard pressed to know whether he was remembering it or learning it for the first time. They stopped at Schillings Bar and Grill for a cool one, and to chat with friends.

Burke was eager to go back to work, and to find out who did it. "Who shot me Elmo?" Burke blurted out one day. "Who killed Smithers?"

"I'm leveling with you Daniel, we don't know. Chief don't want me to get into that with you yet."

"Why not? He thinks I'm too delicate still? Come on, Elmo, give!"

"You're going to get me in trouble if you let on I said anything to you."

"I won't."

"We don't know who shot you, but the word is out on the street that you had been leaning hard on Mark Hamilton concerning the Vann Murder. Lot of people thinks it is absurd that you would be going after him that way. They're talking about how it might have been him that did it."

"Well, that looks like a good bet to me, then, but why Smithers? I guess I can understand how he could come after me based on what you tell me, but why Smithers?"

"I don't know. That's why the chief doesn't want to talk to you about it right now, get you all worked up over gossip, when you should be taking it easy. But that's not the worst of it."

"What do you mean?"

"Doctor Hamilton is in process of filing a lawsuit against the city, and against you, the chief, the mayor, and practically everybody in city government, accusing everybody, you especially, of harassment, and making false, libelous, and slanderous statements about him. His mother is supporting him on it. They say she's out rallying powerful people to their cause. The chief and some people on the other side are trying to quell it, to nip it in the bud. Don't know how it's going to work out, though."

"Jesus! I'm sorry I asked. But that's all ridiculous. I'm the Chief Detective of this town investigating a murder. I haven't harassed him, or even charged him with anything. Where do these people come off?"

"I know, Boss, I'm just telling you to be careful, that's all, and be patient. Hamilton's mother says you got her boy so upset that he's unable to perform his job. He has taken medical leave from the hospital, and is supposed to be under a doctor's care himself somewhere out of town."

"You're kidding me!"

"No, sir, I wish I was. But that's the state of things. So now you know why the chief didn't want to talk business with you, given your delicate condition."

"Yeah, I understand."

<hr />

Burke went back to the hospital for x-rays to see if the fracture lines in his skull were knitting together properly. Even though his recent memory before the incident was still impaired—the doctor explained it in terms of swelling in the area of the brain devoted to short-term memory—his progress otherwise was satisfactory, but he warned him of the remote possibility that some impairment might be permanent.

This proclamation, although casually slipped into the conversation without much emphasis or fanfare by the doctor, startled Burke and struck fear into his heart. In his years of police work in the little town, he was always aware of the possibility of injury or even death, but he had never really believed it would happen to him. Now, the idea that he might suffer permanent impairment hit him hard and sent a chill up his spine.

"It might be beneficial for you to see and talk with people who are knowledgeable of the events which occurred during the time immediately preceding your trauma," the doctor said. "Usually this sort of thing just takes time, but that might speed up the process."

The last thing Burke could remember before he woke up in the hospital was the truck stop where he and Elmo had stopped for coffee coming back from Brockton. So he had Marge talk to him about things that occurred during the few days before he and Dempsey went to Brockton. Then he asked Elmo to go over in detail what they did after the truck stop. Elmo told him everything that transpired from the time the two of them had coffee at the truck stop until Burke left the office that day to meet with Ripley.

"Anything coming back to you?" Dempsey asked.

"Afraid not."

"Why don't you talk to Ripley himself about your visit with him? That might do the trick."

"I'll give him a call."

"If you get it set up I'll drop you off and pick you up when you're finished."

<hr>

"I had no idea what you were going through, Detective Burke," Ripley said. "I'm happy to oblige you." He described the meeting.

"What came of our meeting? Did Hamilton turn up?"

"Yes. Well, sort of, anyway. He contacted his mother, and she called me and said not to worry about him. He was having a really bad time triggered by Miss Vann's murder, as we all suspected. He had to get away, she said. That's all there was to it."

"Hmm, so where is he, then?"

"Actually, I didn't press Doris about exactly where he was. It really was no concern of mine at that point. My impression was that he was at a sanitarium up state somewhere, but Doris wanted to keep it quiet, for obvious reasons. You can understand that, I'm sure."

"Of course. So then, after our meeting broke up, Smithers and I apparently walked out to the parking lot together," Burke said, "where we were ambushed."

"Yes, as far as I know. I didn't see either of you after you left my office"

⊨⊰⊹⊱⊨

After his meeting with Ripley, Burke called Elmo to come and pick him up. As he waited outside on the sidewalk he was thinking of how tired he was of this business of not being able to drive himself, and he was chomping at the bit to get back to work. He felt strong enough to work part time at least, and being back in the midst of things would surely be more conducive to restoring his memory than lying around the house all day. In the car on the way home he discussed it with Elmo: "The doctor says my memory could return at any time. The swelling has gone down in my brain, and the hairline fractures in my skull has healed. so I'm going to ask the doctor to release me to go back to work, light duty, part time, anything— I'm going stir crazy. Besides, there is so much to do, so much up in the air, not that you haven't been doing a great job covering."

"Thanks. Yeah, I agree with you. Seems like it would be better for you, to be active."

"I'm going to talk to the doctor about it, and if he's agreeable I'll ask the chief. I don't expect he would have any objections. Oh, I meant to ask you, anything new turn up on what type of weapon was use to shoot me and Smithers, rifle or pistol or the manufacturer?"

"No. We never found any spent cartridges. Don't know how far away the shooter was, or the exact direction, could have been close up, or far away with a scope. All we got are the two twenty-two caliber slugs they dug out of Smithers, which is standard ammunition, available anywhere."

Elmo turned the car into Burke's driveway.

━╪╾ ╾╪━

When Burke approached his doctor, he was amenable to part time work and so was the chief. A week after he returned to the office, as he shuffled papers and handled routine reports, he had a sudden, brilliant, instantaneous flash of the blossom of bright red blood on the front of Smithers shirt. He leaped up and yelled, "Whoa! What was that?" He startling Dempsey, who leaped up also, and ran across the room "What is it? What's wrong?"

"Jesus, I don't know," Burke said. I had this—this vision. It was Smithers, and there was blood on his shirt."

"No kidding?"

"Yeah, it was weird."

"Your memory is coming back, that's what's happening. You got to be prepared for that so you don't have a heart attack—or give me one."

Burke laughed. "I'll try not to give you a heart attack."

Burke sat back uncomfortably in his chair, nervous, his skin damp, and tried to relax. He got up from his chair, walked to the water fountain in the hallway, took a long drink, straightened up and stretched his body, then walked back to his desk.

"You okay, Boss?"

"Yeah, I feel better now."

That night, another vivid and frightening flashback occurred. He was sleeping alone in the spare bedroom so as not to disturb Marge. The flashback was more like a dream this time, in that it ran for what seemed like a minute. In the dream, he was sitting in the chair in the computer lab, while Smithers ran the computer. Burke waited impatiently, tapping his fingers on the arm of the chair. The scene changed, and Burke was in his canoe at the lake, positioned just below the ripples where the creek runs into the lake, casting his fly into the ripples. A big trout hit the fly, just as a voice screams, "I have It!" and then he awoke.

He called the doctor the next morning and told him what had been happening to him. The doctor said not to worry about it, that it was a good development. Over the next few days, other fragments of the missing time came back to him. Thinking it might accelerate the process, Elmo sat on the other side of the desk from him and retraced the day of the shooting again, from the time when Burke had received the telephone call from Ripley, and he had left the station to meet with him. The bits and pieces began to merge and meld. Suddenly, in his mind's eye he could see Smithers jumping up and shouting, "I have it!" Then he remembering hearing Smithers say that there was a match for Hamilton and Hanford, that they were related to each other. The memory startled him as much as the actual event had. Sweat broke out all over his body, and a sharp stab of fear sliced through him.

"What's wrong, Boss. You look like you seen a ghost."

Get me some water, Elmo, quick."

It dawned upon Burke at that instant, that with Smithers' death, he was the only person in the world who had that knowledge, other than Hamilton himself. He also realized, with alarming clarity, that if that were the case, it behooved Hamilton to silence him, to try again. With Burke out of the way, the case would wither and die. There would be no case.

That was why Hamilton had shot the two of them!

Suddenly, he remembered the tapes and the reports that he had been carrying. They were his proof. *Where were they?*

Dempsey came rushing in with a paper cup of water from the cooler.

"I'm all right, Elmo. I had another flashback. I remember what happened, I think all of it. Listen, when Smithers and I walked out of the building to the parking lot, I carried typewritten sheets of paper, about ten of them, and I carried the tray of backup tapes."

"You mean our backup tapes?"

"The same. I'll explain it all to you later. Right now I have to find those items. They must have been gathered up at the scene by the first responders, or the officer in charge. Who was in charge of the initial investigation? Was it you?"

"The first officer on the scene was uh...I'm trying to think. I was there a little later, as was the chief, and a bunch of other people. It was a couple of Marty's patrolmen. I'm drawing a blank. But I can tell you right now, that no tapes or reports were turned in as evidence."

"Get me the file. I want to review it. See if there is any mention. Wait, come with me. Let's go check the evidence room first. May save a lot of time."

The evidence room, was twelve by twelve feet square, and was protected by iron bars and steel mesh, and strong locks. The keys to those locks were strictly accounted for. It was situated adjacent to the city jail, for reasons of economy, so that the officer on duty could monitor the entrance to the cells and the evidence room simultaneously. Evidence was tagged and identified with whatever case it was associated. It was logged in and logged out, and signed for.

Burke and Dempsey hurried to the evidence room, Burke hopeful, Dempsey not hopeful at all.

"I want to see all the evidence logged in concerning the shooting of myself and Professor Smithers."

The officer walked between two rows of shelves, and emerged moments later with a basket, which he placed on the counter of the steel-mesh Dutch door separating the evidence room from the rest of the world. "Not much to show you, the officer said."

Burke and Dempsey studied the contents of the basket. There was one small manila envelope, with a string which wrapped around a circular tab to keep it closed. Burke took it up, unfastened the string, and looked inside. There were two small bullets, somewhat distorted, and flattened out on the tips.

"This is it?" Burke asked. "I was carrying a tray of computer tapes, and papers when I was shot. Where are they?"

"I don't know what you're talking about, Daniel," the officer said. "There were no tapes or papers logged in here in connection with the shooting. Whatever you had on you, the person who shot and robbed you no doubt took it."

Burke hesitated, then said "Thanks," and turned and walked away.

"Take it easy, Daniel," Dempsey said, when they were out of earshot. Don't start jumping to conclusions, and get yourself worked up. Go back to the office and sit down, and I will go ask Marty about it, and find out which officers were on the scene first. Then I'll bring you the file."

"Okay, you're right. Hurry up, will you?"

Dempsey returned fifteen minutes later. "Officers Bledsoe and Dodson were the officers first on the scene," he said. "Marty said he would have them come by and talk to you when they come in. And here's the case file."

"Thanks, Elmo. What did Marty say about it?"

"Same as me, there were no tapes and no papers"

"I want to go through this file before Bledsoe and Dodson get here. How about you compiling a list of all people who visited the scene of the shooting. Somebody else could have found my things. They could have fallen under a car. Someone could have found it hours later. It wouldn't mean anything to anyone else. They would probably toss it in the trash."

"Okay, and I'll drive out there and look around again."

Bledsoe and Dodson came into the office later.

"You wanted to talk to us, Lieutenant?" Bledsoe asked.

"Yes. I understand you two were first on the scene of my shooting."

"Yes."

"I had a tray of computer tapes and some papers with me. They haven't turned up. Do you know anything about them?"

"No. There was nothing like that around you or Professor Smithers."

"Were there any cars nearby that it could have fallen under?"

"Not close by."

"Did anyone report hearing the shots, or seeing anything suspicious?"

"No."

"All right, thanks a lot"

"You bet."

Burke felt frustration. it was evident that Hamilton took the items while he and Smithers lay on the parking lot pavement in their own blood. Hamilton thought he was dead, too, or he would have pumped another slug or two into his brain. That was very sloppy on his part. That mistake just might prove to be his undoing.

What was most disturbing to Burke was that he knew he could not tell his story to the chief without evidence to back it up. He would get no help there. He could not tell Elmo Dempsey either. He was on his own. He had to get Hamilton before he got him.

Burke picked up the telephone receiver and dialed Samuel Belden's office. "This is Daniel Burke, I need to speak to Mr. Belden."

Belden came on the line. "I need to speak to you, Sam. I'm in real trouble. The family could be in danger."

Burke walked directly from the police station to Belden's office on Main Street. He was promptly shown in. He sat down and began speaking without preliminaries."

"Sam, I have emerged from the fog only this morning, into a world more complicated and dangerous than I knew or suspected since I was shot."

"Your memory has returned?"

"Yes it has."

"That's wonderful, Daniel."

"Yes, it is, but with its return came some rather ominous knowledge. You see, when Smithers and I were shot, I carried evidence in the form of a tray of computer tapes, and reports from computer runs, which, I believe, proved conclusively that Hamilton is our murderer. That evidence has disappeared. No one knows anything about it. But I don't want to get ahead of myself, I want to go back to the discovery of the bones in Bealer Woods and bring you completely up to date with what I know and believe to be true, if that's okay with you."

"Yes. Go ahead."

It didn't take very long for Burke to recount the entire narrative from the time Bobby Moore and his friend from next door found the skull protruding from the dirt and leaves of Bealer Woods, through Burke's involvement with the laboratory services of the college, the investigative work, Hanford and his missing son, all the way up to Burke's and Smithers' discovery the evening they were shot

Belden was a quick study, and grasped everything quickly, nodding and grunting here and there. "You and Smithers found the missing tapes in Hamilton's desk drawer. You ran this tape and came up with proof that Hanford and Hamilton were father and son."

"That's correct. It was there in black and white."

"But now the proof is gone."

"Yes."

"You think Hamilton killed Vann to keep his relationship to Hanford secret.

"Yes, that's what I believe. I believe Hamilton killed to protect his mother. from disgrace and his own reputation from the notoriety.

What about the Hanford fire? You think he did that too? Wanted to kill his own father?

"I don't now—yes, I do believe that, but I can't prove it. I can see where he would hate him for what he did."

Belden frowned and shook his head in bewilderment. "Do you know how crazy that all sounds? I've known that boy all of his life. As for Doris, I knew her when we were children, in elementary and high school. I was a year ahead of her. They moved away when I was a junior in high school. I'm sorry, I just can't see it. From everything you've told me about all those tests on the bones and so forth, I think it's more likely that they were somehow switched."

"I felt the same way, initially," Burke said. "That's why I went to the college the day Sheila was killed. I meant to talk to Smithers about it, but he was not there, neither was Hamilton, so I talked to Sheila. I asked her if there was any way the samples could have been switched, and she convinced me it could not have happened."

"She could have been wrong, that's all I'm saying. That makes far more sense than that Hamilton is Hanford's son." Belden paused, thoughtful, while Burke waited for him to continue. "Did you consider the possibility that someone had it in for Hamilton, and deliberately switched those samples?"

"No, that didn't cross my mind."

Belden thought some more. Burke could see the wheels turning, Belden the attorney and ex-judge was applying his formidable legal mind to a problem of law and logic.

"There is a principle of logical thought," Belden began, "that says you should not overlook the obvious. And another which states that the simplest answer is more than likely the correct one. I'm just saying that there can be other explanations for things. I recommend you be on your guard, but keep an open mind, and don't talk to anybody about any of this. Don't give them any reason to attack you again, to try and discredit you, or kill you. By the way, you asked me to see if I could find out who was behind Newman pressuring you to back off of Hamilton. From what I can glean, the pressure is mainly coming from Doris.

"You mean Doris has that much influence with Newman?"

"Looks that way."

"How come? What's their relationship?"

"I don't know. Maybe they had the hots for each other at one time or another. Like I said before, we all went to the same school when we were kids."

"Sam, I hear what you're saying, and it makes sense, but I had the proof right there in those tapes, and those reports.

"You believe Hamilton saw you and Smithers together in the lab, figured out what you were doing, shot the two of you to silence you and then destroyed the evidence?"

'Yes, that's what I believe. How difficult would it be to get the court to compel these two men to contribute additional DNA samples for analysis? That would prove or disprove the relationship."

"Well, I don't know. I think there would have to be a showing of probable cause. If one or the other of them is guilty of something, I suspect that party would refuse to cooperate. But' let's say the judge could find a basis to compel the two men to submit to the test, and the test results confirmed your suspicion. That still doesn't prove they murdered anybody. Don't you see that? That would make some sensational gossip, to be sure, and people could believe what they wanted to, but that is about all. You have to have evidence of the crime that will stand up in court. By the way, has Newman ordered you off the Vann case?"

"No, he hasn't said that, specifically. He told me to back off Hamilton. It was more of an angry and scared plea than an order, even then. I haven't done anything, really, since I've been back on the job, just light duty and office work. Elmo has been carrying the ball."

"Just watch your step, and your back. Bide your time. We will think of some way out of this mess."

Burke sighed. "Okay, Sam, I'll play it your way for now."

After Burke returned to his office, he sat with an elbow on the arm of his chair, his cheek resting in his hand, staring out the window, and thinking. He was thinking that Sam really didn't believe him, that it was Burke's injuries and trauma that were talking. Well, that may be right, but it also may be wrong. Burke couldn't afford to be wrong. He had his family to think of. They may be in danger. Now that he was back at work, Newman had relaxed the surveillance of the house, only patrolling the neighborhood with greater than normal frequently. Why would Hamilton harm his family? Burke could think of no advantage which would accrue to Hamilton to harm them. Besides, Stanton may have seen the last of him. He was supposed to be upstate taking the rest. Burke wondered if that was true. He could be in Canada by now.

No, in truth, Burke believed he was in more troubled than he was willing to admit to Belden or anybody else. It was a ridiculous situation, knowing what he did, but with his hands tied. Hamilton would be a fool not to try to silence him permanently. He would lay low until he got his strength back, as Belden had advised, but then he would get Hamilton one way or the other before Hamilton got him. If he ever managed to get the young doctor in his sights, he would shoot to kill.

It was a gray, dismal morning in December, and cold, and had been snowing lightly most of the night, and was still dark as Burke drove to the station. The traffic crept along past a few people already out sweeping and shoveling the accumulation from their steps and sidewalks. The Christmas decorations on the houses and stores, and the lights strung diagonally across the streets at the corners of the town square created a Christmas card effect. Burke was back at work full time now. With the holiday season upon him, he was not in a festive mood since there had been no progress in finding the person or persons who had shot him and killed Smithers, nor had there been any progress in solving the Vann murder. None of this surprised Burke, since Newman was either a fool, or a corrupt coward, who deliberately misdirected the resources of the department away from the logical suspect, Mark Hamilton. An uneasy quiet seemed to settled over the department, and the town. Burke was laying plans to change all that.

While Burke was incapacitated, Dempsey had carried the ball, pursuing the investigations, if you could call it that, and following up on the three newspaper stories of missing persons he had gleaned from his search of the statewide newspaper archives. He had accumulated copies of case files, bits and pieces of information from the municipal police departments in the cities where the incidences had occurred, letters from insurance underwriters, ands from personnel officers where the people under investigation had worked. However, because of the unfolding events involving Burke and Smithers, Dempsey had probably not been able to devote the time needed to matters, and Burke certainly had done little else than glance through the material. He decided this morning that he would launch a new effort, would sit down and thoroughly evaluate what Dempsey had accumulated.

When Burke got to the office and announced his wishes, it caught Dempsey by surprise, but he didn't object, he put down his newspaper and began. They set up a long folding table and Dempsey brought the three case files from the cabinet and placed them out on the table. Then he and burke pulled their chairs up to the table, side by side, and Dempsey explained the cases, showing Burke newspaper clippings and other supporting materials as he talked.

The case where the court declared the husband legally dead caught Burke's attention.

"The wife collected a hundred thousand dollars?" Burke asked.

"Yes. Seven years after the husband disappeared."

"Were there policies on any of the other missing people?"

"Yes, there were a few other policies which appear to be routine. I'm still waiting for some information on beneficiaries, and payouts. It's a slow process trying to get other people to do things for you."

"Okay, thanks, Elmo, I want to read the entire case files, so just leave them where they are for now. Did you check with the state bureau of vital statistics for death certificates for all the parties involved?"

"Yes."

"Got any pictures of the missing people?"

"No, no pictures."

"Will you try to get them?"

"Right."

"You've done a good job, Elmo, and I appreciate how you handled things while I was laid up."

"Thanks, Boss."

"That's all I need for now. You can go back to whatever you were doing."

The weather improved in the afternoon and the snow began to melt, but it froze again during the night, and by morning another layer of snow had fallen and the roads were hazardous. The highway patrol, the local police, tow trucks, and ambulances were doing a brisk business. Once again, Burke was at his desk early, his coffee mug in his hand, mulling over his situation, and mapping out his plan of action to find Hamilton. Previously, indecision had placed enormous strain upon him. Now that he had decided what he had to do, he was strangely calm. Midmorning, he went by the city attorney's office for an update on the law suit filed by Hamilton against him, and the city, et al. The city attorney had filed a motion with the court for dismissal of the charges, but the judge had denied it. Now the attorney for Mark Hamilton was engaged in discovery, but it looked to Burke like nobody was in a real hurry to engage in a Court battle. Burke was not too worried about the lawsuit, personally, even though he was named as a defendant. The city attorney, Alan Pruitt, represented him as an official of city government, and Burke saw no necessity to engage additional counsel. Sam Belden, Esq., could jump in on his behalf if the going got tough, but Burke did not expect that to happen. He believed Hamilton was bluffing about the lawsuit. He was guilty of at least three murders and two cases of attempted murder. He knew that Burke knew that he was guilty. If Burke had not survived, Hamilton would be home free. It must be the most frustrating thing in the world for him to know that he had been standing over the bleeding and prostrate body of Burke there in the parking lot, thinking he was dead. He could have finished him off with the greatest of ease. Burke smiled at the irony. Mark had been overconfident of his marksmanship.

Hamilton would not necessarily be in any hurry to kill Burke, because he knew that Burke could not come forward with unsubstantiated charges against him—he had the tapes and the reports. If Burke did accuse him, no one would believe him, and it would lend credence to Hamilton's suit against Burke and the city. Even if some people did believe Burke, there was no evidence that would stand up in court.

What a set-up!

Burke had to find Hamilton and kill him! It was the only way. He would tell Newman nothing beforehand. If he ran into difficulties, he would worry about that then.

Burke wondered if Hamilton had taken anyone into his confidence. *How much did his mother know?* He was clearly something of a "momma's boy." *Had he confided in her? She has to know where he was. Of course! She would be the logical path to her son.*

What about Mr. Hanford? Was Hamilton likely to make another attempt on his life? Burke could see no way that Hanford constituted a threat to him. If Hamilton killed Hanford, it would be purely for vengeance.

All of these thoughts cascaded through Burke's mind as he developed his secret plan of action, to locate and eliminate Hamilton.

First, he would find Mr. Hanford, for either Hanford knew about Hamilton or he didn't. If he did know about him, he would behave differently toward Burke than he would if he didn't, and

Burke would be able to tell which. The first complication arose when Burke called the hospital in Brockton. Mr. Hanford was no longer there. They said he had transferred to a convalescent home in Columbus, but they would not give out the name and address of the place because Mr. Hanford wanted seclusion during his convalescence, and the doctors had agreed.

Burke had no jurisdiction there, and could not compel their cooperation. He had another idea. He called the arson investigator in Brockton to whom he had spoken about the fire at Hanford's house.

"Any new developments in the investigation of the Hanford fire?" Burke asked him.

"I sent you the report, that's all we have. I've filed the case away until we learn something different."

"What's your gut feeling about it, just between us?"

"Just between us, I have little doubt that it was arson."

"Okay, thanks. Listen, they've moved the old man to a convalescence home in Columbus. I need the address. Do you have it?"

"Yeah, hold on."

The man came back on the phone and gave Burke the address, which he wrote in his notebook. The name of the place was the Cherry Hill Convalescent Center.

CHAPTER 10
LOOKING FOR HANFORD

Burke would not call ahead and seek approval to see Hanford, he would go unannounced and take his chances. The issues were too important to risk having the old man refuse to see him beforehand. If necessary, he would try to bluff his way in—flash his badge at the help. That got him in places sometimes where he had no authority to be.

To account for his absence from the office, he took two days off, and asked Marge to go with him. She could help with the driving, and he liked the idea of having her along. He told her without elaboration that he had business to conduct in Columbus, that they could stay overnight, and she could go shopping at one of the fancy new shopping centers while he handled his business.

The roads were clear of snow and ice, the traffic was moderate, and the drive was pleasant. When they got to Columbus, Burke located the convalescent home first, and then found a motel nearby. He ran over in his mind one last time how he planned to approach Hanford. He had given it much thought, and had concluded that the best approach was the most direct one. He would tell Hanford the test results, and ask him if he could explain them. He imagined how the conversation might go. "Mr. Hanford, I have good news for you, and I have bad news for you. First the good news: I've found your missing son. Now for the bad news: Your son just burned down your house, killed your housekeeper, and tried to kill you."

Burke found himself morbidly laughing.

When he got to the receptionist desk at the Cherry Hills Convalescent Center, the woman at the desk advised him that Hanford was seeing no one.

"I am Chief Detective Daniel Burke of the Stanton Police Department," Burke said with authority, as he flipped out his badge and I.D. "I'm here on official police business, concerning Mr. Hanford's missing son. We have spoken before. I'm sure he will want to see me."

"One moment, sir, I'll inform Mr. Burton, the Director of the center. You may speak with him. If you would like to have a seat, I'll let him know you're here."

Burke took a seat in the spacious waiting area, noting that the furniture was new and comfortable and the room was painted a pleasant light mint green. There were large potted plants positioned about in strategic locations. He picked up a magazine with the addressee label snipped from the front cover and leafed through it. It was a travel magazine with an array of tantalizing, exotic destinations.

"Mr. Burke?"

"Detective Burke, Yes."

"I'm Dwayne Burton, the Director of Cherry Hills. Would you like to step into my office?"

Burke followed him into his office and took a proffered chair.

"Detective Burke, I'm sure you know better than most that Mr. Hanford has suffered enormous trauma, both to his body and to his mind. He is only beginning a long process of convalescence, and we have strict instructions not to allow him any visitors."

"Yes, I'm fully aware of his circumstances, Mr. Barton, but my reasons for desiring to see him are most important, not only to me in our ongoing murder investigations, but to him as well. It is imperative that I be allowed to see him, even if very briefly."

"I see. Would you excuse me for a moment, please, Detective?"

Burton picked up the phone, dialed, and spoke briefly and inaudibly. He replaced the receiver. "I've asked our legal counsel to join us, if you don't mind. His office is not very far. He will be here shortly. May I offer you some refreshment while we wait?"

"No, thank you."

While they waited, Burton engaged him in a stream of pleasant conversation. Burke thought him a very cordial man. Presently, a door opened, and a man entered the room.

Burton said, "Detective Burke, this is Mr. Hayden, our attorney."

The two men shook hands, and Hayden took a seat opposite the other men, so that they formed a loose triangle in their seating arrangement.

"Harry, I was explaining the situation with regard to Mr. Hanford, but Detective Burke still feels he needs access to Mr. Hanford. Perhaps you could explain the situation to him better than I."

"Certainly. Detective Burke, let me be clear. You may not see Mr. Hanford under any circumstances at this time. The police in Brockton have cleared Mr. Hanford of any complicity in the fire that killed his housekeeper and nearly took his own life. He is no longer a person of interest to them. I have some familiarity with your involvement in searching for his missing son. Mr. Hanford no longer entertains any hope of finding his son, who has been missing for three decades, and now realizes that his obsession has brought about his near ruin, including his failing health. Merely discussing it now causes him enormous emotional stress. Consequently, he has no interest in having you or anyone else continue in this hopeless quest. His doctors have given us strict written orders. Do you understand, sir?"

"I certainly do, and I appreciate all that you have said, and I would do nothing to jeopardize Mr. Hanford's recovery. As to the other matter, I'm afraid it has progressed beyond Mr. Hanford's discretion at this point. There are certain developments that I am not at liberty to discuss with you which make it necessary for me to speak with him as soon as he is medically able to do so. Are you asserting that he is medically unable to see me?"

"I'm a lawyer, Detective Burke, not a doctor, but that's my understanding of the situation."

"Then perhaps I should take this up with his doctors directly."

"You're free to do as you wish, but unless the local authorities are prepared to charge Mr. Hanford with some offence or crime, you have no jurisdiction here."

The adamancy of the lawyer startled Burke. It was too strong, to the point of bizarre.

"Then, I may have to request a court order."

"We'll fight such a request, I assure you."

"We? I don't understand. I thought you were the attorney for the Center."

"I have nothing further to say to you, Detective. I'm afraid you'll have to excuse us. Mr. Burton and I have matters to attend to."

The two men stood up and waited expectantly for Burke to leave. Burke studied the faces of the two men, dumbfounded by the sternness of their position. "Very well, Gentlemen," Burke said, pleasantly, "thanks for seeing me."

Burke and Marge had dinner that evening at a popular seafood restaurant. Burke had steak and lobster, baked potato with sour cream, and string beans, while Marge had shrimp scampi. It was his first major diet transgression since leaving the hospital. During the convalescence, he had lost his excess body fat, and, due to his new dedication to regular exercise and Marge's insistence on a sane diet, Burke had slimmed down and was much improved in appearance.

He anticipated Marge's objection to his repast: "Look, hon, I have been a good boy. I deserve a break today," he said, before she could lecture him.

As they worked leisurely through their meal, Burke told Marge everything that had transpired at the Convalescent Center.

"I don't know what to make of it," he said, between mouthfuls.

"Maybe the old man is in worse shape than you think."

"Maybe so, but he was released from the hospital. My impression is that he is out of danger. It's been a while, you know, since the fire. No, there's something funny going on. I can feel it."

"You're probably right, you have a nose for such things. Why do you feel such a pressing need to see him in the first place? After those DNA tests came back negative, I thought you were finished with him."

Burke munched thoughtfully, savoring the opulent meal, glancing up at his wife, who waited for him to respond. He had not confided in her what had transpired between him and Smithers the night of the ambush in the parking lot of the college. She knew nothing about what the two of them had discovered about Hamilton and Hanford. When he was coming out of his coma, he didn't remember what happened, and then later, he consciously decided not to tell her. He had been so mentally confused then, that he wasn't confident of his sanity. *What good would it have done to tell Marge about it, anyway?* It would have frightened her much more than she already was, to know that there was someone who was deliberately trying to murder him, rather than that he and Smithers had been the victim of a random robber and killer. She was still shaky over that and the aftermath: the police sentries outside the house, the fear that the killer would try again. Then Newman, once again, had propagated the notion that it was the act of a common criminal—a random happening. It amazed Burke how everyone seemed to accept that, that it was someone just passing though, someone off the bypass on his way from one large city to another, who had stopped at the little town, to rob and kill for drug money, for bread money, or for the thrill of it— just like Sheila Vann. Nobody wanted to accuse one of their own.

Newman and his crowd had come to that, that it was a murder/robbery—the assailant had empties the pockets of both victims and taken their rings and watches—pure and simple. They were posting guards on Burke's house in the off chance that they were wrong, and the killer (or killers) had deliberately selected his two victims, and, being only half-successful, would try to finish the job.

Yes, Marge had held up remarkably well, and now Burke wondered if the time was right to let her in on it all. He would prefer that she not be blind-sided somewhere down the line in case something went terribly wrong.

"There's something I didn't tell you, before, sweetheart. I didn't want to worry you unnecessarily. You had enough on your mind with me all shot up and in the hospital."

"Something to do with Mr. Hanford?"

"Yes."

"What is it?"

Burke sighed and began. He took her through it all.

━┼╀━

The moment Burke got back to work, Newman called him into his office. He was pale, his features contorted. "Burke, I got calls last night at home, complaints about you from several sources. I won't say from whom just yet. They tell me that you went to the Cherry Hill Convalescent Home in Columbus, where Hanford is recovering from his injuries, and tried to strong arm your way in to see him, even after they told you that his doctors would not permit him any visitors. Is this true?"

"Chief, it's true that I went there to see him, but I assure you, I strong armed nobody."

"Do you want to explain to me what the hell you're doing there harassing that old man? What do you want from him?"

"Have you forgotten, Chief? I'm investigating two murders, and my own attempted murder, not to mention the two skeletons from Bealer Woods."

"I haven't forgotten a damn thing, and don't you get smart with me. I haven't authorized you to leave our jurisdiction and strike out on your own. You've already got us sued. You tell me what this near-dead old man has to do with any of this, anyway. Just because you had that cockamamie notion back there where you thought that dead baby was his long lost kid. Well, those laboratory tests dispelled that notion. Now, tell me what you are doing, and I want straight answers."

"He's not out of it, Chief, not by a long shot."

"Did you threaten to get a court order to see him?"

"I mentioned that possibility, but not the way you're suggesting."

"What way, then?"

"You know, Chief, it's standard procedure, when you have reluctant witnesses, for example, to use the old official business routine on them. We do it every day. Why are you making a big deal out of it, now?"

"The big deal is that this man has got important connections. When I start getting calls from Columbus…"

Burke was fuming inside. Here we go again, he thought. He experienced a surge of resentment and defiance. He was tired of pussyfooting around this man.

"So what?" he said, grimly.

"What did you say?"

"You heard me. I said so what if you got calls from Columbus. What are you afraid of?"

Newman glared at him. "Watch yourself, boy."

"No, you watch yourself. For years I've tiptoed around you, and this half-assed department of yours. No more. From this day forward, I'm going to do my job. I'm going to call 'em the way I see 'em. And if you don't like it you know what you can do about it. And, by the way, I'm not a boy, I'm a man."

"You think I won't fire you?"

"You do what you have to do, Chief"

Burke stomped out of the office, went to his office and sat down at his desk and waited to see what the chief was going to do. He turned to the window and watched the kids in the snow-covered playground, all bundled up, as rambunctious as ever.

An hour passed, and still Burke had not received his walking papers. Dempsey strode in, removing his gloves and jacket. He glanced over at Burke and did a double take. "What's wrong?" he asked.

"I may not have much time. I've had it out with Newman. He may fire me. I'm going to stay here until this afternoon. If he still hasn't fired me by then, I'm going to see Doris. I've got to move fast. Doris is the key. She knows where Hamilton is. I'm going to get it out of her one way or another. I'll start by being nice to her, and see what that gets me.

CHAPTER 11

HOT CHOCOLATE WITH DORIS

By the time Burke got to the house shared by Hamilton and his mother it was nearly four o'clock. Under a gray overcast sky, a few of the photocell-controlled street lights had already switched on. The house was on a quiet, tree-lined street in one of the better neighborhoods of Stanton. Burke parked his car around the corner underneath a large leafless tree, so as not to arouse the curiosity of her neighbors. He walked to the house, rang the bell, and waited. He rang it twice more before a door opened in the back of the hall that was visible through the glass in the front door. He saw Doris walking toward the front, drying her hands on a cloth. As she opened the door her face registered surprise. "Why Daniel Burke, what a surprise it is to see you here."

"Good evening, Mrs. Hamilton. I took a chance on catching you at home. I know this is a little awkward under the circumstances, but I have something important I need to discuss with you."

She registered alarm. "Has something happened to my son?"

"No, not yet. That's what I want to talk to you about."

She hesitated only briefly as a look of painful indecision flickered across her face and then was gone, replaced by the perennial slight smile. She opened the door wider, stepped aside, and said,

"Come in." She led him back the way she had come, toward the back of the house.

He had to hand it to Doris. It apparently took a lot of provocation to crack her composure. He couldn't help thinking, that by any objective criteria, Doris Hamilton was the quintessential modern woman, the mature matron. Her eyes wore signs of paunches, and her face bore wrinkles, which her careful makeup no longer concealed. But she was still an attractive woman, and the care with which her hair was always neatly done, with no effort to conceal the gray, and the way she carried herself, conveyed a sense of stately dignity.

"I hope I'm not inconveniencing you too much, calling on you unannounced this way," Burke said.

"I assume this is a business call, Lieutenant Burke. In spite of our current differences, you are still an officer of the law to me, and I think highly of that sweet wife of yours, you know. I was in the sunroom, reading. It's my favorite place this time of day."

She stepped aside once again and motioned him through double French doors into the pleasantly appointed room. Through the large windows that wrapped around two sides of the room, he could see a well-manicured lawn and an array of plants and shrubs beyond the patio. The flower gardens, now dormant, which had stood her in such good stead with the Stanton Garden Club over the years, and a brick walkway, led to a kidney shaped swimming pool, whose water glowed aquamarine from underwater lighting.

"This is truly beautified, Mrs. Hamilton." Burke said.

"Thank you. As I said, this is my favorite spot in the house, where I can look out on my garden and pool. Please sit down Lieutenant Burke—Daniel."

Burke took the chair, marveling to himself how cool Doris appeared, while he suspected that her insides were not quite so cool. "Getting rather cold for the pool, though, isn't it?" He asked.

"Yes, I suppose so. It's heated, of course and, believe it or not, until recently we were still swimming occasionally, making a mad dash for the door when we exit the pool."

The oblique reference to her son, contained in the "we" of her statement, caused her to react noticeably. It was as if she wished to avoid the matter she knew he had come there to discuss.

"I won't keep you very long. I've come to talk to you about Doctor Hamilton."

"First, how are Marge and the children?"

"Oh, they're fine, Mrs. Hamilton, just fine," Burke said.

"That's wonderful. I'm so glad to hear it. I'm afraid our bridge game has been disrupted by all this—unpleasantness. By the way, won't you please call me Doris." she said, as she leaned forward in her chair, and patted his hand, which was resting on his knee. "Being called Mrs. Hamilton makes me feel so very old, and I'll continue to call you Daniel, if that's all right. There's no reason we can't be civil to each other, is there. I think we know each other well enough for that, and we must not let the current misunderstandings destroy our civility, must we?"

"Of course not…, Doris," he said, fidgeting under her touch.

Burke had dreaded the necessity of coming by to talk with Mrs. Hamilton. He had always been ill at ease around her on those few occasions when he was thrust into her presence by circumstances, more often than not, of his wife's making. Marge admired Doris. However, Doris had always been a bit too imperial to suit him, but then, maybe he wasn't being fair.

Now, he was fearful that she could read his thoughts and learn that he intended to kill her rotten-to-the-core son, the doctor if he had to, if he could find him. *Yeah, shoot him down like a dog, just as soon as Doris told him where he was.* So Burke endured her noblesse oblige, let her condescend, while he played the role of the plebian, the peasant. She was the librarian while he was the boisterous little boy. If there had been lines of flux emanating from people, theirs would not have attracted each other, they would have repelled, instead. And it wasn't any single, specific thing that she did or said that he could cite to indict her, it was an aura, or—hell, he didn't know what it was.

"Would you excuse me for a moment, Daniel? Please make yourself at home, I won't be a moment. I have something on the stove." She rose and left the room by a different door than the one they had entered. He could see that it led into the kitchen. As he waited for her return he stood up, stretched, and looked around the room. It really was a pleasant room. Rather on the feminine side, as one might expect. He examined the pictures and certificates on the walls: a high school diploma, a nursing school graduation certificate, groups of people in various poses and situations. One caught his eye—a group of young people with rifles. Hmm, that is interesting, he thought, experiencing a slight chill: a shooting club. He examined the faces looking for Mark Hamilton's, but did not recognize him.

He turned about as Doris reentered the room carrying a serving tray. She put it down on a low table between their chairs, and sat down. Burke resumed his chair opposite. She leaned forward and poured a steaming liquid into two cups on the tray. "I was preparing hot chocolate when you rang, Daniel. I hope you like it. I always have chocolate this time of day during cold weather. It helps me to relax. You do like chocolate, don't you, Daniel? Well, of course you do. Everybody likes chocolate."

"None for me, thanks. I'll only be here a few minutes. I don't want to keep you longer than necessary."

"Oh, nonsense, Daniel, I insist. You'll hurt my feelings if you don't join me. Now, do you take marshmallows with your chocolate?" She said, holding a spoon with a generous amount of marshmallow crème poised over the cup. Not waiting for an answer, she ladled the marshmallow cream onto the brown liquid. It did look very enticing to Burke, especially given his new diet and weight maintenance restrictions. It actually made his mouth water. But, more importantly, if he alienated Doris he might not get the information he wanted. He took the cup.

"All right," she said. Now that we have chatted and have our cocoa to sip, we ought to attend to the matter which brings you here. You say you've come to discuss my son. Well, he isn't here, as you can see, but I expect him any time."

This statement took Burke completely by surprise. It was the last thing he expected to hear from her. "You do?" he stammered. "I was under the impression he was upstate some place."

"Yes, he was." She glanced at her wristwatch. "If you don't mind waiting a few more minutes. While we wait, you and I can visit. It isn't often I have the pleasure of talking with one of our excellent police officers, and one who is investigating a murder. An awful affair—about Miss Vann, I mean. My son, you know, keeps me informed of the goings-on at the hospital, and at the college. Besides, you'd be surprised what one can hear playing bridge at the country club." She paused, shook her head gently from side-to-side, as if in disbelief, "A murder, right here in Stanton. My heavens! That's such big news, isn't it? And dear, sweet, Sheila... I'm sure you are aware that I knew her, quite well in fact."

"I understood that to be the case, yes," he answered. "She dated your son, I believe, at one time. Isn't that correct?"

"Why, yes. She visited our home on more than one occasion. She was a charming, lovely girl, and very bright. Nothing got by her."

Doris Hamilton's manner was calm, hospitable, not like a mother who had any concern for the safety of her son. *Why hasn't she mentioned the attack on me and Smithers, since she brought up the Vann murder? What is going on? Smithers is dead, and I was seriously wounded, and she hasn't even mentioned it. Maybe she considers it bad manners if I don't mention it first.*

He put the thought aside and said, "I've been trying to reach Doctor Hamilton for some time. The people at the college told me they didn't know where he was, that he had not been to work for quite a while."

"I know," she murmured. "It has been quite a while. Professor Ripley told me about your visit. I know why you want to find him."

"You know?"

"Why, yes, Daniel, it follows logically, doesn't it, that you would begin to have suspicions of him. But I assure you, most sincerely, that there is no reason, no reason whatever, for him to want to harm poor Sheila."

"Forgive me ma'am, but...," He wanted to tell her that many other things had transpired since then, other murders, but surely she knew. *How could she not know?*

"Please, won't you remember to call me Doris? By the way, how is the chocolate?"

Her manner was suddenly gay, almost flippant, and struck Burke as inappropriate under the circumstances. She seemed to be stalling for some reason.

"The chocolate is very good," he said, and took another healthy swallow. He glanced at his watch, and back at her. "Where is your son, Mrs. Hamilton?" He said softly.

"Of course, of course, I understand. We must get down to cases. You have your job to do. But, surely you can understand a mother's concern for her only son, who, once again...," she adopted a sterner pose, her index finger of her right hand thrust into the air in front of her, in the manner of a nineteenth-century orator, "is completely innocent of any wrong-doing." Her voice and manner now took on a strangely plaintive air, completely inconsistent with her previous gay outburst.

"Ma'am..., ah..., Doris..." Burke flushed. "I really don't believe Doctor Hamilton is on his way here right now. Why are you doing this? Why are you stalling? Why are you keeping me here? I really must speak with him. Do you know where I can find him, or not?"

"He's gone to be with his father," she said abruptly, a slight, wicked smile distorting her lips.

Startled, Burke stared at her in confusion. She seemed on the verge of confessing to him the very matter that her son had apparently killed to protect her from knowing. "His father? But I understood his father died long ago?"

Her features changed abruptly, once again, this time contorting into an ugly mask, as if she had just transformed into another person. "Not at all," she hissed bitterly, gazing through the picture window at the dancing reflections of the underwater lights from the swimming pool on the surrounding foliage. "He is very much alive. More is the pity. Though I understand, he is rather the worst for wear these days, as they say, ha-ha! Something to do with a fire I believe! Here, I see your cup is empty, let me pour you more chocolate." She leaned forward, reaching once more for the silver pot.

"No thank you, Doris. It was...very delicious. It was..."

"What is it Daniel? Are you uncomfortable? Is something the matter?"

"It—it is a bit warm in here, don't you think?" He was flushed and suddenly nauseous. He tugged clumsily at his collar. "It's...hot in here...could you...?"

It was as if she had not heard him, didn't see his rising discomfort. "No matter," she said, smiling self-assuredly. Then, straightening in her chair, she rested her hands delicately in her lap, her ankles neatly crossed: a neat, prim lady entertaining company.

Burke struggled to rise from the chair while the room swam around him. He stood swaying, clawing at his collar, then he pitched forward and the floor rushed up to slap him hard in the face.

"What...have you ...," he stammered. His hand fumbled instinctively under his coat for his shoulder holster and awkwardly extracted the pistol. Flopping about on the floor like a caught fish, he gasped for breath, as he tried desperately to raise the hand that tenuously held the weapon. He barely felt the grinding, crushing weight of the heel of her shoe when she brought it down on his hand, dislodging the weapon, and he heard, rather than felt, the violent kick which landed in his face, snapping the bridge of his nose. When the lights went out, he heard Doris' pleasant, purring voice say, "I do hope you enjoyed the chocolate, Detective Burke."

Burke eased in and out of consciousness. He tried to move, but couldn't. As cognition returned, he became aware that he was bound by white adhesive tape about the wrists and ankles, and a large piece of tape covered his mouth so that he could not speak. He breathed with difficulty through his broken, bleeding nose. He heard her voice drone on as if in a haze. "Can you still hear me, Detective Burke? I want to tell you a story before you die. Oh yes, you are going to die, you know. I'm so sorry about that, but please don't feel badly toward me. It isn't personal. I have the greatest respect and admiration for public servants such as yourself. I had a son, once, you see, and a husband. However, my husband was weak and irresponsible. He drank and gambled, and God knows what else. One day, while I was away from our house, he got drunk, and because of that my son died—strangled in his crib, all tangled up in the bedding.

"When I came home, I found my drunken husband sitting at the kitchen table, his head in his hands, weeping. The fool hadn't even had the sense to call an ambulance. Oh, he was sorry, he said, he was contrite. It had been an accident, he said. I struck him with a hatchet, which we kept behind the kitchen stove for chopping kindling, with all my might, while he sat at the table, weeping and begging for forgiveness, even as my child lay dead in the other room in his crib. I ran out of the house, got in my car and drove away, aimlessly, out of my mind with grief.

"Then God sent me another son, a sweet little boy. He was sitting alone, waiting for me, in a shopping cart! I knew it was God's handiwork. We returned home, he and I, and I set about making things right. My husband bled remarkably little. It was because the hatchet was wedged in his forehead, I think. I left it there, waited until nightfall, and put the bodies in the trunk of my car. That's what I have planned for you, Daniel. We drove and drove, my son and I, all the way to Stanton, the place of my childhood. I found the wooded area near the river, at the end of Bealer Street—perhaps you know it. It wasn't built up then. It took me hours to dig the grave, with my child playing on his blanket underneath a big beech tree. I dragged my husband's body into the hole. I wanted him face down, facing hell, ha-ha. So, I dislodged the hatchet—I still have the hatchet, by the way, would you like to see it? No? Well, then I placed my dear dead son, and my new son's clothing, beside his father. Then I said a prayer for my son, and cursed his father.

"When it was all over, I collapsed beside my son on the blanket beneath the big beech tree. I was so exhausted that I went to sleep instantly, cuddling my son in my arms. In the morning, I took the hatchet and cut our initial into the bark of the big beach tree, in a big heart—DH loves MH. It's still there today, and you can still read it. I often went to visit my son in the early days, but, now—that was so very long ago, I—I had forgotten. Imagine my astonishment when those kids found the skull, and later when Sheila Vann called here that evening. I had no civic meeting that night, you see, so I took the call from Sheila. The silly girl told me what she had found on the computer. Well, when I got there and saw what she had, I picked up that paper punch. Then later I set fire to the house in Brockton. Yes, Daniel, I did it all, I and I alone. So you see, there is no reason for you to harass my son further, do you understand?"

She paused, becoming agitated. "Oh, I know what you're thinking. You want to take my son away from me again, to lock him away. I told you he was innocent! You fool! You should have stopped when Chief Newman told you to do so! I have no choice now." She stood over Burke unrolling more adhesive tape.

Nauseous, and barely conscious, he watched her, helpless.

She knelt down and brought the tape to his nose. "This will be quick," she said, "and far less messy than the hatchet."

"You will simply disappear, Daniel, don't you see? I'll say that, sure, you came by for a visit, but then you left. Maybe in thirty or forty years, someone will find *your* old moldy skull, ha-ha-ha!"

CHAPTER 12
ELMO'S GREAT ADVENTURE

Quitting time had come and gone, and Dempsey was still at the police station. Burke had not returned, and he had not called. Dempsey had waited 20 minutes after quitting time, and then had tried to reach Burke on both his radio and pager. When Burke was in his car, he always had the radio on, and when he was out of the car, he either carried his transceiver, or his pager, or both. Under the present circumstances, Dempsey knew that something had to be wrong. Burke was in some sort of trouble. Dempsey took off at a run out of the station, nearly upsetting a janitor mopping the hallway, to his car, and drove as rapidly as he dared through the evening traffic. When he arrived in front of the Hamilton house, he didn't see Burke's car. He drove around the block, found it, parked behind it, and ran back to house, then up the walk to the front door. The house was dark, except for a sliver of light underneath the door at the end of a long hall. He didn't knock or ring the bell but ran around the side of the house to the rear, onto the patio. Through the window, he saw Burke lying on the floor, motionless. There was white tape covering his mouth and nose, and his arms and legs were bound. His face was bloody.

"Oh, my god!" Dempsey blurted.

Doris sat on a high back chair, sipping from a cup, as if at a tea party. Between sips, she seemed to be talking to the prone, motionless form on the floor.

Dempsey lunged for the patio door and rattled the handle. It was locked. Hamilton saw him through the glass. She bent down and picked up Burke's revolver, which was on the floor at her feet. As Dempsey smashed a chair through the window and leaped through the opening, Doris leveled the pistol at him and fired. The slug tore into his abdomen. He crumpled up and his legs buckled, but he drew his pistol and fired two shots before he hit the floor. The slugs knocked Hamilton backwards onto the floor, and she lay still.

Dempsey's face was a mask of pain, as he pulled himself slowly and agonizingly over the carpet toward Burke. "Don't pass out!" he yelled to himself. "Don't pass out!" His fingers fumbled with the tape on Burke mouth, and then the lights went out for him too.

Later that night, Burke sat in the waiting room of Stanton hospital. He had a bandage on his nose and a cast on his right hand, and he felt like hell. The x-ray had shown a broken bone in his hand from Mrs. Hamilton's heel. Elmo was in surgery, and Burke had been standing vigil for what seemed like hours. He had asked them at the desk to notify Dempsey's relatives—Burke didn't know who they were—but nobody had arrived. Finally, around ten-thirty, a green-garbed surgeon came through a double swinging door, saw him and said, "Detective Burke?"

Burke leapt to his feet. "Yes."

"Detective Dempsey is going to make it. We had to remove a section of his colon, so I'm afraid he'll be out of commission for a while. He's in critical care now, and still sedated. Once he's out of danger, we'll move him to recovery."

Burke's tense, aching body slumped in relief, and his weariness became evident.

"You better go home and get some rest. You can come back tomorrow morning around ten, if you like. You should be able to see him then."

"All right, Doctor, thank you."

Two uniformed officers had been waiting, while Burk and Dempsey received medical attention. Now, one of them drove Burke home, while the other followed in Burke's car.

He had called Marge earlier from the hospital to tell her he would be late, but he had not told her of his ordeal, nor what condition his face was in. He wanted to tell her in person. As he walked up the front steps, he wasn't looking forward to it.

The following morning Burke arrived at the hospital, shortly after ten. Dempsey was now in a private room. His face was pale and drawn. Cables and tubes monitored his vital functions, and an intravenous tube was taped to his hand. His eyes were open, and he manages a weak smile. Dempsey's grandfather and uncle were in the room. They greeted Burke, and then withdrew to the hallway to allow the two men to talk privately. Burke moved over beside the bed and took his assistant's hand. "Hey, there, pal," he said softly, "how's my favorite detective today?"

"I feel like I just came home from the war and I lost." Dempsey mumbled. "But now that I see your face, I feel better about it."

Burke grinned. "We both earned our pay last night. You saved my life. Thank you."

"Thank you for saving mine. They said this morning that if you had not called the ambulance when you did I would have been a goner. How did you manage to get yourself free? Last time I saw you, you were wrapped up like a Christmas package."

"I came to and saw you lying there in a pool of blood with adhesive tape stuck to your fingers, and saw Doris on the floor across the room. I used a piece of glass from the smashed window to cut through the tape on my wrists." He held up his bandaged wrist to show Dempsey. "I nicked myself a couple of times doing it."

Dempsey tried to adjust his position slightly, and moaned. "That was a bit of work. Oh!" Burke gently patted his hand. "Don't talk anymore. You rest. Is there anything I can get you, before I go?"

"No, I'm fine," he said, bravely.

"I'll be back later."

He left the hospital and drove down town, entered police head-quarters by the back way, then wove his way through members of the force, who crowded around anxious to learn the details of what had happened. "The press is camping out in the lobby, the dis-patcher said, they don't know what's going on, and they're very anxious to talk to you."

Burke winced. "I'm not ready for the press. I still have things to do. Is the Chief in his office?"

"The Chief's not here. He called in sick this morning."

Burke grimaced. He was on his own, it seemed. He would have to decide what to do next. "Damn! Well, I'm going out again," he said, "and I may not be back for the rest of the day. Try to hold the reporters off."

Burke slipped out the back entrance and made it to his car with-out being seen, and drove out of town on the road to Columbus. He drove fast this time, with his siren and lights. An hour and a half later, he pulled into the parking lot of the Cherry Hills Convalescent home. He showed his badge and identification the lady at the desk. If they refused him this time he intended to go directly to the Columbus police to obtain a warrant.

The woman studied his identification. "You were here before, Detective Burk. Mr. Hanford is expecting you. You'll find him in the lounge there." The woman pointed to a large open area to his left"

"Thank you, Ma'am."

Expecting me!

Burke walked to where he could see the entire interior of the room. He saw the two men, Hanford and Hamilton, seated in stuffed chairs toward the back of the room, in what appeared to be a reading area. He walked back toward them. Ten feet from where they sat, Hamilton saw him, and rose from his chair."

"Detective Burke?"

"Hello, Doctor Hamilton, Mr. Hanford, how are you, sir?"

Hanford nodded to him, but didn't speak.

"Doctor Hamilton," Burke spoke slowly, calmly, "I must speak with you privately."

Hamilton excused himself from Hanford and accompanied Burke to a table across the room.

"What's happened? Something is wrong, isn't it?"

"I'm afraid I have bad news for you." Burke paused only for an instant.

"It's Mother. She's dead, isn't she?" Hamilton said

"Yes."

Hamilton seemed to melt. His shoulders lurched forward, his chin on his chest, and he began to weep. Tears rolled down his cheeks. He slumped into his chair. Burke remained silent until Hamilton regained his composure."

"Tell me what happen."

"I can fill you in on our way back to Stanton. I'm afraid you'll have to come with me."

"But I..." Hamilton glanced around at Hanford, who was gazing in their direction, but appeared composed. In fact, he looked in far better condition than the last time Burke had seen him."

"Why don't you make some excuse to you father. I don't want to arrest you. I would prefer if you came voluntarily. I'm sure you agree there are a number of things that need clarification."

"You know about my father?"

"Yes, some of it, but not all. You will have to help me with the rest."

Hamilton thought about it. "Give me a few minutes alone with him, please. I give you my word I will come peacefully then."

"I'll wait outside in my car. I'm just outside the main entrance."

"Thank you, Detective."

CHAPTER 13

DENOUEMENT

The bandage was off Burke's nose, the cut was scabbed over, and the surrounding skin had turned a sickening yellowish-purple, although he still wore a small cast on his hand. Dempsey sat up in bed. He had been reading the Wall Street Journal when Burke entered the hospital room.

"When are they going to let you out of here?" Burke asked.

"Pretty soon, they tell me. It won't be too soon for me. How's everything at the station?"

"Everything's fine. We're doing the best we can while you goof off in here."

"Yeah, sure. That was some surprise about Chief Newman retiring, wasn't it? I can't get over it," said Elmo.

"It was an even greater surprise that he recommended me as his successor instead of Sullivan, and an even greater surprise that the council went along with it."

"It's going to take me a while getting used to calling you Chief, you know, after all these years of calling you, Boss."

"Well, imagine how difficult it's going to be for me, Chief Detective Dempsey."

"You're kidding me. Me, Chief Detective?"

"I'm not kidding you. It's already official. I won't take no for an answer."

Burke could tell that Elmo was pleased. "I see you still got your nose in the financial sheets," he said, nodding toward the newspaper. "What's with you, anyway?"

"Me? Oh, I got to stay on top of things, you know."

"I've always been curious, do you actually invest in the stock market, or is it some kind of hobby with you?"

"Sure, I invest. How about you?"

"I don't have enough left over at the end of the month to invest in anything, much less the stock market. The wife and kids take care of that. I always thought you were putting on airs. What do you invest in, if you don't mind my asking?"

"I buy stocks, mainly, but I dabble a bit in others things. My portfolio is...well, diversified."

"Do okay at it, then, do you?"

"You could say that."

There was a clumsy silence, while Burke's curiosity was getting the better of him. He smiled at Elmo, and Elmo smiled back.

Finally, Elmo said, "Okay, if you promise to keep it to yourself, Chief, and not hold it against me, I'll tell you how well I do."

"What? Oh, I don't want to pry into your personal business. I was just curious, that's all."

"My portfolio is worth over seven hundred thousand dollars, as of the close of the market yesterday."

"Seven hundred thousand dollars!"

"Yeah."

"Jesus, Elmo, you're almost a millionaire."

"Well, actually, Boss, ah, Chief, I am a millionaire. I own real estate, too."

Burke gaped at him, incredulous. Suddenly, he began laughing. "I thought you were dumb, Elmo! I guess I'm the one who's the dummy."

Dempsey joined in the laughing."

Finally, Burke said, "Well, I'm impressed."

"Aren't you going to ask me to prove it?"

"No, I believe you. But I have one more question, you know what it is?"

"Yeah, I think I do. You what to know what I'm doing here, working for the Police Department."

"That's it, exactly."

"I like the work, Chief. I like the people. A man has to be some-where, and he has to be doing something. Where would you have me be, roasting on a beach somewhere? Let me tell you, every year I take a vacation for two or three weeks and go someplace. It's all very interesting, and I enjoy it. I've been all over the world. You didn't know that, did you? But this is my home town. My family is here. This is where my roots are. Beside, a million doesn't go as far as it used to."

"Well, I'm glad you explained it to me, Elmo. I guess I'll have to treat you with a little more respect."

"Have I been complaining? A man doesn't get to work for a real Sherlock Holmes like you every day."

"Or have a Doctor Watson like you for a sidekick. But seriously, Elmo, I was wrong about practically everything. I think it is pure blind luck that things turned out as they did."

"I disagree. You were only wrong a little. You were essentially right. And you stood up against everybody, including me, Newman, the mayor. Give yourself a pat on the back."

⊫╪ ╪⊐

On their drive from Columbus back to Stanton, Burke told Hamilton that Doris had been shot resisting arrest, after she shot a police officer, and that he would learn the detail later. Then he was asked how and when he had learned about his

father, and of Doris Hamilton transgressions. Hamilton suddenly seemed eager to talk, as if it were a catharsis for him, a
purging of long pent up emotions and frustrations. "It was the
visit from Mrs. Halper to my office that evening," he began.
"Only three of us, besides Mrs. Halper herself, knew about her
visit: you, my mother, and I. The night of the fire mother was
out, and came home quite late. Then, when you called and told
me about the fire, I began to have suspicions, and it got me to
thinking about everything from a new and unpleasant perspec-
tive. I spent days at it, and nights driving around in my car,
living on black coffee at all-night cafes. Eventually, it occurred
to me that my mother may have answered the phone that night
when you said Sheila called my house, and that mother could
have gone to the lab. If she went there...why would she? You can
see where I'm going, Detective Burke. Mother had gone to the
lab and ...and...I couldn't deal with the possibility. I would not
allow myself to consider it. I could not accuse my own mother. It
would be the end of my world, don't you see?

"What would be her motive for killing Sheila, that she posed
some threat? What threat and to whom? I could come up with
nothing. Then I reviewed what Sheila had done at the computer
the day she died, and I thought of you, Lieutenant, and your interest in her activities. It dawned on me how she backed up those
tapes. I needed to see those tapes again. My problem then was that
you had the tapes at the police station. I had to know what was
on those tapes. I arranged to get them from the Police Station. I
had help getting them, of course, and I refuse now and forever to
reveal the source of that help. When I ran the tape and saw the
match between my father and me, everything fell into place. It was
then that I confronted my mother. As you would expect, she denied it. I kept at her until she broke down and told me everything.
I was devastated, in shock, nearly out of my mind."

"You still kept it to yourself," Burke said.

"Yes, I did. I thought there might be some way out, some way I hadn't thought of. I'll go to jail for that, I'm sure. Look, my mother loved me—

"She wasn't your mother. She was a kidnapper and a murderer."

"She was my mother to me, the only one I ever knew. What do you expect me to do, hate her? I suppose you think I should have turned her in the moment I knew. Well, I couldn't do that. I just couldn't. I guess that says I'm weak."

He stopped talking and gazed off into space, his eyes filled with tears. "My mother was insane. I could see it at the end. She always saw me as her little boy, all those years, except at rare moments, triggered by something, when she would realize, when it would all come back to her, flooding her brain, and she would get that wild look in her eyes. It used to frighten me. I didn't know what it meant. In her mind, I guess I went back and forth between being Mark Hamilton, her son, to being 'the other.' I'm not sure she ever knew the child's name that she kidnapped until it all finally caught up with her."

"Then, to protect you mother, you decided to murder Smithers and me, as we left the college."

"No! I swear to you I didn't!"

"Are you telling me your mother did that, too? Do you know how tight that pattern was on Smithers' chest? And my ear, and the crease across my skull?"

"She was an expert shooter," Hamilton said. "She even competed in school. She was really quite a remarkable woman."

"That picture on the wall in your sun room, the picture of a rifle team, I thought you were in that picture, but I couldn't find you. She was in the picture."

"Yes."

(Later, the police found the rifle in the trunk of her car, with her prints all over it, along with the tapes, and the papers she had taken from the lab. The hatchet was found in her home.)"

"I'm glad it's over," Hamilton said, "this part of it at least. I'll take my punishment, whatever it is. My poor father, what he has been through."

After the dust settled, Dr. Carlton Hanford, alias Mark Hamilton, moved to Brockton to be near his father. No charges were brought against him.

A few days after he left the hospital, Chief Detective Dempsey received an envelope in the mail from the Nightingale School of Nursing containing biographical information about the woman who had collected the one hundred thousand dollars from the insurance company for her legally dead husband. Along with the biographical information was a picture of a young, smiling Doris Hamilton.

The End

www.ingramcontent.com/pod-product-compliance
Lightning Source LLC
Chambersburg PA
CBHW071311250626
47159CB00004B/1385